He had now entered the skirts of the village. A troop of strange children ran at his heels, hooting after him and pointing at his gray beard. The dogs, too, not one of which he recognized for an old acquaintance, barked at him as he passed. The very village was altered; it was larger and more populous. There were rows of houses which he had never seen before, and those which had been his familiar haunts had disappeared. Strange names were over the doors—strange faces at the windows—everything was strange . . . .

This book was purchased at Sunnyside,
home of Washington Irving

Washington Irving

Rip Van Winkle
and Other Selected Stories

WASHINGTON IRVING

TOR®

A TOM DOHERTY ASSOCIATES BOOK
NEW YORK

This is a work of fiction. All the characters and events portrayed in this book are fictitious, and any resemblance to real people or events is purely coincidental.

RIP VAN WINKLE AND OTHER SELECTED STORIES

All new material copyright © 1993 by Tor Books, Inc.

Cover art by June Oros

A Tor Book
Published by Tom Doherty Associates, Inc.
175 Fifth Avenue
New York, NY 10010

Tor® is a registered trademark of Tom Doherty Associates, Inc.

ISBN: 0-812-52332-6

First Tor edition: January 1993

Printed in the United States of America

0 9 8 7 6 5 4 3 2

CONTENTS

RIP VAN WINKLE

———

A Posthumous Writing of Diedrich Knickerbocker

By Woden, God of Saxons,
From whence comes Wensday, that is Wodensday,
Truth is a thing that ever I will keep
Unto thylke day in which I creep into
My sepulchre——

CARTWRIGHT

[The following Tale was found among the papers of the late Diedrich Knickerbocker, an old gentleman of New York, who was very curious in the Dutch history of the province and the manners of the descendants from its primitive settlers. His historical researches, however, did not lie so much among books as among men, for the former are lamentably scantly on his favorite topics, whereas he found the old burghers, and still more their wives, rich in that legendary lore so invaluable to true history. Whenever, therefore, he happened upon a genuine Dutch family, snugly shut up in its low-roofed farmhouse, under a spreading sycamore, he looked upon it as a little clasped volume of black letter and studied it with the zeal of a bookworm.

The result of all these researchers was a history of the province during the reign of the Dutch governors, which he published some years since. There have been various opinions as to the literary character of his work, and, to tell the truth, it is not a whit better than it should be. Its chief merit is its scrupulous accuracy, which indeed was a little questioned on its first appearance, but has since been completely established, and it is now admitted into all historical collections as a book of unquestionable authority.

The old gentleman died shortly after the publication of his work, and now that he is dead and gone, it cannot do much harm to his memory to say that his time might have been much better employed in weightier labors. He, however, was apt to ride his hobby his own way; and though it did now and then kick up the dust a little in the eyes of his neighbors and grieve the spirit of some friends, for whom he felt the truest deference and affection, yet his errors and follies are remembered "more in sorrow than in anger," and it begins to be suspected that he never intended to injure or offend. But however his memory may be appreciated by critics, it is held dear by many folks, whose good opinion is well worth having; particularly by certain biscuit bakers, who have gone so far as to imprint his likeness on their new-year cakes, and have thus given him a chance for immortality, almost equal to being stamped on a Waterloo Medal, or a Queen Anne's Farthing.]

Whoever has made a voyage up the Hudson must remember the Kaatskill Mountains. They are a dismembered branch of the great Appalachian family, and are seen away to the west of the river, swelling up to a noble height and lording it over the surrounding country. Every change of season, every change of weather, indeed, every hour of the day produces some change in the magical hues and shapes of these mountains, and they are regarded by all the good wives, far and near, as perfect barometers. When the weather is fair and settled, they are clothed in blue and purple, and print their bold outlines on the clear evening sky; but, sometimes, when the rest of the landscape is cloudless, they will gather a hood of gray vapors about their summits, which, in the last rays of the setting sun, will glow and light up like a crown of glory.

At the foot of these fairy mountains, the voyager may have described the light smoke curling up from a village, whose shingle roofs gleam among the trees, just where the blue tints of the upland melt away into the fresh green of the nearer landscape. It is a little village of great antiquity, having been founded by some of the Dutch colonists in the early times of the province, just about the beginning of the government of the good Peter Stuyvesant (may he rest in peace!), and there were some of the houses of the original settlers standing within a few years, built of small yellow bricks brought from Holland, having latticed windows and gable fronts, surmounted with weathercocks.

In that same village, and in one of these very houses (which, to tell the precise truth, was sadly time-worn and weather-beaten), there lived many years since, while the country was yet a province of Great Britain, a simple, good-natured fellow of the name of Rip Van Winkle. He was a descendant of the Van Winkles who figured so gallantly in the chivalrous days of Peter Stuyvesant, and accompanied him to the siege of Fort Christina. He inherited, however, but little of the martial character of his ancestors. I have observed that he was a simple, good-natured man; he was, moreover, a kind neighbor, and an obedient, henpecked husband. Indeed, to the latter circumstance might be owing that meekness of spirit which gained him such universal popularity, for those men are most apt to be obsequious and conciliating abroad who are under the discipline of shrews at home. Their tempers, doubtless, are rendered pliant and malleable in the fiery furnace of domestic tribulation, and a curtain lecture is worth all the sermons in the world for teaching the virtues of patience and long-suffering. A termagant wife may, therefore, in some respects, be considered a tolerable blessing; and if so, Rip Van Winkle was thrice blessed.

Certain it is that he was a great favorite among all the good wives of the village, who, as usual with the amiable sex, took his part in all family squabbles and never failed, whenever they talked those matters over in their evening gossipings, to lay all the blame on Dame Van Winkle. The children of the village, too, would shout with joy whenever he approached. He assisted at their sports, made their playthings, taught them to fly kites and shoot marbles, and told them long stories of ghosts, witches, and Indians. Whenever he went dodging about the village, he was surrounded by a troop of them, hanging on his skirts, clambering on his back, and playing a thousand tricks on him with impunity; and not a dog would bark at him throughout the neighborhood.

The great error in Rip's composition was an insuperable aversion to all kinds of profitable labor. It could not be from the want of assiduity or perseverance, for he would sit on a wet rock, with a rod as long and heavy as a Tartar's lance, and fish all day without a murmur, even though he should not be encouraged by a single nibble. He would carry a fowling piece on his shoulder for hours together, trudging through woods and swamps and up hill and down dale to shoot a few squirrels or wild pigeons. He would never refuse to assist a neighbor even in the roughest toil, and was a foremost man at all country frolics for husking Indian corn or building stone fences; the women of the village, too, used to employ him to run their errands and to do such little odd jobs as their less obliging husbands would not do for them. In a word, Rip was ready to attend to anybody's business but his own; but as to doing family duty and keeping his farm in order, he found it impossible.

In fact, he declared it was of no use to work on his farm; it was the most pestilent little piece of ground in the whole country; everything about it went wrong, and would go wrong, in spite of him. His fences were continually falling to pieces; his cow would either go astray or get among the cabbages; weeds were sure to grow quicker in his fields than anywhere else; the rain always made a point of setting in just as he had some outdoor work to do; so that though his patrimonial estate had dwindled away under his management, acre by acre, until there was little more left than a mere patch of Indian corn and potatoes, yet it was the worst-conditioned farm in the neighborhood.

His children, too, were as ragged and wild as if they belonged to nobody. His son Rip, an urchin begotten in his own likeness, promised to inherit the habits, with the old clothes, of his father. He was generally seen trooping like a colt at his mother's heels, equipped in a pair of his father's cast-off galligaskins, which he had much ado to hold up with one hand as a fine lady does her train in bad weather.

Rip Van Winkle, however, was one of those happy mortals of foolish, well-oiled dispositions who take the world easy, eat white bread or brown, whichever can be got with least thought or trouble, and would rather starve on a penny than work for a pound. If left to himself, he would have whistled life away in perfect contentment; but his wife kept continually dinning in his ears about his idleness, his carelessness, and the ruin he was bringing on his family. Morning, noon, and night, her tongue was incessantly going, and everything he said or did was sure to produce a torrent of household eloquence. Rip had but one way of replying to all lectures of the kind, and that, by frequent use, had grown into a habit. He shrugged his shoulders, shook his head, cast up his eyes, but said nothing. This, however, always provoked a fresh volley from his wife, so that he was fain to draw off his forces and take to the outside of the house—the only side which, in truth, belongs to a henpecked husband.

Rip's sole domestic adherent was his dog, Wolf, who was as much henpecked as his master, for Dame Van Winkle regarded them as companions in idleness, and even looked upon Wolf with an evil eye as the cause of his master's going so often astray. True it is, in all points of spirit befitting an honorable dog, he was an courageous an animal as ever scoured the woods—but what courage can withstand the ever-during and all-besetting terrors of a woman's tongue? The moment Wolf entered the house his crest fell, his tail drooped to the ground, or curled between his legs, he sneaked about with a gallows air, casting many a sidelong glance at Dame Van Winkle, and at the least flourish of a broomstick or ladle he would fly to the door with yelping precipitation.

Times grew worse and worse with Rip Van Winkle as years of matrimony rolled on; a tart temper never mellows with age, and a sharp tongue is the only edged tool that grows keener with constant use. For a long while he used to console himself, when driven from home, by frequenting a kind of perpetual club of the sages, philosophers, and other idle personages of the village, which held its sessions on a bench before a small inn, designated by a rubicund portrait of His Majesty George the Third. Here they used to sit in the shade through a long, lazy summer's day, talking listlessly over village gossip or telling endless sleepy stories about nothing. But it would have been worth any statesman's money to have heard the profound discussions that sometimes took place when by chance an old newspaper fell into their hands from some passing traveler. How solemnly they would listen to the contents, as drawled out by Derrick Van Bummel, the schoolmaster, a dapper, learned little man who was not to be daunted by the most gigantic word in the dictionary; and how sagely they would deliberate upon public events some months after they had taken place.

The opinions of this junto were completely controlled by Nicholas Vedder, a patriarch of the village and landlord of the inn, at the door of which he took his seat from morning till night, just moving sufficiently to avoid the sun and keep in the shade of a large tree, so that the neighbors could tell the hour by his movements as accurately as by a sundial. It is true he was rarely heard to speak, but smoked his pipe incessantly. His adherents, however (for every great man has his adherents), perfectly understood him, and knew how to gather his opinions. When anything that was read or related displeased him, he was observed to smoke his pipe vehemently and to send forth short, frequent, and angry puffs; but when pleased, he would inhale the smoke slowly and tranquilly and emit it in light and placid clouds, and sometimes, taking the pipe from his mouth and letting the fragrant vapor curl about his nose, would gravely nod his head in token of perfect approbation.

From even this stronghold the unlucky Rip was at length routed by his termagant wife, who would suddenly break in upon the tranquillity of the assemblage and call the members all to naught; nor was that august personage, Nicholas Vedder himself, sacred from the daring tongue of this terrible virago, who charged him outright with encouraging her husband in habits of idleness.

Poor Rip was at last reduced almost to despair, and his only alternative, to escape from the labor of the farm and clamor of his wife, was to take gun in hand and stroll away into the woods. Here he would sometimes seat himself at the foot of a tree and share the contents of his wallet with Wolf, with whom he sympathized as a fellow sufferer in persecution. "Poor Wolf," he would say, "thy mistress leads thee a dog's life of it; but never mind, my lad, whilst I live thou shalt never want a friend to stand by thee!" Wolf would wag his tail, look wistfully in his master's face, and if dogs can feel pity, I verily believe he reciprocated the sentiment with all his heart.

In a long ramble of the kind of a fine autumnal day, Rip had unconsciously scrambled to one of the highest parts of the Kaatskill Mountains. He was after his favorite sport of squirrel shooting, and the still solitudes had echoed and re-echoed with the reports of his gun. Panting and fatigued, he threw himself, late in the afternoon, on a green knoll, covered with mountain herbage, that crowned the brow of a precipice. From an opening between the trees he could overlook all the lower country for many a mile of rich woodland. He saw at a distance the lordly Hudson, far, far below him, moving on its silent but majestic course, with the reflection of a purple cloud or the sail of a lagging bark here and there sleeping on its glassy bosom, and at least losing itself in the blue highlands.

On the other side he looked down into a deep mountain glen, wild, lonely, and shagged, the bottom filled with fragments from the impending cliffs, and scarcely lighted by the reflected rays of the setting sun. For some time Rip lay musing on this scene. Evening was gradually advancing; the mountains began to throw their long blue shadows over the valleys. He saw that it would be dark long before he could reach the village, and he heaved a heavy sigh when he thought of encountering the terrors of Dame Van Winkle.

As he was about to descend, he heard a voice from a distance, hallooing, "Rip Van Winkle! Rip Van Winkle!" He looked around, but could see nothing but a crow winging its solitary flight across the mountain. He thought his fancy must have deceived him, and turned again to descend, when he heard the same cry ring through the still evening air, "Rip Van Winkle! Rip Van Winkle!" At the same time Wolf bristled up his back and, giving a low growl, skulked to his master's side, looking fearfully down into the glen. Rip now felt a vague apprehension stealing over him; he looked anxiously in the same direction and perceived a strange figure slowly toiling up the rocks, and bending under the weight of something he carried on his back. He was surprised to see any human being in this lonely and unfrequented place, but supposing it to be some one of the neighborhood in need of his assistance, he hastened down to yield it.

On nearer approach he was still more surprised at the singularity of the stranger's appearance. He was a short, square-built old fellow, with thick, bushy hair and a grizzled beard. His dress was of the antique Dutch fashion—a cloth jerkin strapped around the waist and several pairs of breeches, the outer one of ample volume, decorated with rows of buttons down the sides and bunches at the knees. He bore on his shoulder a stout keg that seemed full of liquor, and made signs for Rip to approach and assist him with the load. Though rather shy and distrustful of this new acquaintance, Rip complied with his usual alacrity, and mutually relieving one another, they clambered up a narrow gully, apparently the dry bed of a mountain torrent. As they ascended, Rip every now and then heard long rolling peals, like distant thunder, that seemed to issue out of a deep ravine, or rather cleft, between lofty rocks, toward which their rugged path conducted. He paused for an instant, but supposing it to be the muttering of one of those transient thunder showers which often take place in mountain heights, he proceeded. Passing through the ravine, they came to a hollow, like a small amphitheater, surrounded by perpendicular precipices, over the brinks of which impending trees shot their branches, so that you only caught glimpses of the azure sky and the bright evening cloud. During the whole time, Rip and his companion had labored on in silence, for though the former marveled greatly what could be the object of carrying a keg of liquor up this wild mountain, yet there was something strange and incomprehensible about the unknown that inspired awe and checked familiarity.

On entering the amphitheater, new objects of wonder were to be seen. On a level spot in the center was a company of odd-looking persons playing at ninepins. They were dressed in a quaint, outlandish fashion; some wore short doublets, others jerkins, with long knives in their belts, and most of them had enormous breeches, of similar style with that of the guide's. Their visages, too, were peculiar; one had a large beard, broad face, and small piggish eyes, the face of another seemed to consist entirely of nose and was surmounted by a white sugarloaf hat set off with a little red cock's tail. They all had beards, of various shapes and colors. There was one who seemed to be the commander. He was a stout old gentleman, with a weather-beaten countenance; he wore a laced doublet, broad belt and hanger, high-crowned hat and feather, red stockings, and high-heeled shoes, with roses in them. The whole group reminded Rip of the figures in an old Flemish painting, in the parlor of Dominie Van Shaick, the village parson, and which had been brought over from Holland at the time of the settlement.

What seemed particularly odd to Rip was that though these folks were evidently amusing themselves, yet they maintained the gravest faces, the most mysterious silence, and were, withal, the most melancholy party of pleasure he had ever witnessed. Nothing interrupted the silness of the scene but the noise of the balls, which, whenever they were rolled, echoed along the mountains like rumbling peals of thunder.

As Rip and his companion approached them, they suddenly desisted from their play and stared at him with such fixed, statuelike gaze and such strange, uncouth, lackluster countenances that his heart turned within him and his knees smote together. His companion now emptied the contents of the keg into large flagons and made signs to him to wait upon the company. He obeyed with fear and trembling; they quaffed the liquor in profound silence and then returned to their game.

By degrees Rip's awe and apprehension subsided. He even ventured, when no eye was fixed upon him, to taste the beverage, which he found had much of the flavor of excellent Hollands. He was naturally a thirsty soul and was soon tempted to repeat the draft. One taste provoked another; and he reiterated his visits to the flagon so often that at length his senses were overpowered, his eyes swam in his head, his head gradually declined, and he fell into a deep sleep.

On waking, he found himself on the green knoll whence he had first seen the old man of the glen. He rubbed his eyes— it was a bright, sunny morning. The birds were hopping and twittering among the bushes, and the eagle was wheeling aloft and breasting the pure mountain breeze. "Surely," thought Rip, "I have not slept here all night." He recalled the occurrences before he fell asleep. The strange man with a keg of liquor— the mountain ravine—the wild retreat among the rocks—the woebegone party at ninepins—the flagon—"Oh! That flagon! That wicked flagon!" thought Rip. "What excuse shall I make to Dame Van Winkle?"

He looked around for his gun, but in place of the clean, well-oiled fowling piece he found an old firelock lying by him, the barrel encrusted with rust, the lock falling off, and the stock worm-eaten. He now suspected that the grave roysters of the mountain had put a trick upon him, and, having dosed him with liquor, had robbed him of his gun. Wolf, too, had disappeared, but he might have strayed away after a squirrel or partridge. He whistled after him and shouted his name, but all in vain;

the echoes repeated his whistle and shout, but no dog was to be seen.

He determined to revisit the scene of the last evening's gambol, and if he met with any of the party, to demand his dog and gun. As he rose to walk, he found himself stiff in the joints and wanting in his usual activity. "These mountain beds do not agree with me," thought Rip, "and if this frolic should lay me up with a fit of the rheumatism, I shall have a blessed time with Dame Van Winkle." With some difficulty he got down into the glen; he found the gully up which he and his companion had ascended the preceding evening, but to his astonishment a mountain stream was now foaming down it, leaping from rock to rock and filling the glen with babbling murmurs. He, however, made shift to scramble up its sides, working his toilsome way through thickets of birch, sassafras, and witch hazel, and sometimes tripped up or entangled by the wild grapevines that twisted their coils or tendrils from tree to tree and spread a kind of network in his path.

At length he reached to where the ravine had opened through the cliffs to the amphitheater, but no traces of such opening remained. The rocks presented a high, impenetrable wall over which the torrent came tumbling in a sheet of feathery foam and fell into a broad, deep basin, black from the shadows of the surrounding forest. Here, then, poor Rip was brought to a stand. He again called and whistled after his dog; he was only answered by the cawing of a flock of idle crows, sporting high in air about a dry tree that overhung a sunny precipice, and who, secure in their elevation, seemed to look down and scoff at the poor man's perplexities. What was to be done? The morning was passing away, and Rip felt famished for want of his breakfast. He grieved to give up his dog and gun; he dreaded to meet his wife, but it would not do to starve among the mountains. He shook his head, shouldered the rusty firelock, and, with a heart full of trouble and anxiety, turned his steps homeward.

As he approached the village he met a number of people, but none whom he knew, which somewhat surprised him, for he had thought himself acquainted with every one in the country around. Their dress, too, was of a different fashion from that to which he was accustomed. They all stared at him with equal marks of surprise, and whenever they cast their eyes upon him invariably stroked their chins. The constant recurrence of this gesture induced Rip, involuntarily, to do the same, when, to his astonishment, he found his beard had grown a foot long!

He had now entered the skirts of the village. A troop of strange children ran at his heels, hooting after him and pointing at his gray beard. The dogs, too, not one of which he recognized for an old acquaintance, barked at him as he passed. The very village was altered; it was larger and more populous. There were rows of houses which he had never seen before, and those which had been his familiar haunts had disappeared. Strange names were over the doors—strange faces at the windows—everything was strange. His mind now misgave him; he began to doubt whether both he and the world around him were not bewitched. Surely this was his native village, which he had left but the day before. There stood the Kaatskill Mountains— there ran the silver Hudson at a distance—there was every hill and dale precisely as it had always been. Rip was sorely perplexed. "That flagon last night," thought he, "has addled my poor head sadly!"

It was with some difficulty that he found the way to his own house, which he approached with silent awe, expecting every moment to hear the shrill voice of Dame Van Winkle. He found the house gone to decay—the roof fallen in, the windows shattered, and the doors off the hinges. A half-starved dog that looked like Wolf was skulking about it. Rip called him by name, but the cur snarled, showed his teeth, and passed on. This was an unkind cut indeed. "My very dog," sighed poor Rip, "has forgotten me!"

He entered the house, which, to tell the truth, Dame Van Winkle had always kept in neat order. It was empty, forlorn, and apparently abandoned. This desolateness overcame all his connubial fears—he called loudly for his wife and children; the lonely chambers rang for a moment with his voice, and then all again was silence.

He now hurried forth and hastened to his old resort, the village inn—but it too was gone. A large, rickety, wooden building stood in its place, with great gaping windows, some of them broken and mended with old hats and petticoats, and over the door was painted, "the Union Hotel, by Jonathan Doolittle." Instead of the great tree that used to shelter the quiet little Dutch inn of yore, there now was reared a tall, naked pole, with something on the top that looked like a red nightcap, and from it was fluttering a flag, on which was a singular assemblage of stars and stripes—all this was strange and incomprehensible. He recognized on the sing, however, the ruby face of King George, under which he had smoked so many a peaceful pipe; but even this was singularly metamorphosed. The red coat was changed for one of blue and buff, a sword was held in the hand instead of a scepter, the head was decorated with a cocked hat, and underneath was painted in large characters, GENERAL WASHINGTON.

There was, as usual, a crowd of folk about the door, but none that Rip recollected. The very character of the people seemed changed. There was a busy, bustling, disputatious tone about it, instead of the accustomed phlegm and drowsy tranquillity. He looked in vain for the sage Nicholas Vedder, with his broad face, double chin, and fair long pipe, uttering clouds of tobacco smoke instead of idle speeches; or Van Bummel, the schoolmaster, doling forth the contents of an ancient newspaper. In place of these, a lean, billious-looking fellow, with his pockets full of handbills, was haranguing vehemently about rights of citizens—elections—members of congress—liberty—Bunker's Hill—heroes of seventy-six—and other words, which were a perfect Babylonish jargon to the bewildered Van Winkle.

The appearance of Rip, with his long, grizzled beard, his rusty fowling piece, his uncouth dress, and an army of women and children at his heels, soon attracted the attention of the tavern politicians. They crowded around him, eying him from head to foot with great curiosity. The orator bustled up to him and, drawing him partly aside, inquired "on which side he voted?" Rip stared in vacant stupidity. Another short but busy little fellow pulled him by the arm, and, rising on tiptoe, inquired in his ear, "whether he was Federal or Democrat?" Rip was equally at a loss to comprehend the question; when a knowing, self-important old gentleman in a sharp cocked hat made his way through the crowd, putting them to the right and left with his elbows as he passed, and, planting himself before Van Winkle, with one arm akimbo, the other resting on his cane, his keen eyes and sharp hat penetrating, as it were, into his very soul, demanded in an austere tone, "what brought him to the election with a gun on his shoulder, and a mob at his heels, and whether he meant to breed a riot in the village?" "Alas! Gentlemen," cried Rip, somewhat dismayed, "I am a poor, quiet man, a native of the place, and a loyal subject of the king. God bless him!"

Here a general shout burst from the bystanders. "A tory! A tory! A spy! A refugee! Hustle him! Away with him!" It was with great difficulty that the self-important man in the cocked hat restored order; and, having assumed a tenfold austerity of brow, demanded again of the unknown culprit what he came there for and whom he was seeking. The poor man humbly assured him that he meant no harm, but merely came there in search of some of his neighbors, who used to keep about the tavern.

"Well—who are they? Name them."

Rip bethought himself a moment, and inquired, "Where's Nicholas Vedder?"

There was a silence for a little while, when an old man replied, in a thin, piping voice, "Nicholas Vedder! Why, he is dead and gone these eighteen years! There was a wooden tombstone in the churchyard that used to tell all about him, but that's rotten and gone too."

"Where's Brom Dutcher?"

"Oh, he went off to the army in the beginning of the war; some say he was killed at the storming of Stony Point—others say he was drowned in a squall at the foot of Antony's Nose. I don't know—he never came back again."

"Where's Van Bummel, the schoolmaster?"

"He went off to the wars, too, was a great militia general, and is now in congress."

Rip's heart died away at hearing of these sad changes in his home and friends, and finding himself thus alone in the world. Every answer puzzled him, too, by treating of such enormous lapses of time and of matters which he could not understand: war—congress—Stony Point. He had no courage to ask after any more friends, but cried out in despair, "Does nobody here know Rip Van Winkle?"

"Oh, Rip Van Winkle!" exclaimed two or three. "Oh, to be sure! That's Rip Van Winkle yonder, leaning against the tree."

Rip looked, and beheld a precise counterpart of himself as he went up the mountain: apparently as lazy, and certainly as ragged. The poor fellow was now completely confounded. He doubted his own identity, and whether he was himself or another man. In the midst of his bewilderment, the man in the cocked hat demanded who he was, and what was his name?

"God knows," exclaimed he, at his wit's end. "I'm not myself—I'm somebody else—that's me yonder—no—that's somebody else got into my shoes—I was myself last night, but I fell asleep on the mountain, and they've changed my gun, and everything's changed, and I'm changed, and I can't tell what's my name, or who I am!"

The bystanders began now to look at each other, nod, wink significantly, and tap their fingers against their foreheads. There was a whisper also about securing the gun and keeping the old fellow from doing mischief, at the very suggestion of which the self-important man in the cocked hat retired with some precipitation. At this critical moment a fresh, comely woman pressed through the throng to get a peep at the gray-bearded man. She had a chubby child in her arms, which, frightened at his looks, began to cry. "Hush, Rip," cried she, "hush, you little fool; the old man won't hurt you." The name of the child, the air of the mother, the tone of her voice, all awakened a train of recollections in his mind. "What is your name, my good woman?" asked he.

"Judith Gardenier."

"And your father's name?"

"Ah, poor man, Rip Van Winkle was his name, but it's twenty years since he went away from home with his gun, and never has been heard of since—his dog came home without him; but whether he shot himself, or was carried away by the Indians, nobody can tell. I was then but a little girl."

Rip had but one question more to ask; but he put it with a faltering voice:

"Where's your mother?"

"Oh, she too had died but a short time since; she broke a blood vessel in a fit of passion at a New England peddler."

There was a drop of comfort, at least, in this intelligence. The honest man could contain himself no longer. He caught his daughter and her child in his arms. "I am your father!" cried he. "Young Rip Van Winkle once—old Rip Van Winkle now! Does nobody know poor Rip Van Winkle?"

All stood amazed, until an old woman, tottering out from among the crowd, put her hand to her brow and, peering under it in his face for a moment, exclaimed, "Sure enough! It is Rip Van Winkle—it is himself! Welcome home again, old neighbor. Why, where have you been these twenty long years?"

Rip's story was soon told, for the whole twenty years had been to him but as one night. The neighbors stared when they heard it; some were seen to wink at each other and put their tongues in their cheeks, and the self-important man in the cocked hat, who, when the alarm was over, had returned to the field, screwed down the corners of his mouth and shook his head—upon which there was a general shaking of the head throughout the assemblage.

It was determined, however, to take the opinion of old Peter Vanderdonk, who was seen slowly advancing up the road. He was a descendant of the historian of that name, who wrote one of the earliest accounts of the province. Peter was the most ancient inhabitant of the village, and well versed in all the wonderful events and traditions of the neighborhood. He recollected Rip at once and corroborated his story in the most satisfactory manner. He assured the company that it was a fact, handed down from his ancestor the historian, that the Kaatskill Mountains had always been haunted by strange beings. That it was affirmed that the great Hendrick Hudson, the first discoverer of the river and country, kept a kind of vigil there every twenty years, with his crew of the *Half Moon*, being permitted in this way to revisit the scenes of his enterprise and keep a guardian eye upon the river and the great city called by his name. That his father had once seen them in their old Dutch dresses playing at ninepins in a hollow of the mountain, and that he himself had heard, one summer afternoon, the sound of their balls, like distant peals of thunder.

To make a long story short, the company broke up and returned to the more important concerns of the election. Rip's daughter took him home to live with her; she had a snug, well-furnished house, and a stout, cheery farmer for a husband, whom Rip recollected for one of the urchins that used to climb upon his back. As to Rip's son and heir, who was the ditto of himself, seen leaning against the tree, he was employed to work on the farm, but evinced a hereditary disposition to attend to anything else but his business.

Rip now resumed his old walks and habits; he soon found many of his former cronies, though all rather the worse for the wear and tear of time, and preferred making friends among the rising generation, with whom he soon grew into great favor.

Having nothing to do at home, and being arrived at that happy age when a man can be idle with impunity, he took his place once more on the bench at the inn door and was reverenced as one of the patriarchs of the village, and a chronicle of the old times "before the war." It was some time before he could get into the regular track of gossip, or could be made to comprehend the strange events that had taken place during his torpor. How that there had been a revolutionary war—

that the country had thrown off the yoke of old England—
and that, instead of being a subject of his Majesty George
the Third, he was now a free citizen of the United States.
Rip, in fact, was no politician—the changes of states and
empires made but little impression on him; but there was
one species of despotism under which he had long groaned,
and that was—petticoat government. Happily that was at an
end; he had got his neck out of the yoke of matrimony and
could go in and out whenever he pleased, without dread-
ing the tyranny of Dame Van Winkle. Whenever her name
was mentioned, however, he shook his head, shrugged his
shoulders, and cast up his eyes, which might pass either for
an expression of resignation to his fate or joy at his deliverance.

He used to tell his story to every stranger that arrived at Mr.
Doolittle's hotel. He was observed, at first, to vary on some
points every time he told it, which was, doubtless, owing to
his having so recently awaked. It at last settled down precisely
to the tale I have related, and not a man, woman, or child in
the neighborhood but knew it by heart. Some always pretended
to doubt the reality of it, and insisted that Rip had been out
of his head, and that this was one point on which he always
remained flighty. The old Dutch inhabitants, however, almost
universally gave it full credit. Even to this day they never hear
a thunderstorm of a summer afternoon about the Kaatskill but
they say Hendrink Hudson and his crew are at their game of
ninepins; and it is a common wish of all henpecked husbands
in the neighborhood, when life hangs heavy on their hands,
that they might have a quieting draft out of Rip Van Winkle's
flagon.

NOTE

The foregoing Tale, one would suspect, had been suggested
to Mr. Knickerbocker by a little German superstition about the
Emperor Frederick *der Rothbart* and the Kypphaüser mountain. The subjoined note, however, which he had appended to

the tale, shows that it is an absolute fact, narrated with his usual fidelity:

"The story of Rip Van Winkle may seem incredible to many, but nevertheless I give it my full belief, for I know the vicinity of our old Dutch settlements to have been very subject to marvelous events and appearances. Indeed, I have heard many stranger stories than this, in the villages along the Hudson, all of which were too well authenticated to admit of a doubt. I have even talked with Rip Van Winkle myself, who, when last I saw him, was a very venerable old man and so perfectly rational and consistent on every other point that I think no conscientious person could refuse to take this into the bargain; nay, I have seen a certificate on the subject taken before a country justice and signed with a cross, in the justice's own handwriting. The story, therefore, is beyond the possibility of doubt.

D.K."

POSTSCRIPT

The following are traveling notes from a memorandum book of Mr. Knickerbocker:

The Kaatsberg, or Catskill Mountains, have always been a region full of fable. The Indians considered them the abode of spirits, who influenced the weather, spreading sunshine or clouds over the landscape, and sending good or bad hunting seasons. They were ruled by an old squaw spirit, said to be their mother. She dwelt on the highest peak of the Catskills and had charge of the doors of day and night, to open and shut them at the proper hour. She hung up the new moons in the skies and cut up the old ones into stars. In times of drought, if properly propitiated, she would spin light summer clouds out of cobwebs and morning dew and send them off from the crest of the mountain, flake after flake, like flakes of carded cotton, to float in the air; until, dissolved by the heat of the sun, they would fall in gentle showers, causing the grass to spring, the fruits to ripen, and the corn to grow an inch an hour. If displeased, however, she would brew up clouds black as ink, sitting in the midst of them like a bottle-bellied spider in the midst of its web; and when these clouds broke, woe betide the valleys!

In old times, say the Indian traditions, there was a kind of Manitou or Spirit, who kept about the wildest recesses of the Catskill Mountains, and took a mischievous pleasure in wreaking all kinds of evils and vexations upon the red men. Sometimes he would assume the form of a bear, a panther, or a deer, lead the bewildered hunter a weary chase through tangled forests and among ragged rocks, and then spring off with a loud ho! ho! leaving him aghast on the brink of a beetling precipice or raging torrent.

The favorite abode of this Manitou is still shown. It is a great rock or cliff on the loneliest part of the mountains, and, from the flowering vines which clamber about it and the wild flowers which abound in its neighborhood, is known by the name of the Garden Rock. Near the foot of it is a small lake, the haunt of the solitary bittern, with water snakes basking in the sun on the leaves of the pond lilies which lie on the surface. This place was held in great awe by the Indians, insomuch that the boldest hunter would not pursue his game within its precincts. Once upon a time, however, a hunter who had lost his way penetrated to the Garden Rock, where he beheld a number of gourds placed in the crotches of trees. One of these he seized and made off with, but in the hurry of his retreat he let it fall among the rocks, when a great stream gushed forth, which washed him away and swept him down precipices, where he was dashed to pieces, and the stream made its way to the Hudson and continues to flow to the present day; being the identical stream known by the name of the Kaaters-kill.

THE AUTHOR'S
ACCOUNT OF HIMSELF

"I am of this mind with Homer, that as the snaile that crept out of her shel was turned eftsoons into a toad, and thereby was forced to make a stoole to sit on; so the traveller that straggleth from his owne country is in a short time transformed into so monstrous a shape, that he is faine to alter his mansion with his manners, and to live where he can, not where he would."—

LYLY'S *Euphues*

I was always fond of visiting new scenes, and observing strange characters and manners. Even when a mere child I began my travels, and made many tours of discovery into foreign parts and unknown regions of my native city, to the frequent alarm of my parents, and the emolument of the town-crier. As I grew, into boyhood, I extended the range of my observations. My holiday afternoons were spent in rambles about the surrounding country. I made myself familiar with all its places famous in history or fable. I knew every spot where a murder or robbery had been committed, or a ghost seen. I visited the neighboring villages, and added greatly to my stock of knowledge by noting their habits and customs, and conversing with their sages and great men. I even journeyed one long summer's day to the summit of the most distant hill, whence I stretched my eye over many a mile of *terra incognita*, and was astonished to find how vast a globe I inhabited.

This rambling propensity strengthened with my years. Books of voyages and travels became my passion, and in devouring their contents, I neglected the regular exercises of the school. How wistfully would I wander about the pierheads in fine weather, and watch the parting ships, bound to distant climes; with what longing eyes would I gaze after their lessening sails, and waft myself in imagination to the ends of the earth!

Further reading and thinking, though they brought this vague inclination into more reasonable bounds, only served to make it more decided. I visited various parts of my own country; and had I been merely a lover of fine scenery, I should have felt little desire to seek elsewhere its gratification, for on no country have the charms of nature been more prodigally lavished. Her mighty lakes, like oceans of liquid silver; her mountains, with their bright aerial tints; her valleys, teeming with wild fertility; her tremendous cataracts, thundering in their solitudes; her boundless plains, waving with spontaneous verdure; her broad deep rivers, rolling in solemn silence to the ocean; her trackless forests, where vegetation puts forth all its magnificence; her skies, kindling with the magic of summer clouds and glorious sunshine;—no, never need an American look beyond his own country for the sublime and beautiful of natural scenery.

But Europe held forth the charms of storied and poetical association. There were to be seen the masterpieces of art, the refinements of highly cultivated society, the quaint peculiarities of ancient and local custom. My native country was full of youthful promise: Europe was rich in the accumulated treasures of age. Her very ruins told the history of times gone by, and every mouldering stone was a chronicle. I longed to wander over the scenes of renowned achievement—to tread, as it were, in the footsteps of antiquity—to loiter about the ruined castle—to meditate on the falling tower—to escape, in short, from the commonplace realities of the present, and lose myself among the shadowy grandeurs of the past.

I had, beside all this, an earnest desire to see the great men of the earth. We have, it is true, our great men in America: not a city but has an ample share of them. I have mingled among them in my time, and been almost withered by the shade into which they cast me; for there is nothing so baleful to a small man as the shade of a great one, particularly the great man of a city. But I was anxious to see the great men of Europe; for I had read in the works of various philosophers, that all animals degenerated in America, and man among the number. A great man of Europe, thought I, must therefore be as superior to a great man of America, as a peak of the Alps to a highland of the Hudson; and in this idea I was confirmed, by observing the comparative importance and swelling magnitude of many English travellers among us, who, I was assured, were very little people in their own country. I will visit this land of wonder, thought I, and see the gigantic race from which I am degenerated.

It has been either my good or evil lot to have my roving passion gratified. I have wandered through different countries, and witnessed many of the shifting scenes of life. I cannot say that I have studied them with the eye of a philosopher, but rather with the sauntering gaze with which humble lovers of the picturesque stroll from the window of one print-shop to another, caught sometimes by the delineations of beauty, sometimes by the distortions of caricature, and sometimes by the loveliness of landscape. As it is the fashion for modern tourists to travel pencil in hand, and bring home their portfolios filled with sketches, I am disposed to get up a few for the entertainment of my friends. When, however, I look over the hints and memorandums I have taken down for the purpose, my heart almost fails me at finding how my idle humor has led me aside from the great objects studied by every regular traveller who would make a book. I fear I shall give equal disappointment with an unlucky landscape-painter, who had travelled on the continent, but, following the bent of his vagrant inclination, had sketched in nooks, and corners, and by-places. His sketch-book was accordingly crowded with cottages, and landscapes, and obscure ruins; but he had neglected to paint St. Peter's, or the Coliseum; the cascade of Terni, or the bay of Naples; and had not a single glacier or volcano in his whole collection.

THE SPECTER BRIDEGROOM

A Traveler's Tale*

He that supper for is dight,
He lyes full cold, I trow, this night!
Yestreen to chamber I him led,
This night Gray-Steel has made his bed.
SIR EGER, SIR GRAHAME, AND SIR GRAY-STEEL

On the summit of one of the heights of the Odenwald, a wild
and romantic tract of Upper Germany that lies not far from
the confluence of the Main and the Rhine, there stood, many,
many years since, the Castle of the Baron Von Landshort. It
is now quite fallen to decay and almost buried among beech
trees and dark firs, above which, however, its old watchtower
may still be seen, struggling, like the former possessor I have

---

*The erudite reader, well versed in good-for-nothing lore, will
perceive that the above Tale must have been suggested to the
old Swiss by a little French anecdote, a circumstance said to
have taken place at Paris.

mentioned, to carry a high head and look down upon the neighboring country.

The baron was a dry branch of the great family of Katz-enellenbogen,* and inherited the relics of the property and all the pride of his ancestors. Though the warlike disposition of his predecessors had much impaired the family possessions, yet the baron still endeavored to keep up some show of former state. The times were peacable, and the German nobles, in general, had abandoned their inconvenient old castles, perched like eagles' nests among the mountains, and had built more convenient residences in the valleys; still the baron remained proudly drawn up in his little fortress, cherishing, with hereditary inveteracy, all the old family feuds, so that he was on ill terms with some of his nearest neighbors on account of disputes that had happened between their great-great-grandfathers.

The baron had but one child, a daughter, but nature, when she grants but one child, always compensates by making it a prodigy, and so it was with the daughter of the baron. All the nurses, gossips, and country cousins assured her father that she had not her equal for beauty in all Germany; and who should know better than they? She had, moreover, been brought up with great care under the superintendence of two maiden aunts, who had spent some years of their early life at one of the little German courts and were skilled in all the branches of knowledge necessary to the education of a fine lady. Under their instructions she became a miracle of accomplishments. By the time she was eighteen she could embroider to admiration and had worked whole histories of the saints in tapestry with such strength of expression in their countenances that they looked like so many souls in purgatory. She could read without great

---

*I.e., CAT'S-ELBOW. The name of a family of those parts very powerful in former times. The appellation, we are told, was given in compliment to a peerless dame of the family, celebrated for her fine arm.

difficulty, and had spelled her way through several church legends and almost all the chivalric wonders of the Heldenbuch. She had even made considerable proficiency in writing, could sign her own name without missing a letter, and so legibly that her aunts could read it without spectacles. She excelled in making little elegant good-for-nothing ladylike knick-knacks of all kinds; was versed in the most abstruse dancing of the day; played a number of airs on the harp and guitar; and knew all the tender ballads of the Minnelieders by heart.

Her aunts, too, having been great flirts and coquettes in their younger days, were admirably calculated to be vigilant guardians and strict censors of the conduct of their niece, for there is no duenna so rigidly prudent and inexorably decorous as a superannuated coquette. She was rarely suffered out of their sight; never went beyond the domains of the castle, unless well attended, or rather well watched; had continual lectures read to her about strict decorum and implicit obedience; and, as to the men—pah!—she was taught to hold them at such a distance, and in such absolute distrust, that, unless properly authorized, she would not have cast a glance upon the handsomest cavalier in the world—no, not if he were even dying at her feet.

The good effects of this system were wonderfully apparent. The young lady was a pattern of docility and correctness. While others were wasting their sweetness in the glare of the world and liable to be plucked and thrown aside by every hand, she was coyly blooming into fresh and lovely womanhood under the protection of those immaculate spinsters, like a rosebud blushing forth among guardian thorns. Her aunts looked upon her with pride and exultation, and vaunted that though all the other young ladies in the world might go astray, yet, thank Heaven, nothing of the kind could happen to the heiress of Katzenellenbogen.

But, however scantily the Baron Von Landshort might be provided with children, his household was by no means a small one, for Providence had enriched him with abundance of poor relations. They, one and all, possessed the affectionate disposition common to humble relatives, were wonderfully attached to the baron, and took every possible occasion to come in swarms and enliven the castle. All family festivals were commemorated by these good people at the baron's expense; and, when they were filled with good cheer they would declare that there was nothing on earth so delightful as these family meetings, these jubilees of the heart.

The baron, though a small man, had a large soul, and it swelled with satisfaction at the consciousness of being the greatest man in the little world about him. He loved to tell long stories about the dark old warriors whose portraits looked grimly down from the walls around, and he found no listeners equal to those that fed at his expense. He was much given to the marvelous, and a firm believer in all those supernatural tales with which every mountain and valley in Germany abounds. The faith of his guests exceeded even his own; they listened to every tale of wonder with open eyes and mouth, and never failed to be astonished, even though repeated for the hundredth time. Thus lived the Baron Von Landshort, the oracle of his table, the absolute monarch of his little territory, and happy, above all things, in the persuasion that he was the wisest man of the age.

At the time of which my story treats there was a great family gathering at the castle, on an affair of the utmost importance: it was to receive the destined bridegroom of the baron's daughter. A negotiation had been carried on between the father and an old nobleman of Bavaria to unite the dignity of their houses by the marriage of their children. The preliminaries had been conducted with proper punctilio. The young people were betrothed without seeing each other, and the time was appointed for the marriage ceremony. The young Count Von Altenburg had been recalled from the army for the purpose, and was actually on his way to the baron's to receive his bride. Missives had even been received from him, from Würzburg, where he was accidentally detained, mentioning the day and hour when he might be expected to arrive.

The castle was in a tumult of preparation to give him a suitable welcome. The fair bride had been decked out with uncommon care. The two aunts had superintended her toilet and quarreled the whole morning about every article of her dress. The young lady had taken advantage of their contest to follow the bent of her own taste, and fortunately it was a good one. She looked as lovely as a youthful bridegroom could desire, and the flutter of expectation heightened the luster of her charms.

The suffusions that mantled her face and neck, the gentle heaving of the bosom, the eye now and then lost in reverie, all betrayed the soft tumult that was going on in her little heart. The aunts were continually hovering around her, for maiden aunts are apt to take great interest in affairs of this nature. They were giving her a world of staid counsel how to deport herself, what to say, and in what manner to receive the expected lover.

The baron was no less busied in preparations. He had, in truth, nothing exactly to do, but he was naturally a fuming bustling little man, and could not remain passive when all the world was in a hurry. He worried from top to bottom of the castle with an air of infinite anxiety; he continually called the servants from their work to exhort them to be diligent; and buzzed about every hall and chamber, as idly restless and importunate as a bluebottle fly on a warm summer's day.

In the meantime the fatted calf had been killed; the forests had rung with the clamor of the huntsmen; the kitchen was crowded with good cheer; the cellars had yielded up whole oceans of *Rhein-wein* and *Ferne-wein*; and even the great Heidelberg tun had been laid under contribution. Everything was ready to receive the distinguished guest with *Saus und Braus* in the true spirit of German hospitality—but the guest delayed to make his appearance. Hour rolled after hour. The sun that had poured his downward rays upon the rich forest of the Odenwald now just gleamed along the summits of the mountains. The baron mounted the highest tower, and strained his eyes in hope of catching a distant sight of the count and his attendants. Once he thought he beheld them; the sound of horns came floating from the valley, prolonged by the mountain echoes. A number of horsemen were seen far below, slowly advancing along the road; but when they had nearly reached the foot of the mountain they suddenly struck off in a different direction. The last ray of sunshine departed—the bats began to flit by in the twilight—the road grew dimmer and dimmer to the view; and nothing appeared stirring in it but now and then a peasant lagging homeward from his labor.

While the old castle of Landshort was in this state of perplexity a very interesting scene was transacting in a different part of the Odenwald.

The young Count Von Altenburg was tranquilly pursuing his route in that sober jog-trot way, in which a man travels toward matrimony when his friends have taken all the trouble and uncertainty of courtship off his hands, and a bride is waiting for him as certainly as a dinner at the end of his journey. He had encountered at Würzburg a youthful companion in arms with whom he had seen some service on the frontiers, Herman Von Starkenfaust, one of the stoutest hands and worthiest hearts of German chivalry, who was now returning from the army. His father's castle was not far distant from the old fortress of Landshort, although an hereditary feud rendered the families hostile and strangers to each other.

In the warmhearted moment of recognition the young friends related all their past adventures and fortunes, and the count gave the whole history of his intended nuptials with a young lady whom he had never seen but of whose charms he had received the most enrapturing descriptions.

As the route of the friends lay in the same direction, they agreed to perform the rest of their journey together; and, that they might do it the more leisurely, set off from Würzburg at an early hour, the count having given directions for his retinue to follow and overtake him.

They beguiled their wayfaring with recollections of their military scenes and adventures; but the count was apt to be a little tedious, now and then, about the reputed charms of his bride, and the felicity that awaited him.

In this way they had entered among the mountains of the Odenwald, and were traversing one of its most lonely and thickly wooded passes. It is well known that the forests of Germany have always been as much infested by robbers as its castles by specters; and at this time the former were particularly numerous, from the hordes of disbanded soldiers wandering about the country. It will not appear extraordinary, therefore, that the cavaliers were attacked by a gang of these stragglers in the midst of the forest. They defended themselves with bravery, but were nearly overpowered, when the count's retinue arrived to their assistance. At sight of them the robbers fled, but not until the count had received a mortal wound. He was slowly and carefully conveyed back to the city of Würzburg, and a friar summoned from a neighboring convent, who was famous for his skill in administering to both soul and body; but half of his skill was superfluous; the moments of the unfortunate count were numbered.

With his dying breath he entreated his friend to repair instantly to the castle of Landshort and explain the fatal cause of his not keeping his appointment with his bride. Though not the most ardent of lovers, he was one of the most punctilious of men, and appeared earnestly solicitous that his mission should be speedily and courteously executed. "Unless this is done," said he, "I shall not sleep quietly in my grave!" He repeated these last words with peculiar solemnity. A request, at a moment so impressive, admitted no hesitation. Starkenfaust endeavored to soothe him to calmness, promised faithfully to execute his wish, and gave him his hand in solemn pledge. The dying man pressed it in acknowledgment, but soon lapsed into delirium—raved about his bride—his engagements—his plighted word; ordered his horse that he might ride to the castle of Landshort; and expired in the fancied act of vaulting into the saddle.

Starkenfaust bestowed a sigh and a soldier's tear on the untimely fate of his comrade, and then pondered on the awkward mission he had undertaken. His heart was heavy and his head perplexed, for he was to present himself an unbidden

guest among hostile people, and to damp their festivity with
tidings fatal to their hopes. Still there were certain whisperings
of curiosity in his bosom to see this far-famed beauty of
Katzenellenbogen, so cautiously shut up from the world, for
he was a passionate admirer of the sex, and there was a dash
of eccentricity and enterprise in his character that made him
fond of all singular adventure.

Previous to his departure he made all due arrangements with
the holy fraternity of the convent for the funeral solemnities of
his friend, who was to be buried in the cathedral of Würzburg,
near some of his illustrious relatives; and the mourning retinue
of the count took charge of his remains.

It is now high time that we should return to the ancient
family of Katzenellenbogen, who were impatient for their
guest, and still more for their dinner; and to the worthy little
baron, whom we left airing himself on the watchtower.

Night closed in, but still no guest arrived. The baron
descended from the tower in despair. The banquet, which
had been delayed from hour to hour, could no longer be
postponed. The meats were already overdone; the cook in an
agony; and the whole household had the look of a garrison that
had been reduced by famine. The baron was obliged reluctantly
to give orders for the feast without the presence of the guest. All
were seated at the table, and just on the point of commencing
when the sound of a horn from without the gate gave notice
of the approach of a stranger. Another long blast filled the old
courts of the castle with its echoes, and was answered by the
warder from the walls. The baron hastened to receive his future
son-in-law.

The drawbridge had been let down, and the stranger was
before the gate. He was a tall, gallant cavalier, mounted on a
black steed. His countenance was pale, but he had a beaming,
romantic eye, and an air of stately melancholy. The baron was
a little mortified that he should have come in this simple,
solitary style. His dignity for a moment was ruffled, and he
felt disposed to consider it a want of proper respect for the
important occasion and the important family with which he

was to be connected. He pacified himself, however, with the conclusion that it must have been youthful impatience which had induced him thus to spur on sooner than his attendants.

"I am sorry," said the stranger, "to break in upon you thus unseasonably—"

Here the baron interrupted him with a world of compliments and greetings, for, to tell the truth, he prided himself upon his courtesy and eloquence. The stranger attempted, once or twice to stem the torrent of words, but in vain, so he bowed his head and suffered it to flow on. By the time the baron had come to a pause, they had reached the inner court of the castle, and the stranger was again about to speak when he was once more interrupted by the appearance of the female part of the family, leading forth the shrinking and blushing bride. He gazed on her for a moment as one entranced; it seemed as if his whole soul beamed forth in the gaze, and rested upon that lovely form. One of the maiden aunts whispered something in her ear; she made an effort to speak; her moist blue eye was timidly raised, gave a shy glance of inquiry on the stranger, and was cast again to the ground. The words died away, but there was a sweet smile playing about her lips and a soft dimpling of the cheek that showed her glance had not been unsatisfactory. It was impossible for a girl of the fond age of eighteen, highly predisposed for love and matrimony, not to be pleased with so gallant a cavalier.

The late hour at which the guest had arrived left no time for parley. The baron was peremptory, and deferred all particular conversation until the morning, and led the way to the untasted banquet.

It was served up in the great hall of the castle. Around the walls hung the hard-favored portraits of the heroes of the house of Katzenellenbogen and the trophies which they had gained in the field and in the chase. Hacked corslets, splintered jousting spears, and tattered banners were mingled with the spoils of sylvan warfare; the jaws of the wolf and the tusks of the boar grinned horribly among cross-bows and battle-axes, and a huge pair of antlers branched immediately over the head of the youthful bridegroom.

The cavalier took but little notice of the company or the entertainment. He scarcely tasted the banquet, but seemed absorbed in admiration of his bride. He conversed in a low tone that could not be overheard—for the language of love is never loud; but where is the female ear so dull that it cannot catch the softest whisper of the lover? There was a mingled tenderness and gravity in his manner that appeared to have a powerful effect upon the young lady. Her color came and went as she listened with deep attention. Now and then she made some blushing reply, and when his eye was turned away, she would steal a sidelong glance at his romantic countenance and heave a gentle sigh of tender happiness. It was evident that the young couple were completely enamored. The aunts, who were deeply versed in the mysteries of the heart, declared that they had fallen in love with each other at first sight.

The feast went on merrily, or at least noisily, for the guests were all blessed with those keen appetites that attend upon light purses and mountain air. The baron told his best and longest stories, and never had he told them so well or with such great effect. If there was anything marvelous, his auditors were lost in astonishment; and if anything facetious, they were sure to laugh exactly in the right place. The baron, it is true, like most great men, was too dignified to utter any joke but a dull one; it was always enforced, however, by a bumper of excellent Hockheimer, and even a dull joke, at one's own table, served up with jolly old wine, is irresistible. Many good things were said by poorer and keener wits that would not bear repeating, except on similar occasions; many sly speeches whispered in ladies ears that almost convulsed them with suppressed laughter; and a song or two roared out by a poor but merry and broad-faced cousin of the baron that absolutely made the maiden aunts hold up their fans.

Amidst all this revelry, the stranger guest maintained a most singular and unseasonable gravity. His countenance assumed a deeper cast of dejection as the evening advanced; and, strange as it may appear, even the baron's jokes seemed only to render him the more melancholy. At times he was lost in thought, and at times there was a perturbed and restless wandering of the eye that bespoke a mind but ill at ease. His conversations with the bride became more and more earnest and mysterious. Lowering clouds began to steal over the fair serenity of her brow, and tremors to run through her tender frame.

All this could not escape the notice of the company. Their gaiety was chilled by the unaccountable gloom of the bridegroom; their spirits were infected; whispers and glances were interchanged, accompanied by shrugs and dubious shakes of the head. The song and the laugh grew less and less frequent; there were dreary pauses in the conversation, which were at length succeeded by wild tales and supernatural legends. One dismal story produced another still more dismal, and the baron nearly frightened some of the ladies into hysterics with the history of the goblin horseman that carried away the fair Leonora; a dreadful story, which has since been put into excellent verse, and is read and believed by all the world.

The bridegroom listened to this tale with profound attention. He kept his eyes steadily fixed on the baron, and, as the story drew to a close, began gradually to rise from his seat, growing taller and taller, until, in the baron's entranced eye, he seemed almost to tower into a giant. The moment the tale was finished, he heaved a deep sigh, and took a solemn farewell of the company. They were all amazement. The baron was perfectly thunderstruck.

"What! Going to leave the castle at midnight? Why, everything was prepared for his reception; a chamber was ready for him if he wished to retire."

The stranger shook his head mournfully and mysteriously. "I must lay my head in a different chamber tonight!"

There was something in this reply and the tone in which it was uttered that made the baron's heart misgive him, but he rallied his forces and repeated his hospitable entreaties.

The stranger shook his head silently, but positively, at every offer; and, waving his farewell to the company, stalked slowly

out of the hall. The maiden aunts were absolutely petrified—
the bride hung her head, and a tear stole to her eye.

The baron followed the stranger to the great court of the
castle, where the black charger stood pawing the earth, and
snorting with impatience. When they had reached the portal,
whose deep archway was dimly lighted by a cresset, the stranger paused, and addressed the baron in a hollow tone of voice,
which the vaulted roof rendered still more sepulchral.

"Now that we are alone," said he, "I will impart to you
the reason of my going. I have a solemn, an indispensable
engagement——"

"Why," said the baron, "cannot you send someone in your
place?"

"It admits of no substitute—I must attend it in person—I
must away to Würzburg cathedral——"

"Ay," said the baron, plucking up spirit, "but not until
tomorrow—tomorrow you shall take your bride there."

"No! no!" replied the stranger, with tenfold solemnity, "my
engagement is with no bride—the worms! The worms expect
me! I am a dead man—I have been slain by robbers—my body
lies at Würzburg—at midnight I am to be buried—the grave is
waiting for me—I must keep my appointment!"

He sprang on his black charger, dashed over the drawbridge,
and the clattering of his horse's hoofs was lost in the whistling
of the night blast.

The baron returned to the hall in the utmost consternation
and related what had passed. Two ladies fainted outright, others sickened at the idea of having banqueted with a specter. It
was the opinion of some that this might be the wild huntsman,
famous in German legend. Some talked of mountain sprites,
of wood demons, and of other supernatural beings, with which
the good people of Germany have been so grievously harassed
since time immemorial. One of the poor relations ventured to
suggest that it might be some sportive evasion of the young
cavalier, and that the very gloominess of the caprice seemed to
accord with so melancholy a personage. This, however, drew
on him the indignation of the whole company, and especially

of the baron, who looked upon him as little better than an infidel, so that he was fain to abjure his heresy as speedily as possible and come into the faith of the true believers.

But whatever may have been the doubts entertained, they were completely put to an end by the arrival, next day, of regular missives, confirming the intelligence of the young count's murder, and his interment in Würzburg cathedral.

The dismay at the castle may well be imagined. The baron shut himself up in his chamber. The guests, who had come to rejoice with him, could not think of abandoning him in his distress. They wandered about the courts, or collected in groups in the hall, shaking their heads and shrugging their shoulders at the troubles of so good a man; and sat longer than ever at table, and ate and drank more stoutly than ever, by way of keeping up their spirits. But the situation of the widowed bride was the most pitiable. To have lost a husband before she had even embraced him—and such a husband! If the very specter could be so gracious and noble, what must have been the living man? She filled the house with lamentations.

On the night of the second day of her widowhood, she had retired to her chamber, accompanied by one of her aunts, who insisted on sleeping with her. The aunt, who was one of the best tellers of ghost stories in all Germany, had just been recounting one of her longest, and had fallen asleep in the very midst of it. The chamber was remote, and overlooked a small garden. The niece lay pensively gazing at the beams of the rising moon, as they trembled on the leaves of an aspen tree before the lattice. The castle clock had just tolled midnight when a soft strain of music stole up from the garden. She rose hastily from her bed, and stepped lightly to the window. A tall figure stood among the shadows of the trees. As it raised its head, a beam of moonlight fell upon the countenance. Heaven on earth! She beheld the Specter Bridegroom! A loud shriek at that moment burst upon her ear, and her aunt, who had been awakened by the music and had followed her silently to the window, fell into her arms. When she looked again, the specter had disappeared.

Of the two females, the aunt now required the more sooth-
ing, for she was perfectly beside herself with terror. As to the
young lady, there was something, even in the specter of her
lover, that seemed endearing. There was still the semblance
of manly beauty; and though the shadow of a man is but little
calculated to satisfy the affections of a lovesick girl, yet, where
the substance is not to be had, even that is consoling. The aunt
declared she would never sleep in that chamber again; the
niece, for once, was refractory, and declared as strongly that
she would sleep in no other in the castle. The consequence was
that she had to sleep in it alone; but she drew a promise from
her aunt not to relate the story of the specter, lest she should
be denied the only melancholy pleasure left her on earth—that
of inhabiting the chamber over which the guardian shade of
her lover kept its nightly vigils.

How long the good old lady would have observed this promise is uncertain, for she dearly loved to talk of the marvelous,
and there is a triumph in being the first to tell a frightful story;
it is, however, still quoted in the neighborhood, as a memo-
rable instance of female secrecy, that she kept it to herself
for a whole week, when she was suddenly absolved from all
further restraint by intelligence brought to the breakfast table
one morning that the young lady was not to be found. Her
room was empty—the bed had not been slept in—the window
was open, and the bird had flown!

The astonishment and concern with which the intelligence
was received can only be imagined by those who have witnessed
the agitation which the mishaps of a great man cause among his
friends. Even the poor relations paused for a moment from the
indefatigable labors of the trencher, when the aunt, who had at
first been struck speechless, wrung her hands, and shrieked out,
"The goblin! The goblin! She's carried away by the goblin."

In a few words she related the fearful scene of the garden,
and concluded that the specter must have carried off his bride.
Two of the domestics corroborated the opinion, for they had
heard the clattering of a horse's hoofs down the mountain
about midnight, and had no doubt that it was the specter on his

black charger, bearing her away to the tomb. All present were struck with the direful probability, for events of the kind are extremely common in Germany, as many well-authenticated histories bear witness.

What a lamentable situation was that of the poor baron! What a heart-rending dilemma for a fond father, and a member of the great family of Katzenellenbogen! His only daughter had either been rapt away to the grave, or he was to have some wood demon for a son-in-law, and, perchance, a troop of goblin grandchildren. As usual, he was completely bewildered, and all the castle in an uproar. The men were ordered to take horse and scour every road and path and glen of the Odenwald. The baron himself had just drawn on his jack boots, girded on his sword, and was about to mount his steed to sally forth on the doubtful quest when he was brought to a pause by a new apparition. A lady was seen approaching the castle, mounted on a palfrey, attended by a cavalier on horseback. She galloped up to the gate, sprang from her horse, and, falling at the baron's feet, embraced his knees. It was his lost daughter and her companion—the Specter Bridegroom! The baron was astounded. He looked at his daughter, then at the specter, and almost doubted the evidence of his senses. The latter, too, was wonderfully improved in his appearance since his visit to the world of spirits. His dress was splendid, and set off a noble figure of manly symmetry. He was no longer pale and melancholy. His fine countenance was flushed with the glow of youth, and joy rioted in his large dark eye.

The mystery was soon cleared up. The cavalier (for, in truth, as you must have known all the while, he was no goblin) announced himself as Sir Herman Von Starkenfaust. He related his adventure with the young count. He told how he had hastened to the castle to deliver the unwelcome tidings, but that the eloquence of the baron had interrupted him in every attempt to tell his tale. How the sight of the bride had completely captivated him, and that to pass a few hours near her he had tacitly suffered the mistake to continue. How he had been sorely perplexed in what way to make a decent retreat, until the baron's goblin stories had suggested his eccentric exit. How, fearing the feudal hostility of the family, he had repeated his visits by stealth—had haunted the garden beneath the young lady's window—had wooed—had won—had borne away in triumph—and, in a word, had wedded the fair.

Under any other circumstances the baron would have been inflexible, for he was tenacious of paternal authority and devoutly obstinate in all family feuds; but he loved his daughter; he had lamented her as lost; he rejoiced to find her still alive; and, though her husband was of a hostile house, yet, thank Heaven, he was not a goblin. There was something, it must be acknowledged, that did not exactly accord with his notions of strict veracity, in the joke the knight had passed upon him of his being a dead man; but several old friends present, who had served in the wars, assured him that every stratagem was excusable in love, and that the cavalier was entitled to especial privilege, having lately served as a trooper.

Matters, therefore, were happily arranged. The baron pardoned the young couple on the spot. The revels at the castle were resumed. The poor relations overwhelmed this new member of the family with loving kindness; he was so gallant, so generous—and so rich. The aunts, it is true, were somewhat scandalized that their system of strict seclusion and passive obedience should be so badly exemplified, but attributed it all to their negligence in not having the windows grated. One of them was particularly mortified at having her marvelous story marred, and that the only specter she had ever seen should turn out a counterfeit; but the niece seemed perfectly happy at having found him substantial flesh and blood—and so the story ends.

THE WIFE

The treasures of the deep are not so precious
As are the conceal'd comforts of a man
Locked up in woman's love. I scent the air
Of blessings, when I come but near the house.
What a delicious breath marriage sends forth . . .
The violet bed's not sweeter.

MIDDLETON

I have often had occasion to remark the fortitude with which women sustain the most overwhelming reverses of fortune. Those disasters which break down the spirit of a man and prostrate him in the dust seem to call forth all the energies of the softer sex, and give such intrepedity and elevation to their character that at times it approaches to sublimity. Nothing can be more touching than to behold a soft and tender female, who had been all weakness and dependence and alive to every trivial roughness while treading the prosperous paths of life, suddenly rising in mental force to be the comforter and support of her husband under misfortune, and abiding with unshrinking firmness the bitterest blasts of adversity.

As the vine, which has long twined its graceful foliage about the oak and been lifted by it into sunshine, will, when the hardy plant is rifted by the thunderbolt, cling around it with its caressing tendrils and bind up its shattered boughs, so is it beautifully ordered by Providence, that woman, who is the mere dependent and ornament of man in his happier hours, should be his stay and solace when smitten with sudden calamity, winding herself into the rugged recesses of his nature, tenderly supporting the drooping head, and binding up the broken heart.

I was once congratulating a friend, who had around him a blooming family, knit together in the strongest affection. "I can wish you no better lot," said he, with enthusiasm, "than to have a wife and children. If you are prosperous, there they are to share your prosperity; if otherwise, there they are to comfort you." And, indeed, I have observed that a married man falling into misfortune is more apt to retrieve his situation in the world than a single one, partly because he is more stimulated to exertion by the necessities of the helpless and beloved beings who depend upon him for subsistence, but chiefly because his spirits are soothed and relieved by domestic endearments, and his self-respect kept alive by finding that, though all abroad is darkness and humiliation, yet there is still a little world of love at home, of which he is the monarch. Whereas a single man is apt to run to waste and self-neglect, to fancy himself lonely and abandoned, and his heart to fall to ruin like some deserted mansion for want of an inhabitant.

These observations call to mind a little domestic story, of which I was once a witness. My intimate friend, Leslie, had married a beautiful and accomplished girl who had been brought up in the midst of fashionable life. She had, it is true, no fortune, but that of my friend was ample; and he delighted in the anticipation of indulging her in every elegant pursuit and administering to those delicate tastes and fancies that spread a kind of witchery about the sex. "Her life," said he, "shall be like a fairy tale."

The very difference in their characters produced a harmonious combination: he was of a romantic and somewhat serious cast; she was all life and gladness. I have often noticed the mute rapture with which he would gaze upon her in company, of which her sprightly powers made her the delight; and how, in the midst of applause, her eye would still turn to him, as if there alone she sought favor and acceptance. When leaning on his arm, her slender form contrasted finely with his tall, manly person. The fond confiding air with which she looked up to him seemed to call forth a flush of triumphant pride and cherishing tenderness, as if he doted on his lovely burden for its very helplessness. Never did a couple set forward on the flowery path of early and well-suited marriage with a fairer prospect of felicity.

It was the misfortune of my friend, however, to have embarked his property in large speculations; and he had not been married many months when, by a succession of sudden disasters, it was swept from him, and he found himself reduced almost to penury. For a time he kept his situation to himself, and went about with a haggard countenance and a breaking heart. His life was but a protracted agony; and what rendered it more insupportable was the necessity of keeping up a smile in the presence of his wife, for he could not bring himself to overwhelm her with the news. She saw, however, with the quick eyes of affection that all was not well with him. She marked his altered looks and stifled sighs, and was not to be deceived by his sickly and vapid attempts at cheerfulness. She tasked all her sprightly powers and tender blandishments to win him back to happiness, but she only drove the arrow deeper into his soul. The more he saw cause to love her, the more torturing was the thought that he was soon to make her wretched. A little while, thought he, and the smile will vanish from that cheek—the song will die away from those lips—the luster of those eyes will be quenched with sorrow; and the happy heart, which now beats lightly in that bosom, will be weighed down like mine, by the cares and miseries of the world.

At length he came to me one day and related his whole situation in a tone of the deepest despair. When I heard him through, I inquired, "Does your wife know all this?" At the question he burst into an agony of tears. "For God's sake!" cried he, "if you have any pity on me, don't mention my wife; it is the thought of her that drives me almost to madness!"

"And why not?" said I. "She must know it sooner or later; you cannot keep it long from her, and the intelligence may break upon her in a more startling manner than if imparted by yourself, for the accents of those we love soften the hardest tidings. Besides, you are depriving yourself of the comforts of her sympathy; and not merely that, but also endangering the only bond that can keep hearts together—an unreserved community of thought and feeling. She will soon perceive that something is secretly preying upon your mind; and true love will not brook reserve; it feels undervalued and outraged when even the sorrows of those it loves are concealed from it."

"Oh, but, my friend! To think what a blow I am to give to all her future prospects—how I am to strike her very soul to the earth by telling her that her husband is a beggar! That she is to forego all the elegancies of life—all the pleasures of society—to shrink with me into indigence and obscurity! To tell her that I have dragged her down from the sphere in which she might have continued to move in constant brightness—the light of every eye—the admiration of every heart! How can she bear poverty? She has been brought up in all the refinements of opulence. How can she bear neglect? She has been the idol of society. Oh! It will break her heart—it will break her heart!"

I saw his grief was eloquent, and I let it have its flow, for sorrow relieves itself by words. When his paroxysm had subsided and he had relapsed into moody silence, I resumed the subject gently, and urged him to break his situation at once to his wife. He shook his head mournfully but positively.

"But how are you to keep it from her? It is necessary she should know it, that you may take the steps proper to the alteration of your circumstances. You must change your style of living—nay," observing a pang to pass across his countenance, "don't let that afflict you. I am sure you have never placed your happiness in outward show—you have yet friends, warm friends, who will not think the worse of you for being less splendidly lodged; and surely it does not require a palace to be happy with Mary——"

"I could be happy with her," cried he, convulsively, "in a hovel! I could go down with her into poverty and the dust! I could—I could—God bless her! God bless her!" cried he, bursting into a transport of grief and tenderness.

"And believe me, my friend," said I, stepping up and grasping him warmly by the hand, "believe me, she can be the same with you. Aye, more: it will be a source of pride and triumph to her—it will call forth all the latent energies and fervent sympathies of her nature, for she will rejoice to prove that she loves you for yourself. There is in every true woman's heart a spark of heavenly fire, which lies dormant in the broad daylight of prosperity, but which kindles up, and beams and blazes in the dark hour of adversity. No man knows what the wife of his bosom is—no man knows what a ministering angel she is—until he has gone with her through the fiery trials of this world."

There was something in the earnestness of my manner and the figurative style of my language that caught the excited imagination of Leslie. I knew the auditor I had to deal with; and following up the impression I had made, I finished by persuading him to go home and unburden his sad heart to his wife.

I must confess, notwithstanding all I had said, I felt some little solicitude for the result. Who can calculate on the fortitude of one whose life has been a round of pleasures? Her gay spirits might revolt at the dark downward path of low humility suddenly pointed out before her, and might cling to the sunny regions in which they had hitherto reveled. Besides, ruin in fashionable life is accompanied by so many galling mortifications, to which in other ranks it is a stranger. In short,

I could not meet Leslie the next morning without trepidation. He had made the disclosure.

"And how did she bear it?"

"Like an angel! It seemed rather to be a relief to her mind, for she threw her arms around my neck and asked if this was all that had lately made me unhappy. But, poor girl," added he, "she cannot realize the change we must undergo. She has no idea of poverty but in the abstract; she has only read of it in poetry, where it is allied to love. She feels as yet no privation; she suffers no loss of accustomed conveniences nor elegancies. When we come practically to experience its sordid cares, its paltry wants, its petty humiliations—then will be the real trial."

"But," said I, "now that you have got over the severest task, that of breaking it to her, the sooner you let the world into the secret the better. The disclosure may be mortifying, but then it is a single misery, and soon over; whereas you otherwise suffer it, in anticipation, every hour in the day. It is not poverty so much as pretense that harasses a ruined man—the struggle between a proud mind and an empty purse—the keeping up a hollow show that must soon come to an end. Have the courage to appear poor and you disarm poverty of its sharpest sting." On this point I found Leslie perfectly prepared. He had no false pride himself, and as to his wife, she was only anxious to conform to their altered fortunes.

Some days afterward he called upon me in the evening. He had disposed of his dwelling house and taken a small cottage in the country, a few miles from town. He had been busied all day in sending out furniture. The new establishment required few articles, and those of the simplest kind. All the splendid furniture of his late residence had been sold, excepting his wife's harp. That, he said, was too closely associated with the idea of herself; it belonged to the little story of their loves, for some of the sweetest moments of their courtship were those when he had leaned over that instrument and listened to the melting tones of her voice. I could not but smile at this instance of romantic gallantry in a doting husband.

He was now going out to the cottage, where his wife had been all day superintending its arrangement. My feelings had become strongly interested in the progress of this family story, and, as it was a fine evening, I offered to accompany him.

He was wearied with the fatigues of the day, and as he walked out fell into a fit of gloomy musing.

"Poor Mary!" at length broke, with a heavy sigh, from his lips.

"And what of her?" asked I. "Has anything happened to her?"

"What," said he, darting an impatient glance. "Is it nothing to be reduced to this paltry situation—to be caged in a miserable cottage—to be obliged to toil almost in the menial concerns of her wretched habitation?"

"Has she then repined at the change?"

"Repined! She has been nothing but sweetness and good humor. Indeed, she seems in better spirits than I have ever known her; she has been to me all love, and tenderness, and comfort!"

"Admirable girl!" exclaimed I. "You call yourself poor, my friend; you never were so rich—you never knew the boundless treasures of excellence you possess in that woman."

"Oh! But, my friend, if this first meeting at the cottage were over, I think I could then be comfortable. But this is her first day of real experience; she has been introduced into a humble dwelling, she has been employed all day in arranging its miserable equipments, she has for the first time known the fatigues of domestic employment, she has for the first time looked around her on a home destitute of everything elegant— almost of everything convenient—and may now be sitting down, exhausted and spiritless, brooding over a prospect of future poverty."

There was a degree of probability in this picture that I could not gainsay, so we walked on in silence.

After turning from the main road up a narrow lane so thickly shaded with forest trees as to give it a complete air of seclusion, we came in sight of the cottage. It was humble enough in its appearance for the most pastoral poet, and yet it had a pleasing rural look. A wild vine had overrrun one end with a profusion of foliage; a few trees threw their branches gracefully over it, and I observed several pots of flowers tastefully disposed about the door and on the grass plot in front. A small wicket gate opened upon a footpath that wound through some shrubbery to the door. Just as we approached, we heard the sound of music—Leslie grasped my arm; we paused and listened. It was Mary's voice singing, in a style of the most touching simplicity, a little air of which her husband was peculiarly fond.

I felt Leslie's hand tremble on my arm. He stepped forward to hear more distinctly. His step made a noise on the gravel walk. A bright, beautiful face glanced out at the window and vanished, a light footstep was heard, and Mary came tripping forth to meet us; she was in a pretty rural dress of white, a few wild flowers were twisted in her fine hair, a fresh bloom was on her cheek, her whole countenance beamed with smiles—I had never seen her look so lovely.

"My dear George," cried she, "I am so glad you are come! I have been watching and watching for you, and running down the lane, and looking out for you. I've set out a table under a beautiful tree behind the cottage, and I've been gathering some of the most delicious strawberries, for I know you are fond of them—and we have such excellent cream—and everything is so sweet and still here. . . . Oh!" said she, putting her arm within his and looking up brightly in his face. "Oh, we shall be so happy!"

Poor Leslie was overcome. He caught her to his bosom, he folded his arms around her, he kissed her again and again—he could not speak, but the tears gushed into his eyes; and he has often assured me that, though the world has since gone prosperously with him, and his life has, indeed, been a happy one, yet never has he experienced a moment of more exquisite felicity.

THE VOYAGE

Ships, ships, I will descrie you
  Amidst the main,
I will come and try you,
What you are protecting,
And projecting,
  Whats your end and aim.
One goes abroad for merchandise and trading,
Another stays to keep his country from invading,
A third is coming home with rich and wealthy lading.
  Halloo! my fancie, whither wilt thou go?

OLD POEM

To an American visiting Europe, the long voyage he has to
make is an excellent preparative. The temporary absence of
worldly scenes and employments produces a state of mind
peculiarly fitted to receive new and vivid impressions. The vast
space of waters that separates the hemispheres is like a blank
page in existence. There is no gradual transition, by which, as
in Europe, the features and population of one country blend

almost imperceptibly with those of another. From the moment you lose sight of the land you have left, all is vacancy until you step on the opposite shore and are launched at once into the bustle and novelties of another world.

In traveling by land, there is a continuity of scene and a connected succession of persons and incidents that carry on the story of life and lessen the effect of absence and separation. We drag, it is true, "a lengthening chain" at each remove of our pilgrimage; but the chain is unbroken: we can trace it back link by link, and we feel that the last still grapples us to home. But a wide sea voyage severs us at once. It makes us conscious of being cast loose from the secure anchorage of settled life, and sent adrift upon a doubtful world. It interposes a gulf, not merely imaginary but real, between us and our homes—a gulf subject to tempest and fear and uncertainty, rendering distance palpable and return precarious.

Such, at least, was the case with myself. As I saw the last blue line of my native land fade away like a cloud in the horizon, it seemed as if I had closed one volume of the world and its concerns, and had time for meditation before I opened another. That land, too, now vanishing from my view, which contained all most dear to me in life; what vicissitudes might occur in it, what changes might take place in me before I should visit it again! Who can tell, when he sets forth to wander, whither he may be driven by the uncertain currents of existence, or when he may return, or whether it may be his lot to revisit the scenes of his childhood?

I said that at sea all is vacancy; I should correct the expression. To one given to daydreaming and fond of losing himself in reveries, a sea voyage is full of subjects for meditation; but then they are the wonders of the deep and of the air, and rather tend to abstract the mind from worldly themes. I delighted to loll over the quarter railing, or climb to the maintop, of a calm day, and muse for hours together on the tranquil bosom of a summer's sea; to gaze upon the piles of golden clouds just peering above the horizon, fancy them some fairy realms, and people them with a creation of my own; to watch the gentle undulating billows, rolling their silver volumes, as if to die away on those happy shores.

There was a delicious sensation of mingled security and awe with which I looked down from my giddy height on the monsters of the deep at their uncouth gambols. Shoals of porpoises tumbling about the bow of the ship, the grampus slowly heaving his huge form above the surface, or the ravenous shark, darting, like a specter, through the blue waters. My imagination would conjure up all that I had heard or read of the watery world beneath me, of the finny herds that roam its fathomless valleys, of the shapeless monsters that lurk among the very foundations of the earth, and of those wild phantasms that swell the tales of fishermen and sailors.

Sometimes a distant sail, gliding along the edge of the ocean, would be another theme of idle speculation. How interesting this fragment of a world, hastening to rejoin the great mass of existence! What a glorious monument of human invention, which has in a manner triumphed over wind and wave; has brought the ends of the world into communion; has established an interchange of blessings, pouring into the sterile regions of the north all the luxuries of the south; has diffused the light of knowledge and the charities of cultivated life; and has thus bound together those scattered portions of the human race, between which nature seemed to have thrown an insurmountable barrier.

We one day descried some shapeless object drifting at a distance. At sea, everything that breaks the monotony of the surrounding expanse attracts attention. It proved to be the mast of a ship that must have been completely wrecked, for there were the remains of handkerchiefs by which some of the crew had fastened themselves to this spar to prevent their being washed off by the waves. There was no trace by which the name of the ship could be ascertained. The wreck had evidently drifted about for many months; clusters of shellfish had fastened about it, and long seaweeds flaunted at its sides. But where, thought I, is the crew? Their struggle has long been over—they have gone down amidst the roar of the tempest—their bones lie whitening among the caverns of the deep. Silence, oblivion, like the waves, have closed over them, and no one can tell the story of their end. What sighs have been wafted after that ship! What prayers offered up at the deserted fireside of home! How often has the mistress, the wife, the mother, pored over the daily news, to catch some casual intelligence of this rover of the deep! How has expectation darkened into anxiety—anxiety into dread—and dread into despair! Alas! Not one memento may ever return for love to cherish. All that may ever be known is that she sailed from her port, "and was never heard of more!"

The sight of this wreck, as usual, gave rise to many dismal anecdotes. This was particularly the case in the evening, when the weather, which had hitherto been fair, began to look wild and threatening, and gave indications of one of those sudden storms which will sometimes break in upon the serenity of a summer voyage. As we sat around the dull light of a lamp in the cabin that made the gloom more ghastly, everyone had his tale of shipwreck and disaster. I was particularly struck with a short one related by the captain.

"As I was once sailing," said he, "in a fine, stout ship across the banks of Newfoundland, one of those heavy fogs which prevail in those parts rendered it impossible for us to see far ahead even in the daytime; but at night the weather was so thick that we could not distinguish any object at twice the length of the ship. I kept lights at the masthead, and a constant watch forward to look out for fishing smacks, which are accustomed to lie at anchor on the banks. The wind was blowing a smacking breeze, and we were going at a great rate through the water. Suddenly the watch gave the alarm of 'a sail ahead!' It was scarcely uttered before we were upon her. She was a small schooner, at anchor, with her broadside toward us. The crew were all asleep, and had neglected to hoist a light. We struck her just amidships. The force, the size, the weight of our vessel bore her down below the waves; we passed over her and were hurried on our course. As the crashing wreck was sinking beneath us, I had a glimpse of two or three half-naked wretches rushing from her cabin; they just started from their beds to be swallowed shrieking by the waves. I heard their drowning cry mingling with the wind. The blast that bore it to our ears swept us out of all farther hearing. I shall never forget that cry! It was some time before we could put the ship about, she was under such headway. We returned, as nearly as we could guess, to the place where the smack had anchored. We cruised about for several hours in the dense fog. We fired signal guns and listened if we might hear the halloo of any survivors, but all was silent—we never saw or heard anything of them more."

I confess these stories, for a time, put an end to all my fine fancies. The storm increased with the night. The sea was lashed into tremendous confusion. There was a fearful, sullen sound of rushing waves and broken surges. Deep called unto deep. At times the black column of clouds overhead seemed rent asunder by flashes of lightning, which quivered along the foaming billows and made the succeeding darkness doubly terrible. The thunders bellowed over the wild waste of waters, and were echoed and prolonged by the mountain waves. As I saw the ship staggering and plunging among these roaring caverns, it seemed miraculous that she regained her balance or preserved her buoyancy. Her yards would dip into the water: her bow was almost buried beneath the waves. Sometimes an impending surge appeared ready to overwhelm her, and nothing but a dexterous movement of the helm preserved her from the shock.

When I retired to my cabin, the awful scene still followed me. The whistling of the wind through the rigging sounded like funereal wailings. The creaking of the masts, the straining and groaning of bulkheads as the ship labored in the weltering sea were frightful. As I heard the waves rushing along the sides of the ship and roaring in my very ear, it seemed as if Death were raging around this floating prison, seeking for his prey: the mere starting of a nail, the yawning of a seam, might give him entrance.

A fine day, however, with a tranquil sea and favoring breeze, soon put all these dismal reflections to flight. It is impossible to

resist the gladdening influence of fine weather and fair wind
at sea. When the ship is decked out in her canvas, every sail
swelled, and careering gaily over the curling waves, how
lofty, how gallant she appears—how she seems to lord it over
the deep!

I might fill a volume with the reveries of a sea voyage, for
with me it is almost a continual reverie—but it is time to get
to shore.

It was a fine sunny morning when the thrilling cry of
"land!" was given from the masthead. None but those who
have experienced it can form an idea of the delicious throng of
sensations which rush into an American's bosom when he first
comes in sight of Europe. There is a volume of associations
with the very name. It is the land of promise, teeming with
everything of which his childhood has heard or on which his
studious years have pondered.

From that time until the moment of arrival, it was all feverish excitement. The ships of war that prowled like guardian
giants along the coast; the headlands of Ireland, stretching
out into the channel; the Welsh mountains, towering into the
clouds; all were objects of intense interest. As we sailed up the
Mersey, I reconnoitered the shores with a telescope. My eye
dwelt with delight on neat cottages, with their trim shrubberies
and green grass plots. I saw the moldering ruin of an abbey
overrun with ivy, and the taper spire of a village church rising
from the brow of a neighboring hill—all were characteristic of
England.

The tide and wind were so favorable that the ship was
enabled to come at once to the pier. It was thronged with people; some, idle lookers-on, others, eager expectants of friends
or relatives. I could distinguish the merchant to whom the
ship was consigned. I knew him by his calculating brow
and restless air. His hands were thrust into his pockets; he
was whistling thoughtfully, and walking to and fro, a small
space having been accorded him by the crowd, in deference
to his temporary importance. There were repeated cheerings
and salutations interchanged between the shore and the ship

as friends happened to recognize each other. I particularly noticed one young woman of humble dress but interesting demeanor. She was leaning forward from among the crowd; her eye hurried over the ship as it neared the shore to catch some wished-for countenance. She seemed disappointed and agitated, when I heard a faint voice call her name. It was from a poor sailor who had been ill all the voyage and had excited the sympathy of everyone on board. When the weather was fine, his messmates had spread a mattress for him on deck in the shade, but of late his illness had so increased that he had taken to his hammock, and only breathed a wish that he might see his wife before he died. He had been helped on deck as we came up the river, and was now leaning against the shrouds, with a countenance so wasted, so pale, so ghastly that it was no wonder even the eye of affection did not recognize him. But at the sound of his voice, her eye darted on his features; it read, at once, a whole volume of sorrow; she clasped her hands, uttered a faint shriek, and stood wringing them in silent agony.

All now was hurry and bustle. The meetings of acquaintances—the greetings of friends—the consultations of men of business. I alone was solitary and idle. I had no friend to meet, no cheering to receive. I stepped upon the land of my forefathers—but felt that I was a stranger in the land.

THE DEVIL AND TOM WALKER

A few miles from Boston in Massachusetts, there is a deep inlet, winding several miles into the interior of the country from Charles Bay, and terminating in a thickly-wooded swamp or morass. On one side of this inlet is a beautiful dark grove; on the opposite side the land rises abruptly from the water's edge into a high ridge, on which grow a few scattered oaks of great age and immense size. Under one of these gigantic trees, according to old stories, there was a great amount of treasure buried by Kidd the pirate. The inlet allowed a facility to bring the money in a boat secretly and at night to the very foot of the hill; the elevation of the place permitted a good lookout to be kept that no one was at hand; while the remarkable trees formed good landmarks by which the place might easily be found again. The old stories add, moreover, that the devil presided at the hiding of the money, and took it under his guardianship; but this, it is well known, he always does with buried treasure, particularly when it has been ill-gotten. Be that as it may, Kidd never returned to recover his wealth; being shortly after seized at Boston, sent out to England, and there hanged for a pirate.

About the year 1727, just at the time that earthquakes were prevalent in New England, and shook many tall sinners down upon their knees, there lived near this place a meagre, miserly fellow, of the name of Tom Walker. He had a wife as miserly as himself: they were so miserly that they even conspired to cheat each other. Whatever the woman could lay hands on, she hid away; a hen could not cackle but she was on the alert to secure the new-laid egg. Her husband was continually prying about to detect her secret hoards, and many and fierce were the conflicts that took place about what ought to have been common property. They lived in a forlorn-looking house that stood alone, and had an air of starvation. A few straggling savin-trees, emblems of sterility, grew near it; no smoke ever curled from its chimney; no traveller stopped at its door. A miserable horse, whose ribs were as articulate as the bars of a gridiron, stalked about a field, where a thin carpet of moss, scarcely covering the ragged beds of puddingstone, tantalized and balked his hunger; and sometimes he would lean his head over the fence, look piteously at the passerby, and seem to petition deliverance from this land of famine.

The house and its inmates had altogether a bad name. Tom's wife was a tall termagant, fierce of temper, loud of tongue, and strong of arm. Her voice was often heard in wordy warfare with her husband; and his face sometimes showed signs that their conflicts were not confined to words. No one ventured, however, to interfere between them. The lonely wayfarer shrunk within himself at the horrid clamor and clapper-clawing; eyed the den of discord askance; and hurried on his way, rejoicing, if a bachelor; in his celibacy.

One day that Tom Walker had been to a distant part of the neighborhood, he took what he considered a short cut homeward, through the swamp. Like most short cuts, it was an ill-chosen route. The swamp was thickly grown with great gloomy pines and hemlocks, some of them ninety feet high, which made it dark at noonday, and a retreat for all the owls of the neighborhood. It was full of pits and quagmires, partly covered with weeds and mosses, where the green surface often betrayed the traveller into a gulf of black, smothering mud: there were also dark and stagnant pools, the abodes of the tadpole, the bull-frog, and the water-snake; where the trunks of pines and hemlocks lay half drowned, half rotting, looking like alligators sleeping in the mire.

Tom had long been picking his way cautiously through this treacherous forest; stepping from tuft to tuft of rushes and roots, which afforded precarious footholds among deep sloughs; or pacing carefully, like a cat, along the prostrate trunks of trees; startled now and then by the sudden screaming of the bittern, or the quacking of wild duck rising on the wind from some solitary pool. At length he arrived at a firm piece of ground, which ran out like a peninsula into the deep bosom of the swamp. It had been one of the strongholds of the Indians during their wars with the first colonists. Here they had thrown up a kind of fort, which they had looked upon as almost impregnable and had used as a place of refuge for their squaws and children. Nothing remained of the old Indian fort but a few embankments, gradually sinking to the level of the surrounding earth, and already overgrown in part by oaks and other forest trees, the foliage of which formed a contrast to the dark pines and hemlocks of the swamp.

It was late in the dusk of evening when Tom Walker reached the old fort, and he paused there awhile to rest himself. Any one but he would have felt unwilling to linger in this lonely, melancholy place, for the common people had a bad opinion of it, from the stories handed down from the time of the Indian wars; when it was asserted that the savages held incantations here, and made sacrifices to the evil spirit.

Tom Walker, however, was not a man to be troubled with any fears of the kind. He reposed himself for some time on the trunk of a fallen hemlock, listening to the boding cry of the tree-toad, and delving with his walking-staff into a mound of black mould at his feet. As he turned up the soil unconsciously, his staff struck against something hard. He raked it out of the vegetable mould, and lo! a cloven skull, with an Indian tomahawk buried deep in it, lay before him. The rust on the weapon showed the time that had elapsed since this death-blow had been given. It was a dreary memento of the fierce struggle that had taken place in this last foothold of the Indian warriors.

"Humph!" said Tom Walker, as he gave it a kick to shake the dirt from it.

"Let that skull alone!" said a gruff voice. Tom lifted up his eyes, and beheld a great black man seated directly opposite him, on the stump of a tree. He was exceedingly surprised, having neither heard nor seen any one approach; and he was still more perplexed on observing, as well as the gathering gloom would permit, that the stranger was neither Negro nor Indian. It is true he was dressed in a rude half Indian garb, and had a red belt or sash swathed round his body! but his face was neither black nor copper-color, but swarthy and dingy, and begrimed with soot, as if he had been accustomed to toil among fires and forges. He had a shock of coarse black hair, that stood out from his head in all directions, and bore an axe on his shoulder.

He scowled for a moment at Tom with a pair of great red eyes.

"What are you doing on my grounds?" said the black man, with a hoarse, growling voice.

"Your grounds!" said Tom, with a sneer, "no more your grounds than mine; they belong to Deacon Peabody."

"Deacon Peabody be d——d," said the stranger, "as I flatter myself he will be, if he does not look more to his own sins and less to those of his neighbors. Look yonder, and see how Deacon Peabody is faring."

Tom looked in the direction that the stranger pointed, and beheld one of the great trees, fair and flourishing without, but rotten at the core, and saw that it had been nearly hewn through, so that the first high wind was likely to blow it down. On the bark of the tree was scored the name of Deacon Peabody, an eminent man, who had waxed wealthy by driving shrewd bargains with the Indians. He now looked around, and found most of the tall trees marked with the name of some great man of the colony, and all more or less scored by the axe. The one on which he had been seated, and which had evidently just been hewn down, bore the name of Crowninshield; and he recollected a mighty rich man of that name, who made a vulgar display of wealth, which it was whispered he had acquired by buccaneering.

"He's just ready for burning!" said the black man, with a growl of triumph. "You see I am likely to have a good stock of firewood for winter."

"But what right have you," said Tom, "to cut down Deacon Peabody's timber?"

"The right of a prior claim," said the other. "This woodland belonged to me long before one of your white-faced race put foot upon the soil."

"And pray, who are you, if I may be so bold?" said Tom.

"Oh, I go by various names. I am the wild huntsman in some countries; the black miner in others. In this neighborhood I am he to whom the red men consecrated this spot, and in honor of whom they now and then roasted a white man, by way of sweet-smelling sacrifice. Since the red men have been exterminated by you white savages, I amuse myself by presiding at the persecutions of Quakers and Anabaptists; I am the great patron and prompter of slave-dealers, and the grand-master of the Salem witches."

"The upshot of all which is, that, if I mistake not," said Tom, sturdily, "you are he commonly called Old Scratch."

"The same, at your service!" replied the black man, with a half civil nod.

Such was the opening of this interview, according to the old story; though it has almost too familiar an air to be credited. One would think that to meet with such a singular personage, in this wild, lonely place, would have shaken any man's nerves; but Tom was a hard-minded fellow, not easily daunted, and he had lived so long with a termagant wife, that he did not even fear the devil.

It is said that after this commencement they had a long and earnest conversation together, as Tom returned homeward. The black man told him of great sums of money buried by Kidd the pirate, under the oak-trees on the high ridge, not far from the morass. All these were under his command, and protected by his power, so that none could find them but such as propitiated his favor. These he offered to place within Tom Walker's reach, having conceived an especial kindness for him; but they were to be had only on certain conditions. What these conditions were may be easily surmised, though Tom never disclosed them publicly. They must have been very hard, for he required time to think of them, and he was not a man to stick at trifles when money was in view. When they had reached the edge of the swamp, the stranger paused. "What proof have I that all you have been telling me is true?" said Tom. "There's my signature," said the black man, pressing his finger on Tom's forehead. So saying, he turned off among the thickest of the swamp, and seemed, as Tom said, to go down, down, down, into the earth, until nothing but his head and shoulders could be seen, and so on, until he totally disappeared.

When Tom reached home, he found the black print of a finger burnt, as it were, into his forehead, which nothing could obliterate.

The first news his wife had to tell him was the sudden death of Absalom Crowninshield, the rich buccaneer. It was announced in the papers with the usual flourish, that "A great man had fallen in Israel."

Tom recollected the tree which his black friend had just hewn down, and which was ready for burning. "Let the free-booter roast," said Tom; "who cares!" He now felt convinced that all he had heard and seen was no illusion.

He was not prone to let his wife into his confidence; but as this was an uneasy secret, he willingly shared it with her. All her avarice was awakened at the mention of hidden gold, and she urged her husband to comply with the black man's terms, and secure what would make them wealthy for life. However Tom might have felt disposed to sell himself to the devil, he was determined not to do so to oblige his wife; so he flatly refused, out of the mere spirit of contradiction. Many and bitter were the quarrels they had on the subject; but the more she talked, the more resolute was Tom not to be damned to please her.

At length she determined to drive the bargain on her own account, and if she succeeded, to keep all the gain to herself. Being of the same fearless temper as her husband, she set off for the old Indian fort towards the close of a summer's day. She was many hours absent. When she came back, she was reserved and sullen in her replies. She spoke something of a black man, whom she met about twilight hewing at the root of a tall tree. He was sulky, however, and would not come to terms; she was to go again with a propitiatory offering, but what it was she forbore to say.

The next evening she set off again for the swamp, with her apron heavily laden. Tom waited and waited for her, but in vain; midnight came, but she did not make her appearance: morning, noon, night returned, but still she did not come. Tom now grew uneasy for her safety, especially as he found she had carried off in her apron the silver tea-pot and spoons, and every portable article of value. Another night elapsed, another morning came; but no wife. In a word, she was never heard of more.

What was her real fate nobody knows, in consequence of so many pretending to know. It is one of those facts which have become confounded by a variety of historians. Some asserted that she lost her way among the tangled mazes of the swamp, and sank into some pit or slough; others, more uncharitable, hinted that she had eloped with the household booty, and made off to some other province; while others surmised that the tempter had decoyed her into a dismal quagmire, on the top of which her hat was found lying. In confirmation of this, it was said a great black man, with an axe on his shoulder, was seen late that very evening coming out of the swamp, carrying a bundle tied in a check apron, with an air of surly triumph.

The most current and probable story, however, observes, that Tom Walker grew so anxious about the fate of his wife and his property, that he set out at length to seek them both at the Indian fort. During a long summer's afternoon he searched about the gloomy place, but no wife was to be seen. He called her name repeatedly, but she was nowhere to be heard. The bittern alone responded to his voice, as they flew screaming by; or the bullfrog croaked dolefully from a neighboring pool. At length, it is said, just in the brown hour of twilight, when the owls began to hoot, and the bats to flit about, his attention was attracted by the clamor of carrion crows hovering about a cypress-tree. He looked up, and beheld a bundle tied in a check apron, and hanging in the branches of the tree, with a great vulture perched hard by, as if keeping watch upon it. He leaped with joy; for he recognized his wife's apron, and supposed it to contain the household valuables.

"Let us get hold of the property," said he, consolingly to himself, "and we will endeavor to do without the woman."

As he scrambled up the tree, the vulture spread its wide wings, and sailed off screaming, into the deep shadows of the forest. Tom seized the checked apron, but, woful sight! found nothing but a heart and liver tied up in it!

Such, according to this most authentic old story, was all that was to be found of Tom's wife. She had probably attempted to deal with the black man as she had been accustomed to deal with her husband; but though a female scold is generally considered a match for the devil, yet in this instance she appears to have had the worst of it. She must have died game, however; for it is said Tom noticed many prints of cloven feet stamped upon the tree, and found handfuls of hair, that looked as if they had been plucked from the coarse black shock of the woodman. Tom knew his wife's prowess by experience. He shrugged his shoulders, as he looked at the signs of a fierce, clapper-clawing. "Egad," said he to himself, "Old Scratch must have had a tough time of it!"

Tom consoled himself for the loss of his property with the loss of his wife, for he was a man of fortitude. He even felt something like gratitude towards the black woodman, who, he considered, had done him a kindness. He sought, therefore, to cultivate a further acquaintance with him, but for some time without success; the old black-legs played shy, for whatever people may think, he is not always to be had for calling for: he knows how to play his cards when pretty sure of his game.

At length, it is said, when delay had whetted Tom's eagerness to the quick, and prepared him to agree to anything rather than not gain the promised treasure, he met the black man one evening in his usual woodman's dress, with his axe on his shoulder, sauntering along the swamp, and humming a tune. He affected to receive Tom's advances with great indifference, made brief replies, and went on humming his tune.

By degrees, however, Tom brought him to business, and they began to haggle about the terms on which the former was to have the pirate's treasure. There was one condition which need not be mentioned, being generally understood in all cases where the devil grants favors; but there were others about which, though of less importance, he was inflexibly obstinate. He insisted that the money found through his means should be employed in his service. He proposed, therefore, that Tom should employ it in the black traffic; that is to say, that he should fit out a slave-ship. This, however, Tom resolutely refused: he was bad enough in all conscience; but the devil himself could not tempt him to turn slave-trader.

Finding Tom so squeamish on this point, he did not insist upon it, but proposed, instead, that he should turn usurer; the devil being extremely anxious for the increase of usurers, looking upon them as his peculiar people.

To this no objections were made, for it was just to Tom's taste.

"You shall open a broker's shop in Boston next month," said the black man.

"I'll do it to-morrow if you wish," said Tom Walker.

"You shall lend money at two per cent a month."

"Egad, I'll charge four!" replied Tom Walker.

"You shall extort bonds, foreclose mortgages, drive the merchants to bankruptcy"—

"I'll drive them to the d——l," cried Tom Walker.

"You are the usurer for my money!" said black-legs with delight. "When will you want the rhino?"

"This very night."

"Done!" said the devil.

"Done!" said Tom Walker.—So they shook hands and struck a bargain.

A few days time saw Tom Walker seated behind his desk in a counting-house in Boston.

His reputation for a ready-moneyed man, who would lend money out for a good consideration, soon spread abroad. Everybody remembers the time of Governor Belcher, when money was particularly scarce. It was a time of paper credit. The country had been deluged with government bills, the famous Land Bank had been established; there had been a rage for speculating; the people had run mad with schemes for new settlements; for building cities in the wilderness; land-jobbers went about with maps of grants, and townships, and Eldorados, lying nobody knew where, but which everybody was ready to purchase. In a word, the great speculating fever which breaks out every now and then in the country, had raged to an alarming degree, and everybody was dreaming of making sudden fortunes from nothing. As usual the fever had subsided; the dream had gone off, and the imaginary fortunes with it; the patients were left in doleful plight, and the whole country resounded with the consequent cry of "hard times."

At this propitious time of public distress did Tom Walker set up as usurer in Boston. His door was soon thronged by customers. The needy and adventurous; the gambling speculator; the dreaming land-jobber; the thriftless tradesman; the merchant with cracked credit; in short, every one driven to raise money by desperate means and desperate sacrifices, hurried to Tom Walker.

Thus Tom was the universal friend of the needy, and acted like a "friend in need"; that is to say, he always exacted good

pay and good security. In proportion to the distress of the appli-
cant was the hardness of his terms. He accumulated bonds and
mortgages; gradually squeezed his customers closer and closer:
and sent them at length, dry as a sponge, from his door.

In this way he made money hand over hand; became a rich
and mighty man, and exalted his cocked hat upon 'Change.
He built himself, as usual, a vast house, out of ostentation;
but left the greater part of it unfinished and unfurnished, out
of parsimony. He even set up a carriage in the fullness of his
vain-glory, though he nearly starved the horses which drew
it; and as the ungreased wheels groaned and screeched on the
axle-trees, you would have thought you heard the souls of the
poor debtors he was squeezing.

As Tom waxed old, however, he grew thoughtful. Having
secured the good things of this world, he began to feel anxious
about those of the next. He thought with regret on the bargain
he had made with his black friend, and set his wits to work
to cheat him out of the conditions. He became, therefore, all
of a sudden, a violent church-goer. He prayed loudly and
strenuously, as if heaven were to be taken by force of lungs.
Indeed, one might always tell when he had sinned most during
the week, by the clamor of his Sunday devotion. The quiet
Christians who had been modestly and steadfastly traveling
Zionward, were struck with self-reproach at seeing themselves
so suddenly outstripped in their career by this new-made con-
vert. Tom was as rigid in religious as in money matters; he was
a stern supervisor and censurer of his neighbors, and seemed
to think every sin entered up to their account became a credit
on his own side of the page. He even talked of the expediency
of reviving the persecution of Quakers and Anabaptists. In a
word, Tom's zeal became as notorious as his riches.

Still, in spite of all this strenuous attention to forms, Tom
had a lurking dread that the devil, after all, would have his
due. That he might not be taken unawares, therefore, it is
said he always carried a small Bible in his coat-pocket. He
had also a great folio Bible on his counting house desk, and
would frequently be found reading it when people called on

business; on such occasions he would lay his green spectacles in the book, to mark the place, while he turned round to drive some usurious bargain.

Some say that Tom grew a little crack-brained in his old days, and that, fancying his end approaching, he had his horse new shod, saddled and bridled, and buried with his feet uppermost; because he supposed that at the last day the world would be turned upside-down; in which case he should find his horse standing ready for mounting, and he was determined at the worst to give his old friend a run for it. This, however, is probably a mere old wives' fable. If he really did take such a precaution, it was totally superfluous; at least so says the authentic old legend, which closes his story in the following manner:

One hot summer afternoon in the dog-days, just as a terrible black thunder gust was coming up, Tom sat in his counting-house, in his white cap and India silk morning gown. He was on the point of foreclosing a mortgage, by which he would complete the ruin of an unlucky land-speculator for whom he had professed the greatest friendship. The poor land-jobber begged him to grant a few months' indulgence. Tom had grown testy and irritated, and refused another day.

"My family will be ruined and brought upon the parish," said the land-jobber. "Charity begins at home," replied Tom; "I must take care of myself in these hard times."

"You have made so much money out of me," said the speculator.

Tom lost his patience and his piety. "The devil take me," said he, "if I have made a farthing!"

Just then there were three loud knocks at the street door. He stepped out to see who was there. A black man was holding a black horse, which neighed and stamped with impatience.

"Tom, you're come for," said the black fellow, gruffly. Tom shrank back, but too late. He had left his little Bible at the bottom of his coat-pocket, and his big Bible on the desk buried under the mortgage he was about to foreclose; never was a sinner taken more unawares. The black man whisked him like a child into the saddle, gave the horse the lash, and away he galloped, with Tom on his back, in the midst of the thunderstorm. The clerks stuck their pens behind their ears, and stared after him from the windows. Away went Tom Walker, dashing down the streets; his white cap bobbing up and down; his morning-gown fluttering in the wind, and his steed striking fire out of the pavement at every bound. When the clerks turned to look for the black man, he had disappeared.

Tom Walker never returned to foreclose the mortgage. A countryman, who lived on the border of the swamp, reported that in the height of the thundergust he had heard a great clattering of hoofs and a howling along the road, and running to the window caught sight of a figure, such as I have described, on a horse that galloped like mad across the fields, over the hills, and down into the black hemlock swamp towards the old Indian fort; and that shortly after a thunder-bolt falling in that direction seemed to set the whole forest in a blaze.

The good people of Boston shook their heads and shrugged their shoulders, but had been so much accustomed to witches and goblins, and tricks of the devil, in all kinds of shapes, from the first settlement of the colony, that they were not so much horror-struck as might have been expected. Trustees were appointed to take charge of Tom's effects. There was nothing, however, to administer upon. On searching his coffers, all his bonds and mortgages were found reduced to cinders. In place of gold and silver, his iron chest was filled with chips and shavings; two skeletons lay in his stable instead of his half-starved horses, and the very next day his great house took fire and burnt to the ground.

Such was the end of Tom Walker and his ill-gotten wealth. Let all griping money-brokers lay this story to heart. The truth of it is not to be doubted. The very hole under the oak-trees whence he dug Kidd's money is to be seen to this day; and the neighboring swamp and old Indian fort are often haunted in stormy nights by a figure on horseback, in morning-gown and white cap, which is doubtless the troubled spirit of the usurer. In fact the story has resolved itself into a proverb; prevalent throughout New England, of "The Devil and Tom Walker."

THE ADVENTURE OF THE MASON

"There was once upon a time a poor mason, or bricklayer, in Granada, who kept all the saints' days and holidays, and Saint Monday into the bargain, and yet, with all his devotion, he grew poorer and poorer, and could scarcely earn bread for his numerous family. One night, he was roused from his first sleep by a knocking at his door. He opened it, and beheld before him a tall, meagre, cadaverous-looking priest.

" 'Hark ye, honest friend!' said the stranger; 'I have observed that you are a good Christian, and one to be trusted; will you undertake a job this very night?'

" 'With all my heart, Señor Padre, on condition that I am paid accordingly.'

" 'That you shall be; but you must suffer yourself to be blindfolded.'

"To this the mason made no objection. So, being hood-winked, he was led by the priest through various rough lanes and winding passages, until they stopped before the portal of a house. The priest then applied a key, turned a creaking lock, and opened what sounded like a ponderous door. They entered, the door was closed and bolted, and the mason was conducted through an echoing corridor and a spacious hall to an interior part of the building. Here the bandage was removed from his eyes, and he found himself in a *patio*, or court, dimly lighted by a single lamp. In the centre was the dry basin of an old Moorish fountain, under which the priest requested him to form a small vault, bricks and mortar being at hand for the purpose. He accordingly worked all night, but without finishing the job. Just before daybreak the priest put a piece of gold into his hand, and having again blindfolded him, conducted him back to his dwelling.

" 'Are you willing,' said he, 'to return and complete your work?'

" 'Gladly, Señor Padre, provided I am so well paid.'

" 'Well, then, to-morrow at midnight I will call again.'

"He did so, and the vault was completed.

" 'Now,' said the priest, 'you must help me to bring forth the bodies that are to be buried in this vault.'

"The poor mason's hair rose on his head at these words: he followed the priest, with trembling steps, into a retired chamber of the mansion, expecting to behold some ghastly spectacle of death, but was relieved on perceiving three or four portly jars standing in one corner. They were evidently full of money, and it was with great labor that he and the priest carried them forth and consigned them to their tomb. The vault was then closed, the pavement replaced, and all traces of the work were obliterated. The mason was again hoodwinked and led forth by a route different from that by which he had come. After they had wandered for a long time through a perplexed maze of lanes and alleys, they halted. The priest then put two pieces of gold into his hand: 'Wait here,' said he, 'until you hear the cathedral bell toll for matins. If you presume to uncover your eyes before that time, evil will befall you': so saying, he departed. The mason waited faithfully, amusing himself, by weighing the gold pieces in his hand, and clinking them against each other. The moment the cathedral bell rang its matin peal, he uncovered his eyes, and found himself on the banks of the Xenil, whence he made the best of his way home, and revelled with his family for a whole fortnight on the profits of his two nights' work; after which he was as poor as ever.

"He continued to work a little, and pray a good deal, and keep saints' days and holidays, from year to year, while his family grew up as gaunt and ragged as a crew of gypsies. As he was seated one evening at the door of his hovel, he was accosted by a rich old curmudgeon, who was noted for owning many houses, and being a griping landlord. The man of money eyed him for a moment from beneath a pair of anxious shagged eyebrows.

" 'I am told, friend, that you are very poor.'

" 'There is no denying the fact, Señor,—it speaks for itself.'

" 'I presume, then, that you will be glad of a job, and will work cheap.'

" 'As cheap, my master, as any mason in Granada.'

" 'That's what I want. I have an old house fallen into decay, which costs me more money than it is worth to keep it in repair, for nobody will live in it; so I must contrive to patch it up and keep it together at as small expense as possible.'

"The mason was accordingly conducted to a large deserted house that seemed going to ruin. Passing through several empty halls and chambers, he entered an inner court, where his eye was caught by an old Moorish fountain. He paused for a moment, for a dreaming recollection of the place came over him.

" 'Pray,' said he, 'who occupied this house formerly?'

" 'A pest upon him!' cried the landlord; 'it was an old miserly priest, who cared for nobody but himself. He was said to be immensely rich, and, having no relations, it was thought, he would leave all his treasures to the Church. He died suddenly, and the priests and friars thronged to take possession of his wealth, but nothing could they find but a few ducats in a leathern purse. The worst luck has fallen on me, for, since his death, the old fellow continued to occupy my house without paying rent, and there is no taking the law of a dead man. The people pretend to hear the clinking of gold all night in the chamber where the old priest slept, as if he were counting over his money, and sometimes a groaning and moaning about the court. Whether true or false, these stories have brought a bad name on my house, and not a tenant will remain in it.'

" 'Enough,' said the mason sturdily; 'let me live in your house rent-free until some better tenant present and I will engage to put it in repair, and to quiet the troubled spirit that disturbs it. I am a good Christian and a poor man, and am not to be daunted by the Devil himself, even though he should come in the shape of a big bag of money!'

"The offer of the honest mason was gladly accepted; he moved with his family into the house, and fulfilled all his engagements. By little and little he restored it to its former state; the clinking of gold was no more heard at night in the chamber of the defunct priest, but began to be heard by day in the pocket of the living mason. In a word, he increased rapidly in wealth, to the admiration of all his neighbors, and became one of the richest men in Granada: he gave large sums to the Church, by way, no doubt, of satisfying his conscience, and never revealed the secret of the vault until on his deathbed to his son and heir."

THE GOVERNOR
AND THE NOTARY

In former times there ruled, as governor of the Alhambra, a doughty old cavalier, who, from having lost one arm in the wars, was commonly known by the name of El Gobernador Manco, or "the one-armed governor." He in fact prided himself upon being an old soldier, wore his moustaches curled up to his eyes, a pair of campaigning boots, and a toledo as long as a spit, with his pocket-handkerchief in the basket-hilt.

He was, moreover, exceedingly proud and punctilious, and tenacious of all his privileges and dignities. Under his sway the immunities of the Alhambra, as a royal residence and domain, were rigidly exacted. No one was permitted to enter the fortress with firearms, or even with a sword or staff, unless he were of a certain rank; and every horseman was obliged to dismount at the gate, and lead his horse by the bridle. Now as the hill of the Alhambra rises from the very midst of the city of Granada, being, as it were, an excrescence of the capital, it must at all times be somewhat irksome to the captain-general, who commands the province, to have thus an *imperium in imperio*, a petty independent post in the very centre of his domains. It was rendered the more galling, in the present instance, from the irritable jealousy of the old governor, that took fire on the least question of authority and jurisdiction; and from the loose vagrant character of the people who had gradually nestled themselves within the fortress, as in a sanctuary, and thence carried on a system of roguery and depredation at the expense of the honest inhabitants of the city.

Thus there was a perpetual feud and heart-burning between the captain-general and the governor, the more virulent on the part of the latter, inasmuch as the smallest of two neighboring potentates is always the most captious about his dignity. The stately palace of the captain-general stood in the Plaza Nueva, immediately at the foot of the hill of the Alhambra; and here was always a bustle and parade of guards, and domestics, and city functionaries. A beetling bastion of the fortress overlooked the palace and public square in front of it; and on this bastion the old governor would occasionally strut backwards and forwards, with his toledo girded by his side, keeping a wary eye down upon his rival, like a hawk reconnoitring his quarry from his nest in a dry tree.

Whenever he descended into the city, it was in grand parade; on horseback, surrounded by his guards; or in his state coach, an ancient and unwieldy Spanish edifice of carved timber and gilt leather, drawn by eight mules, with running footmen, outriders, and lackeys; on which occasions he flattered himself he impressed every beholder with awe and admiration as viceregent of the king; though the wits of Granada, particularly those who loitered about the palace of the captain-general, were apt to sneer at his petty parade, and, in allusion to the vagrant character of his subjects, to greet him with the appellation of "the king of the beggars." One of the most fruitful sources of dispute between these two doughty rivals was the right claimed by the governor to have all things passed free of duty through the city that were intended for the use of himself or his garrison. By degrees this privilege had given rise to extensive smuggling. A nest of *contrabandistas* took up their abode in the hovels of the fortress and the numerous caves in its vicinity, and drove a thriving business under the connivance of the soldiers of the garrison.

The vigilance of the captain-general was aroused. He consulted his legal adviser and factotum, a shrewd, meddlesome *escribano*, or notary, who rejoiced in an opportunity of perplexing the old potentate of the Alhambra, and involving him in a maze of legal subtleties. He advised the captain-general to insist upon the right of examining every convoy passing through the gates of his city, and penned a long letter for him in vindication of the right. Governor Manco was a straightforward cut-and-thrust old soldier, who hated an *escribano* worse than the devil, and this one in particular worse than all other *escribanos*.

"What!" said he, curling up his moustaches fiercely, "does the captain-general set his man of the pen to practise confusions upon me? I'll let him see an old soldier is not to be baffled by schoolcraft."

He seized his pen and scrawled a short letter in a crabbed hand, in which, without deigning to enter into argument, he insisted on the right of transit free of search, and denounced vengeance on any custom-house officer who should lay his unhallowed hand on any convoy protected by the flag of the Alhambra. While this question was agitated between the two pragmatical potentates, it so happened that a mule laden with supplies for the fortress arrived one day at the gate of Xenil, by which it was to traverse a suburb of the city on its way to the Alhambra. The convoy was headed by a testy old corporal, who had long served under the governor, and was a man after his own heart; as rusty and stanch as an old Toledo blade.

As they approached the gate of the city, the corporal placed the banner of the Alhambra on the pack-saddle of the mule, and drawing himself up to a perfect perpendicular, advanced with his head dressed to the front, but with the wary sideglance of a cur passing through hostile ground and ready for a snap and a snarl.

"Who goes there?" said the sentinel at the gate.

"Soldier of the Alhambra!" said the corporal, without turning his head.

"What have you in charge?"

"Provisions for the garrison."

"Proceed."

The corporal marched straight forward, followed by the convoy, but had not advanced many paces before a posse of custom-house officers rushed out of a small toll-house.

"Hallo there!" cried the leader. "Muleteer, halt, and open those packages."

The corporal wheeled round and drew himself up in battle array. "Respect the flag of the Alhambra," said he; "these things are for the governor."

"A *figo* for the governor and a *figo* for his flag. Muleteer, halt, I say."

"Stop the convoy at your peril!" cried the corporal, cocking his musket. "Muleteer, proceed."

The muleteer gave his beast a hearty thwack; the custom-house officer sprang forward and seized the halter; whereupon the corporal levelled his piece and shot him dead.

The street was immediately in an uproar.

The old corporal was seized, and after undergoing sundry kicks, and cuffs, and cudgellings, which are generally given impromptu by the mob in Spain as a foretaste of the after penalties of the law, he was loaded with irons and conducted to the city prison, while his comrades were permitted to proceed with the convoy, after it had been well rummaged, to the Alhambra.

The old governor was in a towering passion when he heard of this insult to his flag and capture of his corporal. For a time he stormed about the Moorish halls, and vapored about the bastions, and looked down fire and sword upon the palace of the captain-general. Having vented the first ebullition of his wrath, he despatched a message demanding the surrender of the corporal, as to him alone belonged the right of sitting in judgement of the offences of those under his command. The captain-general, aided by the pen of the delighted *escribano*, replied at great length, arguing that, as the offence had been committed within the walls of his city, and against one of his civil officers, it was clearly within his proper jurisdiction.

The governor rejoined by a repetition of his demand; the captain-general gave a surrejoinder of still greater length and legal acumen; the governor became hotter and more peremptory in his demands, and the captain-general cooler and more copious in his replies; until the old lion-hearted soldier absolutely roared with fury at being thus entangled in the meshes of legal controversy.

While the subtle *escribano* was thus amusing himself at the expense of the governor, he was conducting the trial of the corporal, who, mewed up in a narrow dungeon of the prison, had merely a small grated window at which to show his iron-bound visage and receive the consolations of his friends.

A mountain of written testimony was diligently heaped up, according to Spanish form, by the indefatigable *escribano*; the corporal was completely overwhelmed by it. He was convicted of murder, and sentenced to be hanged.

It was in vain the governor sent down remonstrance and menace from the Alhambra. The fatal day was at hand, and the corporal was put *in capilla*, that is to say, in the chapel of the prison, as is always done with culprits the day before execution, that they may mediate on their approaching end and repent them of their sins.

Seeing things drawing to extremity, the old governor determined to attend to the affair in person. For this purpose he ordered out his carriage of state, and, surrounded by his guards, rumbled down the avenue of the Alhambra into the city. Driving to the house of the *escribano*, he summoned him to the portal.

The eye of the old governor gleamed like a coal at beholding the smirking man of the law advancing with an air of exultation.

"What is this I hear," cried he, "that you are about to put to death one of my soldiers?"

"All according to law—all in strict form of justice," said the self-sufficient *escribano*, chuckling and rubbing his hands; "I can show your Excellency the written testimony in the case."

"Fetch it hither," said the governor. The *escribano* bustled into his office, delighted with having another opportunity of displaying his ingenuity at the expense of the hard-headed veteran. He returned with a satchel full of papers, and began to read a long deposition with professional volubility. By this time a crowd had collected, listening with outstretched necks and gaping mouths.

"Prithee, man, get into the carriage, out of this pestilent throng, that I may the better hear thee," said the governor.

The *escribano* entered the carriage, when, in a twinkling, the door was closed, the coachman smacked his whip,—mules, carriage, guards, and all dashed off at a thundering rate, leaving the crowd in gaping wonderment; nor did the governor pause until he had lodged his prey in one of the strongest dungeons of the Alhambra.

He then sent down a flag of truce in military style, proposing a cartel, or exchange of prisoners,—the corporal for the notary. The pride of the captain-general was piqued; he returned a contemptuous refusal, and forthwith caused a gallows, tall and strong, to be erected in the centre of the Plaza Nueva for the execution of the corporal.

"Oho! is that the game?" said Governor Manco. He gave orders, and immediately a gibbet was reared on the verge of the great beetling bastion that overlooked the Plaza. "Now," said he, in a message to the captain-general, "hang my soldier when you please; but at the same time that he is swung off in the square, look up to see your *escribano* dangling against the sky."

The captain-general was inflexible; troops were paraded in the square; the drums beat, the bell tolled. An immense multitude of amateurs gathered together to behold the execution. On the other hand, the governor paraded his garrison on the bastion, and tolled the funeral dirge of the notary from the Torre de la campana, or Tower of the Bell.

The notary's wife pressed through the crowd with a whole progeny of little embryo *escribanos* at her heels, and throwing herself at the feet of the captain-general, implored him not to sacrifice the life of her husband, and the welfare of herself and her numerous little ones, to a point of pride; "for you know the old governor too well," said she, "to doubt that he will put his threat into execution, if you hang the soldier."

The captain-general was overpowered by her tears and lamentations, and the clamors of her callow brood. The corporal was sent up to the Alhambra, under a guard, in his gallows garb, like a hooded friar, but with head erect and a face of iron. The *escribano* was demanded in exchange, according to the cartel. The once bustling and self-sufficient man of the law was drawn forth from his dungeon more dead than alive. All his flippancy and conceit had evaporated; his hair, it is said, had nearly turned gray with affright, and he had a downcast, dogged look, as if he still felt the halter round his neck.

The old governor stuck his one arm akimbo, and for a moment surveyed him with an iron smile. "Henceforth, my friend," said he, "moderate your zeal in hurrying others to the gallows; be not too certain of your safety, even though you should have the law on your side; and above all, take care how you play off your schoolcraft another time upon an old soldier."

THE GRAND PRAIRIE—
A BUFFALO HUNT

After proceeding about two hours in a southerly direction, we emerged towards mid-day from the dreary belt of the Cross Timber, and to our infinite delight beheld "the Great Prairie," stretching to the right and left before us. We could distinctly trace the meandering course of the Main Canadian, and various smaller streams, by the strips of green forests that bordered them. The landscape was vast and beautiful. There is always an expansion of feeling in looking upon these boundless and fertile wastes; but I was doubly conscious of it after emerging from our "close dungeon of innumerous boughs."

From a rising ground Beatte pointed out the place he and his comrades had killed the buffaloes; and we beheld several black objects moving in the distance, which he said were part of the herd. The Captain determined to shape his course to a woody bottom about a mile distant, and to encamp there for a day for two, by way of having a regular buffalo-hunt, and getting a supply of provisions. As the troop defiled along the slope of the hill towards the campaign ground, Beatte proposed to my mess-mates and myself, that we should put ourselves under his guidance, promising to take us where we should have plenty of sport. Leaving the line of march, therefore, we diverged towards the prairie; traversing a small valley, and ascending a gentle swell of land. As we reached the summit, we beheld a gang of wild horses about a mile off. Beattle was immediately on the alert, and no longer thought of buffalo hunting. He was mounted on his powerful half wild horse, with a lariat coiled at the saddle-bow, and set off in pursuit; while we remained on a rising ground watching his manoeuvres with great solicitude. Taking advantage of a strip of woodland, he stole quietly along, so as to get close to them before he was perceived. The moment they caught sight of him a grand scamper took place. We watched him skirting along the horizon like a privateer in full chase of a merchantman; at length he passed over the brow of a ridge, and down a shallow valley; in a few moments he was on the opposite hill, and close upon one of the horses. He was soon head and head, and appeared to be trying to noose his prey; but they both disappeared again behind the hill, and we saw no more of them. It turned out afterwards that he had noosed a powerful horse, but could not hold him, and had lost his lariat in the attempt.

While we were waiting for his return, we perceived two buffalo descending a slope, towards a stream, which wound through a ravine fringed with trees. The young Count and myself endeavored to get near them under covert of the trees. They discovered us while we were yet three or four hundred yards off, and turning about, retreated up the rising ground. We urged our horses across the ravine, and gave chase. The immense weight of head and shoulders causes the buffalo to labor heavily up-hill; but it accelerates his descent. We had the advantage, therefore, and gained rapidly upon the fugitives, though it was difficult to get our horses to approach them, their very scent inspiring them with terror. The Count, who had a double-barrelled gun loaded with ball, fired, but it missed. The bulls now altered their course, and galloped down-hill with headlong rapidity. As they ran in different directions, we each singled one and separated. I was provided with a brace of veteran brass-barrelled pistols, which I had borrowed at Fort Gibson, and which had evidently seen some service. Pistols are very effective in buffalo hunting, as the hunter can ride up close to the animal, and fire it while at full speed; whereas the long heavy rifles used on the frontier, cannot be easily managed, nor discharged with accurate aim from horseback. My object, therefore, was to get within pistol-shot of the buffalo. This was no very easy matter. I was well mounted on a horse of excellent speed and bottom, that seemed eager for the chase, and soon overtook the game; but the moment he came nearly parallel, he would keep sheering off, with ears forked and pricked forward, and every symptom of aversion and alarm. It was no wonder. Of all animals, a buffalo, when close pressed by the hunter, has an aspect the most diabolical. His two short black horns curve out of a huge frontlet of shaggy hair; his eyes glow like coals; his mouth is open; his tongue parched and drawn up into a half crescent; his tail is erect, and tufted and whisking about in the air; he is a perfect picture of mingled rage and terror.

It was with difficulty I urged my horse sufficiently near, when, taking aim, to my chagrin both pistols missed fire. Unfortunately the locks of these veteran weapons were so much worn, that in the gallop the priming had been shaken out of the pans. At the snapping of the last pistol I was close upon the buffalo, when, in his despair, he turned round with a sudden snort, and rushed upon me. My horse wheeled about as if on a pivot, made a convulsive spring, and, as I had been leaning on one side with pistol extended, I came near being thrown at the feet of the buffalo.

Three or four bounds of the horse carried us out of the reach of the enemy, who, having merely turned in desperate self-defence, quickly resumed his flight. As soon as I could gather in my panic-stricken horse, and prime the pistols afresh, I again spurred in pursuit of the buffalo, who had slackened his speed to take breath. On my approach he again set off full tilt, heaving himself forward with a heavy rolling gallop, dashing with headlong precipitation through brakes and ravines, while several deer and wolves, startled from their coverts by his thundering career, ran helter-skelter to right and left across the waste.

A gallop across the prairies in pursuit of game is by no means so smooth a career as those may imagine who have only the idea of an open level plain. It is true, the prairies of the hunting ground are not so much entangled with flowering plants and long herbage as the lower prairies, and are principally covered with short buffalo-grass; but they are diversified by hill and dale, and where most level, are apt to be cut up by deep rifts and ravines, made by torrents after rains; and which, yawning from an even surface, are almost like pitfalls in the way of the hunter, checking him suddenly when in full career, or subjecting him to the risk of limb and life. The plains, too, are beset by burrowing-holes of small animals, in which the horse is apt to sink to the fetlock, and throw both himself and his rider. The late rain had covered some parts of the prairie, where the ground was hard, with a thin sheet of water, through which the horse had to splash his way. In other parts there were innumerable shallow hollows, eight or ten feet in diameter, made by the buffaloes, who wallow in sand and mud like swine. These being filled with water, shone like mirrors, so that the horse was continually leaping over them or springing on one side. We had reached, too, a rough part of the prairie, very much broken and cut up; the buffalo, who was running for life, took no heed to his course, plunging down break-neck ravines, where it was necessary to skirt the borders in search of a safer descent. At length we came to where a winter stream had torn a deep chasm across the whole prairie, leaving open jagged rocks, and forming a long glen bordered by steep crumbling cliffs of mingled stone and clay. Down one of these the buffalo flung himself, half tumbling, half leaping, and then scuttled along the bottom; while I, seeing all further pursuit useless, pulled up, and gazed quietly after him from the border of the cliff, until he disappeared amidst the windings of the ravine.

Nothing now remained but to turn my steed and rejoin my companions. Here at first was some little difficulty. The ardor of the chase had betrayed me into a long, heedless gallop. I now found myself in the midst of a lonely waste, in which the prospect was bounded by undulating swells of land, naked and uniform, where, from the deficiency of landmarks and distinct features, an inexperienced man may become bewildered, and lose his way as readily as in the wastes of the ocean. The day, too, was overcast, so that I could not guide myself by the sun; my only mode was to retrace the track my horse had made in coming, though this I would often lose sight of, where the ground was covered with parched herbage.

To one unaccustomed to it, there is something inexpressibly lonely in the solitude of a prairie. The loneliness of a forest seems nothing to it. There the view is shut in by trees, and the imagination is left free to picture some livelier scene beyond. But here we have an immense extent of landscape without a sign of human existence. We have the consciousness of being far, far beyond the bounds of human habitation; we feel as if moving in the midst of a desert world. As my horse lagged slowly back over the scenes of our late scamper, and the delirium of the chase had passed away, I was peculiarly sensible to these circumstances. The silence of the waste was now and then broken by the cry of a distant flock of pelicans, stalking like spectres about a shallow pool; sometimes by the sinister croaking of a raven in the air, while occasionally a scoundrel wolf would scour off from before me, and, having attained a safe distance, would sit down and howl and whine with tones that gave a dreariness to the surrounding solitude.

After pursuing my way for some time, I descried a horseman on the edge of a distant hill, and soon recognized him to be the Count. He had been equally unsuccessful with myself; we were shortly after rejoined by our worthy comrade, the Virtuoso, who, with spectacle on nose, had made two or three ineffectual shots from horseback.

We determined not to seek the camp until we had made one more effort. Casting our eyes about the surrounding waste, we descried a herd of buffalo about two miles distant, scattered apart, and quietly grazing near a small strip of trees and bushes. It required but little stretch of fancy to picture them so many cattle grazing on the edge of a common, and that the grove might shelter some lonely farm-house.

We now formed our plan to circumvent the herd, and by getting on the other side of them, to hunt them in the direction where we knew our camp to be situated: otherwise, the pursuit might take us to such a distance as to render it impossible to find our way back before nightfall. Taking a wide circuit, therefore, we moved slowly and cautiously, pausing occasionally when we saw any of the herd desist from grazing. The wind fortunately set from them, otherwise they might have scented us and have taken the alarm. In this way we succeeded in getting round the herd without disturbing it. It consisted of about forty head; bulls, cows, and calves. Separating to some distance from each other, we now approached slowly in a parallel line, hoping by degrees to steal near without exciting attention. They began, however, to move off quietly, stopping at every step or two to graze, when suddenly a bull, that, unobserved by us, had been taking his siesta under a clump of trees to our left, roused himself from his lair, and hastened to join his companions. We were still at a considerable distance, but the game had taken the alarm. We quickened our pace; they broke into a gallop, and now commenced a full chase.

As the ground was level, they shouldered along with great speed, following each other in a line; two or three bulls bringing up the rear, the last of whom, from his enormous size and venerable frontlet, and beard of sunburnt hair, looked like the patriarch of the herd, and as if he might long have reigned the monarch of the prairie.

There is a mixture of the awful and the comic in the look of these huge animals, as they bear their great bulk forwards, with an up and down motion of the unwieldy head and shoulders, their tail cocked up like the cue of a Pantaloon in a pantomime, the end whisking about in a fierce yet whimsical style, and their eyes glaring venomously with an expression of fright and fury.

For some time I kept parallel with the line, without being able to force my horse within pistol-shot, so much had he been alarmed by the assault of the buffalo in the preceding chase. At length I succeeded, but was again balked by my pistols missing fire. My companions, whose horses were less fleet and more wayworn, could not overtake the herd; at length Mr. L., who was in the rear of the line, and losing ground, levelled his double-barrelled gun, and fired a long raking shot. It struck a buffalo just above the loins, broke its backbone, and brought it to the ground. He stopped and alighted to dispatch his prey, when, borrowing his gun, which had yet a charge remaining in it, I put my horse to his speed, again overtook the herd which was thundering along, pursued by the Count. With my present weapon there was no need of urging my horse to such close quarters; galloping along parallel, therefore, I singled out a buffalo, and by a fortunate shot brought it down on the spot. The ball had struck a vital part; it could not move from the place where it fell, but lay there struggling in mortal agony, while the rest of the herd kept on their headlong career across the prairie.

Dismounting, I now fettered my horse to prevent his straying, and advanced to contemplate my victim. I am nothing of a sportsman; I had been prompted to this unwonted exploit by the magnitude of the game and the excitement of an adventurous chase. Now that the excitement was over, I could not but look with commiseration upon the poor animal that lay struggling and bleeding at my feet. His very size and importance, which had before inspired me with eagerness, now increased my compunction. It seemed as if I had inflicted pain in proportion to the bulk of my victim, and as if there were a hundred-fold greater waste of life than there would have been in the destruction of an animal of inferior size.

To add to these after-qualms of conscience, the poor animal lingered in his agony. He had evidently received a mortal wound, but death might be long in coming. It would not do to leave him here to be torn piecemeal while yet alive, by the wolves that had already snuffed his blood, and were skulking and howling at a distance, and waiting for my departure; and by the ravens that were flapping about, croaking dismally in the air. It became now an act of mercy to give him his quietus, and put him out of his misery. I primed one of the pistols, therefore, and advanced close up to the buffalo. To inflict a wound thus in cold blood, I found a totally different thing from firing in the heat of the chase. Taking aim, however, just behind the fore-shoulder, my pistol for once proved true; the ball must have passed through the heart, for the animal gave one convulsive throe and expired.

While I stood meditating and moralizing over the wreck I had so wantonly produced, with my horse grazing near me, I was rejoined by my fellow-sports-man the Virtuoso, who, being a man of universal adroitness, and withal more experienced and hardened in the gentle art of "venerie," soon managed to carve out the tongue of the buffalo, and delivered it to me to bear back to the camp as a trophy.

RURAL LIFE IN ENGLAND

Oh! friendly to the best pursuits of man,
Friendly to thought, to virtue, and to peace,
Domestic life in rural pleasures past!

COWPER

The stranger who would form a correct opinion of the English character must not confine his observations to the metropolis. He must go forth into the country; he must sojourn in villages and hamlets; he must visit castles, villas, farmhouses, cottages; he must wander through parks and gardens; along hedges and green lanes; he must loiter about country churches; attend wakes and fairs and other rural festivals; and cope with the people in all their conditions, and all their habits and humors.

In some countries the large cities absorb the wealth and fashion of the nation; they are the only fixed abodes of elegant and intelligent society, and the country is inhabited almost entirely by boorish peasantry. In England, on the contrary, the metropolis is a mere gathering place, or general rendezvous,

of the polite classes, where they devote a small portion of the
year to a hurry of gaiety and dissipation, and, having indulged
this kind of carnival, return again to the apparently more
congenial habits of rural life. The various orders of society
are therefore diffused over the whole surface of the kingdom,
and the most retired neighborhoods afford specimens of the
different ranks.

The English, in fact, are strongly gifted with the rural feeling. They possess a quick sensibility to the beauties of nature
and a keen relish for the pleasures and employments of the
country. This passion seems inherent in them. Even the inhabitants of cities, born and brought up among brick walls and
bustling streets, enter with facility into rural habits and evince
a tact for rural occupation. The merchant has his snug retreat in
the vicinity of the metropolis, where he often displays as much
pride and zeal in the cultivation of his flower garden and the
maturing of his fruits as he does in the conduct of his business
and the success of a commercial enterprise. Even those less
fortunate individuals who are doomed to pass their lives in
the midst of din and traffic contrive to have something that
shall remind them of the green aspect of nature. In the most
dark and dingy quarters of the city, the drawing-room window
resembles frequently a bank of flowers; every spot capable of
vegetation has its grass plot and flower bed; and every square
its mimic park, laid out with picturesque taste and gleaming
with refreshing verdure.

Those who see the Englishman only in town are apt to form
an unfavorable opinion of his social character. He is either
absorbed in business or distracted by the thousand engagements that dissipate time, thought, and feeling in this huge
metropolis. He has, therefore, too commonly a look of hurry
and abstraction. Wherever he happens to be, he is on the point
of going somewhere else; at the moment he is talking on one
subject, his mind is wandering to another; and while paying a
friendly visit, he is calculating how he shall economize time so
as to pay the other visits allotted in the morning. An immense
metropolis, like London, is calculated to make men selfish and

uninteresting. In their casual and transient meetings, they can but deal briefly in commonplaces. They present but the cold superficies of character—its rich and genial qualities have no time to be warmed into a flow.

It is in the country that the Englishman gives scope to his natural feelings. He breaks loose gladly from the cold formalities and negative civilities of town, throws off his habits of shy reserve, and becomes joyous and freehearted. He manages to collect around him all the conveniences and elegancies of polite life, and to banish its restraints. His country seat abounds with every requisite, either for studious retirement, tasteful gratification, or rural exercise. Books, paintings, music, horses, dogs, and sporting implements of all kinds are at hand. He puts no constraint either upon his guests or himself, but in the true spirit of hospitality provides the means of enjoyment, and leaves everyone to partake according to his inclination.

The taste of the English in the cultivation of land and in what is called landscape gardening is unrivaled. They have studied Nature intently, and discover an exquisite sense of her beautiful forms and harmonious combinations. Those charms, which in other countries she lavishes in wild solitudes, are here assembled around the haunts of domestic life. They seem to have caught her coy and furtive graces and spread them, like witchery, about their rural abodes.

Nothing can be more imposing than the magnificence of English park scenery. Vast lawns that extend like sheets of vivid green, with here and there clumps of gigantic trees, heaping up rich piles of foliage; the solemn pomp of groves and woodland glades, with the deer trooping in silent herds across them, the hare, bounding away to the covert, or the pheasant, suddenly bursting upon the wing; the brook, taught to wind in natural meanderings or expand into a glassy lake; the sequestered pool, reflecting the quivering trees, with the yellow leaf sleeping on its bosom, and the trout roaming fearlessly about its limpid waters, while some rustic temple or sylvan statue, grown green and dank with age, gives an air of classic sanctity to the seclusion.

These are but a few of the features of park scenery; but what most delights me is the creative talent with which the English decorate the unostentatious abodes of middle life. The rudest habitation, the most unpromising and scanty portion of land, in the hands of an Englishman of taste becomes a little paradise. With a nicely discriminating eye, he seizes at once upon its capabilities and pictures in his mind the future landscape. The sterile spot grows into loveliness under his hand; and yet the operations of art which produce the effect are scarcely to be perceived. The cherishing and training of some trees, the cautious pruning of others, the nice distribution of flowers and plants of tender and graceful foliage, the introduction of a green slope of velvet turf, the partial opening to a peep of blue distance or silver gleam of water, all these are managed with a delicate tact, a pervading yet quiet assiduity, like the magic touchings with which a painter finishes up a favorite picture.

The residence of people of fortune and refinement in the country has diffused a degree of taste and elegance in rural economy that descends to the lowest class. The very laborer, with his thatched cottage and narrow slip of ground, attends to their embellishment. The trim hedge, the grass plot before the door, the little flower bed bordered with snug box, the wood-bine trained up against the wall and hanging its blossoms about the lattice, the pot of flowers in the window, the holly, providently planted about the house to cheat winter of its dreariness and to throw in a semblance of green summer to cheer the fireside, all these bespeak the influence of taste, flowing down from high sources and pervading the lowest levels of the public mind. If ever Love, as poets sing, delights to visit a cottage, it must be the cottage of an English peasant.

The fondness for rural life among the higher classes of the English has had a great and salutary effect upon the national character. I do not know a finer race of men than the English gentlemen. Instead of the softness and effeminacy which characterize the men of rank in most countries, they exhibit a union of elegance and strength, a robustness of frame and freshness of complexion which I am inclined to attribute to their living so much in the open air and pursuing so eagerly the invigorating recreations of the country. These hardy exercises produce also a healthful tone of mind and spirits, and a manliness and simplicity of manners, which even the follies and dissipations of the town cannot easily pervert and can never entirely destroy. In the country, too, the different orders of society seem to approach more freely, to be more disposed to blend and operate favorably upon each other. The distinctions between them do not appear to be so marked and impassable as in the cities. The manner in which property has been distributed into small estates and farms has established a regular gradation from the nobleman, through the classes of gentry, small landed proprietors, and substantial farmers, down to the laboring peasantry; and while it has thus banded the extremes of society together, has infused into each intermediate rank a spirit of independence. This, it must be confessed, is not so universally the case at present as it was formerly, the larger estates having, in late years of distress, absorbed the smaller, and, in some parts of the country, almost annihilated the sturdy race of small farmers. These, however, I believe, are but casual breaks in the general system I have mentioned.

In rural occupation there is nothing mean and debasing. It leads a man forth among scenes of natural grandeur and beauty; it leaves him to the workings of his own mind, operated upon by the purest and most elevating of external influences. Such a man may be simple and rough, but he cannot be vulgar. The man of refinement, therefore, finds nothing revolting in an intercourse with the lower orders in rural life, as he does when he casually mingles with the lower orders of cities. He lays aside his distance and reserve and is glad to waive the distinctions of rank and to enter into the honest, heartfelt enjoyments of common life. Indeed, the very amusements of the country bring men more and more together, and the sound of hound and horn blends all feelings into harmony. I believe this is one great reason why the nobility and gentry are more popular among the inferior orders in England than they are in any other country, and why the latter have endured so many excessive pressures and extremities without repining more generally at the unequal distribution of fortune and privilege.

To this mingling of cultivated and rustic society may also be attributed the rural feeling that runs through British literature; the frequent use of illustrations from rural life; those incomparable descriptions of nature that abound in the British poets, that have continued down from "the Flower and the Leaf" of Chaucer and have brought into our closets all the freshness and fragrance of the dewy landscape. The pastoral writers of other countries appear as if they had paid Nature an occasional visit, and become acquainted with her general charms; but the British poets have lived and reveled with her—they have wooed her in her most secret haunts—they have watched her minutest caprices. A spray could not tremble in the breeze, a leaf could not rustle to the ground, a diamond drop could not patter in the stream, a fragrance could not exhale from the humble violet, nor a daisy unfold its crimson tints to the morning, but it has been noticed by these impassioned and delicate observers, and wrought up into some beautiful morality.

The effect of this devotion of elegant minds to rural occupations has been wonderful on the face of the country. A great part of the island is rather level, and would be monotonous were it not for the charms of culture; but it is studded and gemmed, as it were, with castles and palaces, and embroidered with parks and gardens. It does not abound in grand and sublime prospects, but rather in little home scenes of rural repose and sheltered quiet. Every antique farmhouse and moss-grown cottage is a picture; and as the roads are continually winding, and the view is shut in by groves and hedges, the eye is delighted by a continual succession of small landscapes of captivating loveliness.

The great charm, however, of English scenery is the moral feeling that seems to pervade it. It is associated in the mind with ideas of order, of quiet, of sober, well-established principles, of hoary usage and reverent custom. Everything seems to be the growth of ages of regular and peaceful existence. The old church of remote architecture, with its low, massive portal, its gothic tower, its windows rich with tracery and painted glass in scrupulous preservation, its stately monuments of warriors and worthies of the olden time, ancestors of the present lords of the soil, its tombstones, recording successive generations of sturdy yeomanry whose progeny still plow the same fields and kneel at the same altar; the parsonage, a quaint, irregular pile, partly antiquated, but repaired and altered in the tastes of various ages and occupants; the stile and footpath leading from the churchyard, across pleasant fields, and along shady hedgerows, according to an immemorial right of way; the neighboring village, with its venerable cottages, its public green sheltered by trees, under which the forefathers of the present race have sported; the antique family mansion, standing apart in some little rural domain, but looking down with a protecting air on the surrounding scene: all these common features of English landscape evince a calm and settled security, a hereditary transmission of home-bred virtues and local attachments that speak deeply and touchingly for the moral character of the nation.

It is a pleasing sight of a Sunday morning, when the bell is sending its sober melody across the quiet fields, to behold the peasantry in their best finery, with ruddy faces and modest cheerfulness, thronging tranquilly along the green lanes to church; but it is still more pleasing to see them in the evenings, gathering about their cottage doors and appearing to exult in the humble comforts and embellishments which their own hands have spread around them.

It is this sweet home feeling, this settled repose of affection in the domestic scene, that is, after all, the parent of the steadiest virtues and purest enjoyments; and I cannot close these desultory remarks better than by quoting the words of a modern English poet, who has depicted it with remarkable felicity:

> Through each gradation, from the castled hall,
> The city dome, the villa crown'd with shade,
> But chief from modest mansions numberless,

In town or hamlet, shelt'ring middle life,
Down to the cottaged vale, and straw-roof'd shed;
This western isle hath long been famed for scenes
Where bliss domestic finds a dwelling-place;
Domestic bliss, that, like a harmless dove,
(Honor and sweet endearment keeping guard,)
Can center in a little quiet nest
All that desire would fly for through the earth;
That can, the world eluding, be itself
A world enjoy'd; that wants no witnesses
But its own sharers, and approving heaven;
That, like a flower deep hid in rocky cleft,
*Smiles, though 'tis looking only at the sky.**

---

*From a poem on the death of the Princess Charlotte, by the Reverend Rann Kennedy, A.M.

THE ART OF BOOKMAKING

"If that severe doom of Synesius be true—'It is a greater offence to steal dead men's labor, than their clothes,' what shall become of most writers?"

BURTON'S ANATOMY OF MELANCHOLY

I have often wondered at the extreme fecundity of the press, and how it comes to pass that so many heads on which nature seemed to have inflicted the curse of barrenness should teem with voluminous productions. As a man travels on, however, in the journey of life, his objects of wonder daily diminish and he is continually finding out some very simple cause for some great matter of marvel. Thus have I chanced, in my peregrinations about this great metropolis, to blunder upon a scene which unfolded to me some of the mysteries of the bookmaking craft, and at once put an end to my astonishment.

I was one summer's day loitering through the great saloons of the British Museum with that listlessness with which one is apt to saunter about a museum in warm weather, sometimes lolling over the glass cases of minerals, sometimes studying the hieroglyphics on an Egyptian mummy, and sometimes trying, with nearly equal success, to comprehend the allegorical paintings on the lofty ceilings. While I was gazing about in this idle way, my attention was attracted to a distant door, at the end of a suite of apartments. It was closed, but every now and then it would open and some strange-favored being, generally clothed in black, would steal forth and glide through the rooms, without noticing any of the surrounding objects. There was an air of mystery about this that piqued my languid curiosity, and I determined to attempt the passage of that strait and to explore the unknown regions beyond. The door yielded to my hand with that facility with which the portals of enchanted castles yield to the adventurous knight-errant. I found myself in a spacious chamber, surrounded with great cases of venerable books. Above the cases, and just under the cornice, were arranged a great number of black-looking portraits of ancient authors. About the room were placed long tables, with stands for reading and writing, at which sat many pale, studious personages, poring intently over dusty volumes, rummaging among moldy manuscripts, and taking copious notes of their contents. A hushed stillness reigned through this mysterious apartment, excepting that you might hear the racing of pens over sheets of paper, or occasionally, the deep sigh of one of these sages as he shifted his position to turn over the page of an old folio, doubtless arising from that hollowness and flatulency incident to learned research.

Now and then one of these personages would write something on a small slip of paper and ring a bell, whereupon a familiar would appear, take the paper in profound silence, glide out of the room, and return shortly loaded with ponderous tomes, upon which the other would fall tooth and nail with famished voracity. I had no longer a doubt that I had happened upon a body of Magi, deeply engaged in the study of occult sciences. The scene reminded me of an old Arabian tale, of a philosopher shut up in an enchanted library, in the bosom of a mountain, which opened only once a year, where he made the spirits of the place bring him books of all kinds of dark knowledge, so that at the end of the year, when the magic portal once more swung open on its hinges, he issued forth so versed in forbidden lore as to be able to soar above the heads of the multitude and to control the powers of nature.

My curiosity being now fully aroused, I whispered to one of the familiars, as he was about to leave the room, and begged an interpretation of the strange scene before me. A few words were sufficient for the purpose. I found that these mysterious personages, whom I had mistaken for Magi, were principally authors, and in the very act of manufacturing books. I was, in fact, in the reading room of the great British Library— an immense collection of volumes of all ages and languages, many of which are now forgotten, and most of which are sel- dom read; one of these sequestered pools of obsolete literature to which modern authors repair and draw buckets full of classic lore, or "pure English, undefiled," wherewith to swell their own scanty rills of thought.

Being now in possession of the secret, I sat down in a corner and watched the process of this book manufactory. I noticed one lean, bilious-looking wight, who sought none but the most worm-eaten volumes, printed in black letter. He was evidently constructing some work of profound erudition that would be purchased by every man who wished to be thought learned, placed upon a conspicuous shelf of his library, or laid open upon his table, but never read. I observed him, now and then, draw a large fragment of biscuit out of his pocket and gnaw; whether it was his dinner, or whether he was endeavoring to keep off that exhaustion of the stomach produced by much pondering over dry works, I leave to harder students than myself to determine.

There was one dapper little gentleman in bright-colored clothes, with a chirping, gossiping expression of countenance, who had all the appearance of an author on good terms with his bookseller. After considering him attentively, I recognized in him a diligent getter-up of miscellaneous works which bustled off well with the trade. I was curious to see how he manufactured his wares. He made more stir and show of business than any of the others, dipping into various books, fluttering over the leaves of manuscripts, taking a morsel out of one, a morsel out of another, "line upon line, precept upon precept, here a little and there a little." The contents of his book seemed to be as heterogeneous as those of the witches' caldron in *Macbeth*. It was here a finger and there a thumb, toe of frog and blind-worm's sting, with his own gossip poured in like "baboon's blood," to make the medley "slab and good."

After all, thought I, may not this pilfering disposition be implanted in authors for wise purposes; may it not be the way in which Providence has taken care that the seeds of knowledge and wisdom shall be preserved from age to age, in spite of the inevitable decay of the works in which they were first produced? We see that nature has wisely, though whimsically, provided for the conveyance of seeds from clime to clime, in the maws of certain birds, so that animals, which, in themselves, are little better than carrion, and apparently the lawless plunderers of the orchard and the cornfield, are, in fact, Nature's carriers to disperse and perpetuate her blessings. In like manner, the beauties and fine thoughts of ancient and obsolete authors are caught up by these flights of predatory writers and cast forth again to flourish and bear fruit in a remote and distant tract of time. Many of their works, also, undergo a kind of metempsychosis and spring up under new forms. What was formerly a ponderous history revives in the shape of a romance, an old legend changes into a modern play, and a sober philosophical treatise furnishes the body for a whole series of bouncing and sparkling essays. Thus it is in the clearing of our American woodlands; where we burn down a forest of stately pines, a progeny of dwarf oaks start up in their place, and we never see the prostrate trunk of a tree moldering into soil, but it gives birth to a whole tribe of fungi.

Let us not, then, lament over the decay and oblivion into which ancient writers descend; they do but submit to the great law of nature, which declares that all sublunary shapes of matter shall be limited in their duration, but which decrees, also, that their elements shall never perish. Generation after generation, both in animal and vegetable life, passes away, but the vital principle is transmitted to posterity and the species continue to flourish. Thus, also, do authors beget authors, and having produced a numerous progeny, in a good old age they sleep with their fathers, that is to say, with the authors who preceded them—and from whom they had stolen.

While I was indulging in these rambling fancies, I had leaned my head against a pile of reverend folios. Whether it was owing to the soporific emanations from these works, or to the profound quiet of the room, or to the lassitude arising from much wandering, or to an unlucky habit of napping at improper times and places with which I am grievously afflicted, so it was that I fell into a doze. Still, however, my imagination continued busy, and indeed the same scene remained before my mind's eye, only a little changed in some of the details. I dreamed that the chamber was still decorated with the portraits of ancient authors, but that the number was increased. The long tables had disappeared, and in place of the sage Magi I beheld a ragged, threadbare throng, such as may be seen plying about the great repository of cast-off clothes, Monmouth Street. Whenever they seized upon a book, by one of those incongruities common to dreams, methought it turned into a garment of foreign or antique fashion, with which they proceeded to equip themselves. I noticed, however, that no one pretended to clothe himself from any particular suit, but took a sleeve from one, a cape from another, a skirt from a third, thus decking himself out piecemeal, while some of his original rags would peep out from among his borrowed finery.

There was a portly, rosy, well-fed parson, whom I observed ogling several moldy polemical writers through an eyeglass. He soon contrived to slip on the voluminous mantle of one of the old fathers, and, having purloined the gray beard of another, endeavored to look exceedingly wise; but the smirking commonplace of his countenance set at naught all the trappings

of wisdom. One sickly looking gentleman was busied embroi-
dering a very flimsy garment with gold thread drawn out of
several old court dresses of the reign of Queen Elizabeth.
Another had trimmed himself magnificently from an illuminated manuscript, had stuck a nosegay in his bosom, culled
from "The Paradise of Daintie Devices," and having put Sir
Philip Sidney's hat on one side of his head, strutted off with an
exquisite air of vulgar elegance. A third, who was but of puny
dimensions, had bolstered himself out bravely with the spoils
from several obscure tracts of philosophy so that he had a very
imposing front; but he was lamentably tattered in rear, and I
perceived that he had patched his small clothes with scraps of
parchment from a Latin author.

There were some well-dressed gentlemen, it is true, who only
helped themselves to a gem or so, which sparkled among their
own ornaments without eclipsing them. Some, too, seemed to
contemplate the costumes of the old writers, merely to imbibe
their principles of taste, and to catch their air and spirit; but
I grieve to say that too many were apt to array themselves
from top to toe in the patchwork manner I have mentioned.
I shall not omit to speak of one genius, in drab breeches and
gaiters and an Arcadian hat, who had a violent propensity to
the pastoral, but whose rural wanderings had been confined
to the classic haunts of Primrose Hill and the solitudes of the
Regent's Park. He had decked himself in wreaths and ribbons
from all the old pastoral poets, and, hanging his head on one
side, went about with a fantastical lackadaisical air, "babbling
about green fields." But the personage that most struck my
attention was a pragmatical old gentleman, in clerical robes,
with a remarkably large and square but bald head. He entered
the room wheezing and puffing, elbowed his way through the
throng with a look of sturdy self-confidence, and having laid
hands upon a thick Greek quarto, clapped it upon his head and
swept majestically away in a formidable frizzled wig.

In the height of this literary masquerade, a cry suddenly
resounded from every side of "Thieves! thieves!" I looked,
and lo! the portraits about the wall became animated! The old

authors thrust out, first a head, then a shoulder from the canvas, looked down curiously for an instant upon the motley throng, and then descended with fury in their eyes to claim their rifled property. The scene of scampering and hubbub that ensued baffles all description. The unhappy culprits endeavored in vain to escape with their plunder. On one side might be seen half a dozen old monks, stripping a modern professor; on another, there was sad devastation carried into the ranks of modern dramatic writers. Beaumont and Fletcher, side by side, raged around the field like Castor and Pollux, and sturdy Ben Jonson enacted more wonders than when a volunteer with the army in Flanders. As to the dapper little compiler of farragos, mentioned some time since, he had arrayed himself in as many patches and colors as Harlequin, and there was as fierce a contention of claimants about him as about the dead body of Patroclus. I was grieved to see many men to whom I had been accustomed to look up with awe and reverence fain to steal off with scarce a rag to cover their nakedness. Just then my eye was caught by the pragmatical old gentleman in the Greek grizzled wig, who was scrambling away in sore affright with half a score of authors in full cry after him! They were close upon his haunches. In a twinkling off went his wig; at every turn some strip of raiment was peeled away, until in a few moments, from his domineering pomp, he shrunk into a little, pursy "chopped bald shot" and made his exit with only a few tags and rags fluttering at his back.

There was something so ludicrous in the catastrophe of this learned Theban that I burst into an immoderate fit of laughter, which broke the whole illusion. The tumult and the scuffle were at an end. The chamber resumed its usual appearance. The old authors shrunk back into their picture frames and hung in shadowy solemnity along the walls. In short, I found myself wide awake in my corner, with the whole assemblage of bookworms gazing at me with astonishment. Nothing of the dream had been real, but my burst of laughter, a sound never before heard in that grave sanctuary, and so abhorrent to the ears of wisdom as to electrify the fraternity.

The librarian now stepped up to me and demanded whether I had a card of admission. At first I did not comprehend him, but I soon found that the library was a kind of literary "preserve," subject to game laws, and that no one must presume to hunt there without special license and permission. In a word, I stood convicted of being an arrant poacher, and was glad to make a precipitate retreat, lest I should have a whole pack of authors let loose upon me.

THE WIDOW AND HER SON

Pittie olde age, within whose silver haires
Honour and reverence evermore have rain'd.
                    MARLOWE'S TAMBURLAINE

Those who are in the habit of remarking such matters must have noticed the passive quiet of an English landscape on Sunday. The clacking of the mill, the regularly recurring stroke of the flail, the din of the blacksmith's hammer, the whistling of the plowman, the rattling of the cart, and all other sounds of rural labor are suspended. The very farm dogs bark less frequently, being less disturbed by passing travelers. At such times I have almost fancied the winds sunk into quiet, and that the sunny landscape, with its fresh green tints melting into blue haze, enjoyed the hallowed calm.

Sweet day, so pure, so calm, so bright,
The bridal of the earth and sky.

Well was it ordained that the day of devotion should be a day of rest. The holy repose which reigns over the face of nature has its moral influence; every restless passion is charmed down, and we fell the natural religion of the soul gently springing up within us. For my part, there are feelings that visit me in a country church, amid the beautiful serenity of nature, which I experience nowhere else; and if not a more religious, I think I am a better man on Sunday than on any other day of the seven.

During my recent residence in the country, I used frequently to attend at the old village church. Its shadowy aisles, its moldering monuments, its dark oaken paneling, all reverend with the gloom of departed years, seemed to fit it for the haunt of solemn mediation; but being in a wealthy, aristocratic neighborhood, the glitter of fashion penetrated even into the sanctuary, and I felt myself continually thrown back upon the world by the frigidity and pomp of the poor worms around me. The only being in the whole congregation who appeared thoroughly to feel the humble and prostrate piety of a true Christian was a poor, decrepit old woman bending under the weight of years and infirmities. She bore the traces of something better than abject poverty. The lingerings of decent pride were visible in her appearance. Her dress, though humble in the extreme, was scrupulously clean. Some trivial respect, too, had been awarded her, for she did not take her seat among the village poor, but sat alone on the steps of the altar. She seemed to have survived all love, all friendship, all society, and to have nothing left her but the hopes of heaven. When I saw her feebly rising and bending her aged form in prayer, habitually conning her prayerbook, which her palsied hand and failing eyes would not permit her to read but which she evidently knew by heart, I felt persuaded that the faltering voice of that poor woman arose to heaven far before the response of the clerk, the swell of the organ, or the chanting of the choir.

I am fond of loitering about country churches, and this was so delightfully situated that it frequently attracted me. It stood on a knoll, around which a small stream made a beautiful bend and then wound its way through a long reach of soft meadowy scenery. The church was surrounded by yew trees which seemed almost coeval with itself. Its tall Gothic spire shot up lightly from among them, with rooks and crows generally wheeling about it. I was seated there one still, sunny morning, watching two laborers who were digging a grave. They had chosen one of the most remote and neglected corners of the churchyard, where, from the number of nameless graves around, it would appear that the indigent and friendless were huddled into the earth. I was told that the new-made grave was for the only son of a poor widow. While I was mediating on the distinctions of worldly rank, which extend thus down into the very dust, the toll of the bell announced the approach of the funeral. They were the obsequies of poverty, with which pride had nothing to do. A coffin of the plainest materials, without pall or other covering, was borne by some of the villagers. The sexton walked before with an air of cold indifference. There were not mock mourners in the trappings of affected woe, but there was one real mourner who feebly tottered after the corpse. It was the aged mother of the deceased—the poor old woman whom I had seen seated on the steps of the altar. She was supported by a humble friend who was endeavoring to comfort her. A few of the neighboring poor had joined the train, and some children of the village were running hand in hand, now shouting with unthinking mirth and now pausing to gaze, with childish curiosity, on the grief of the mourner.

As the funeral train approached the grave, the parson issued from the church porch, arrayed in the surplice, with prayerbook in hand, and attended by the clerk. The service, however, was a mere act of charity. The deceased had been destitute and the survivor was penniless. It was shuffled through, therefore, in form, but coldly and unfeelingly. The well-fed priest moved but a few steps from the church door; his voice could scarcely be heard at the grave, and never did I hear the funeral service, that sublime and touching ceremony, turned into such a frigid mummery of words.

I approached the grave. The coffin was placed on the ground. On it were inscribed the name and age of the deceased—

"George Somers, aged 26 years." The poor mother had been assisted to kneel down at the head of it. Her withered hands were clasped, as if in prayer, but I could perceive by a feeble rocking of the body and a convulsive motion of her lips that she was gazing on the last relics of her son with the yearnings of a mother's heart.

Preparations were made to deposit the coffin in the earth. There was that bustling stir which breaks so harshly on the feelings of grief and affection; directions given in the cold tones of business, the striking of spades into sand and gravel, which, at the grave of those we love, is, of all sounds, the most withering. The bustle around seemed to waken the mother from a wretched reverie. She raised her glazed eyes and looked about with a faint wildness. As the men approached with cords to lower the coffin into the grave, she wrung her hands and broke into an agony of grief. The poor woman who attended her took her by the arm, endeavoring to raise her from the earth and to whisper something like consolation—"Nay, now—nay, now—don't take it so sorely to heart." She could only shake her head and wring her hands, as one not to be comforted.

As they lowered the body into the earth, the creaking of the cords seemed to agonize her; but when, on some accidental obstruction, there was a justling of the coffin, all the tenderness of the mother burst forth, as if any harm could come to him who was far beyond the reach of worldly suffering.

I could see no more—my heart swelled into my throat—my eyes filled with tears—I felt as if I were acting a barbarous part in standing by and gazing idly on this scene of maternal anguish. I wandered to another part of the churchyard, where I remained until the funeral train had dispersed.

When I saw the mother slowly and painfully quitting the grave, leaving behind her the remains of all that was dear to her on earth and returning to silence and destitution, my heart ached for her. What, thought I, are the distresses of the rich! They have friends to soothe—pleasures to beguile—a world to divert and dissipate their griefs. What are the sorrows of the young! Their growing minds soon close above the wound—

their elastic spirits soon rise beneath the pressure—their green and ductile affections soon twine around new objects. But the sorrows of the poor, who have no outward appliances to soothe; the sorrows of the aged, with whom life at best is but a wintry day, and who can look for no aftergrowth of joy; the sorrows of a widow, aged, solitary, destitute, mourning over an only son, the last solace of her years: these are indeed sorrows which make us feel the impotency of consolation.

It was some time before I left the churchyard. On my way homeward I met with the woman who had acted as comforter; she was just returning from accompanying the mother to her lonely habitation, and I drew from her some particulars connected with the affecting scene I had witnessed.

The parents of the deceased had resided in the village from childhood. They had inhabited one of the neatest cottages, and by various rural occupations and the assistance of a small garden, had supported themselves creditably and comfortably and led a happy and a blameless life. They had one son, who had grown up to be the staff and pride of their age. "Oh, sir!" said the good woman, "he was such a comely lad, so sweet-tempered, so kind to everyone around him, so dutiful to his parents! It did one's heart good to see him of a Sunday, dressed out in his best, so tall, so straight, so cheery, supporting his old mother to church—for she was always fonder of leaning on George's arm than on her good man's; and, poor soul, she might well be proud of him, for a finer lad there was not in the country round."

Unfortunately, the son was tempted, during a year of scarcity and agricultural hardship, to enter into the service of one of the small craft that plied on a neighboring river. He had not been long in this employ when he was entrapped by a press gang and carried off to sea. His parents received tidings of his seizure, but beyond that they could learn nothing. It was the loss of their main prop. The father, who was already infirm, grew heartless and melancholy and sunk into his grave. The widow, left lonely in her age and feebleness, could no longer support herself and came upon the parish. Still there was a kind feeling toward her throughout the village, and a certain respect as being one of the oldest inhabitants. As no one applied for the cottage in which she had passed so many happy days, she was permitted to remain in it, where she lived solitary and almost helpless. The few wants of nature were chiefly supplied from the scanty productions of her little garden, which the neighbors would now and then cultivate for her. It was but a few days before the time at which these circumstances were told me that she was gathering some vegetables for her repast when she heard the cottage door which faced the garden suddenly opened. A stranger came out and seemed to be looking eagerly and wildly around. He was dressed in seaman's clothes, was emaciated and ghastly pale, and bore the air of one broken by sickness and hardships. He saw her and hastened toward her, but his steps were faint and faltering; he sank on his knees before her and sobbed like a child. The poor woman gazed upon him with a vacant and wandering eye—"Oh, my dear, dear mother! Don't you know your son? Your poor boy, George?" It was indeed the wreck of her once noble lad, who, shattered by wounds, by sickness and foreign imprisonment, had, at length, dragged his wasted limbs homeward, to repose among the scenes of his childhood.

I will not attempt to detail the particulars of such a meeting, where joy and sorrow were so completely blended. Still he was alive! He was come home! He might yet live to comfort and cherish her old age! Nature, however, was exhausted in him, and if anything had been wanting to finish the work of fate, the desolation of his native cottage would have been sufficient. He stretched himself on the pallet on which his widowed mother had passed many a sleepless night, and he never rose from it again.

The villagers, when they heard that George Somers had returned, crowded to see him, offering every comfort and assistance that their humble means afforded. He was too weak, however, to talk—he could only look his thanks. His mother was his constant attendant, and he seemed unwilling to be helped by any other hand.

There is something in sickness that breaks down the pride of manhood, that softens the heart and brings it back to the feelings of infancy. Who that has languished, even in advanced life, in sickness and despondency, who that has pined on a weary bed in the neglect and loneliness of a foreign land but has thought on the mother "that looked on his childhood," that smoothed his pillow and administered to his helplessness? Oh! There is an enduring tenderness in the love of a mother to her son that transcends all other affections of the heart. It is neither to be chilled by selfishness, nor daunted by danger, nor weakened by worthlessness, nor stifled by ingratitude. She will sacrifice every comfort to his convenience, she will surrender every pleasure to his enjoyment, she will glory in his fame and exult in his prosperity; and, if misfortune overtake him, he will be the dearer to her from misfortune; and if disgrace settle upon his name, she will still love and cherish him in spite of his disgrace; and if all the world beside cast him off, she will be all the world to him.

Poor George Somers had known what it was to be in sickness, and none to soothe—lonely and in prison, and none to visit him. He could not endure his mother from his sight; if she moved away, his eye would follow her. She would sit for hours by his bed, watching him as he slept. Sometimes he would start from a feverish dream and look anxiously up until he saw her bending over him, when he would take her hand, lay it on his bosom, and fall asleep, with the tranquillity of a child. In this way he died.

My first impulse on hearing this humble tale of affliction was to visit the cottage of the mourner and administer pecuniary assistance and, if possible, comfort. I found, however, on inquiry that the good feelings of the villagers had prompted them to do everything that the case admitted; and as the poor know best how to console each other's sorrows, I did not venture to intrude.

The next Sunday I was at the village church when, to my surprise, I saw the poor old woman tottering down the aisle to her accustomed seat on the steps of the altar.

She had made an effort to put on something like mourning for her son; and nothing could be more touching than this struggle between pious affection and utter poverty: a black ribbon or so, a faded black handkerchief, and one or two more such humble attempts to express by outward signs that grief which passes show. When I looked around upon the storied monuments, the stately hatchments, the cold marble pomp with which grandeur mourned magnificently over departed pride, and turned to this poor widow, bowed down by age and sorrow, at the altar of her God and offering up the prayers and praises of a pious though a broken heart, I felt that this living monument of real grief was worth them all.

I related her story to some of the wealthy members of the congregation, and they were moved by it. They exerted themselves to render her situation more comfortable and to lighten her afflictions. It was, however, but smoothing a few steps to the grave. In the course of a Sunday or two after, she was missed from her usual seat at church, and before I left the neighborhood I heard, with a feeling of satisfaction, that she had quietly breathed her last and had gone to rejoin those she loved, in that world where sorrow is never known and friends are never parted.

THE MUTABILITY OF LITERATURE

A Colloquy in Westminster Abbey

> *I know that all beneath the moon decays,*
> *And what by mortals in this world is brought,*
> *In time's great period shall return to nought.*
> *I know that all the muse's heavenly lays,*
> *With toil of sprite which are so dearly bought,*
> *As idle sounds, of few or none are sought,*
> * That there is nothing lighter than mere praise.*
> DRUMMOND OF HAWTHORNDEN

There are certain half-dreaming moods of mind in which we naturally steal away from noise and glare and seek some quiet haunt, where we may indulge our reveries and build our air castles undisturbed. In such a mood I was loitering about the old gray cloisters of Westminster Abbey, enjoying that luxury of wandering thought which one is apt to dignify with the name of reflection, when suddenly an interruption of madcap boys from Westminster School, playing at football, broke in upon the monastic stillness of the place, making the vaulted passages and moldering tombs echo with their merriment. I sought to take refuge from their noise by penetrating still deeper into the solitudes of the pile, and applied to one of the vergers for admission to the library. He conducted me through a portal rich with the crumbling sculpture of former ages, which opened upon a gloomy passage leading to the chapter house and the chamber in which doomsday book is deposited. Just within the passage is a small door on the left. To this the verger applied a key; it was double-locked, and opened with some difficulty, as if seldom used. We now ascended a dark, narrow staircase, and, passing through a second door, entered the library.

I found myself in a lofty antique hall, the roof supported by massive joists of old English oak. It was soberly lighted by a row of Gothic windows at a considerable height from the floor and which apparently opened upon the roofs of the cloisters. An ancient picture of some reverend dignitary of the church in his robes hung over the fireplace. Around the hall and in a small gallery were the books, arranged in carved oaken cases. They consisted principally of old polemical writers, and were much more worn by time than use. In the center of the library was a solitary table with two or three books on it, an inkstand without ink, and a few pens parched by long disuse. The place seemed fitted for quiet study and profound meditation. It was buried deep among the massive walls of the abbey and shut up from the tumult of the world. I could only hear now and then the shouts of the schoolboys faintly swelling from the cloisters and the sound of a bell tolling for prayers, echoing soberly along the roofs of the abbey. By degrees the shouts of merriment grew fainter and fainter, and at length died away; the bell ceased to toll, and a profound silence reigned through the dusky hall.

I had taken down a little thick quarto, curiously bound in parchment, with brass clasps, and seated myself at the table in a venerable elbow chair. Instead of reading, however, I was beguiled by the solemn monastic air and lifeless quiet of the place into a train of musing. As I looked around upon the old volumes in their moldering covers, thus ranged on the shelves, and apparently never disturbed in their repose, I could not but consider the library a kind of literary catacomb, where authors,

like mummies, are piously entombed and left to blacken and
molder in dusty oblivion.

How much, thought I, has each of these volumes, now
thrust aside with such indifference, cost some aching head!
How many weary days! How many sleepless nights! How
have their authors buried themselves in the solitude of cells
and cloisters, shut themselves up from the face of man and
the still more blessed face of nature, and devoted themselves
to painful research and intense reflection! And all for what?
To occupy an inch of dusty shelf—to have the title of their
works read now and then in a future age by some drowsy
churchman or casual straggler like myself, and in another age
to be lost, even to remembrance. Such is the amount of this
boasted immortality. A mere temporary rumor, a local sound,
like the tone of that bell which has just tolled among these
towers, filling the ear for a moment—lingering transiently in
echo—and then passing away like a thing that was not.

While I sat half-murmuring, half-meditating these unprofitable speculations with my head resting on my hand, I was
thrumming with the other hand upon the quarto, until I accidentally loosened the clasps; when, to my utter astonishment,
the little book gave two or three yawns, like one awaking from
a deep sleep, then a husky hem, and at length began to talk. At
first its voice was very hoarse and broken, being much troubled
by a cobweb which some studious spider had woven across it,
and having probably contracted a cold from long exposure to
the chills and damps of the abbey. In a short time, however,
it became more distinct, and I soon found it an exceedingly
fluent conversable little tome. Its language, to be sure, was
rather quaint and obsolete, and its pronunciation, what, in the
present day, would be deemed barbarous; but I shall endeavor,
as far as I am able, to render it in modern parlance.

It began with railings about the neglect of the world—about
merit being suffered to languish in obscurity and other such
commonplace topics of literary repining, and complained bit-
terly that it had not been opened for more than two centuries.
That the dean only looked now and then into the library,

sometimes took down a volume or two, trifled with them for a few moments, and then returned them to their shelves. "What a plague do they mean," said the little quarto, which I began to perceive was somewhat choleric, "what a plague do they mean by keeping several thousand volumes of us shut up here, and watched by a set of old vergers, like so many beauties in a harem, merely to be looked at now and then by the dean? Books were written to give pleasure and to be enjoyed; and I would have a rule passed that the dean should pay each of us a visit at least once a year; or if he is not equal to the task, let them once in a while turn loose the whole school of Westminster among us, that at any rate we may now and then have an airing."

"Softly, my worthy friend," replied I, "you are not aware how much better you are off than most books of your generation. By being stored away in this ancient library, you are like the treasured remains of those saints and monarchs, which lie enshrined in the adjoining chapels, while the remains of your contemporary mortals, left to the ordinary course of nature, have long since returned to dust."

"Sir," said the little tome, ruffling his leaves and looking big, "I was written for all the world, not for the bookworms of an abbey. I was intended to circulate from hand to hand, like other great contemporary works; but here have I been clasped up for more than two centuries, and might have silently fallen a prey to these worms that are playing the very vengeance with my intestines if you had not by chance given me an opportunity of uttering a few last words before I go to pieces."

"My good friend," rejoined I, "had you been left to the circulation of which you speak you would long ere this have been no more. To judge from your physiognomy, you are now well stricken in years; very few of your contemporaries can be at present in existence, and those few owe their longevity to being immured like yourself in old libraries, which, suffer me to add, instead of likening to harems, you might more properly and gratefully have compared to those infirmaries attached to religious establishments for the benefit of the old and decrepit and where, by quiet fostering and no employment, they often endure to an amazingly good-for-nothing old age. You talk of your contemporaries as if in circulation—where do we meet with their works? What do we hear of Robert Grosseteste, of Lincoln? No one could have toiled harder than he for immortality. He is said to have written nearly two hundred volumes. He built, as it were, a pyramid of books to perpetuate his name. But, alas! the pyramid has long since fallen, and only a few fragments are scattered in various libraries, where they are scarcely disturbed even by the antiquarian. What do we hear of Giraldus Cambrensis, the historian, antiquary, philosopher, theologian, and poet? He declined two bishoprics that he might shut himself up and write for posterity; but posterity never inquires after his labors. What of Henry of Huntingdon, who, besides a learned history of England, wrote a treatise on the contempt of the world, which the world has revenged by forgetting him? What is quoted of Joseph of Exeter, styled the miracle of his age in classical composition? Of his three great heroic poems one is lost forever, excepting a mere fragment; the others are known only to a few of the curious in literature; and as to his love verses and epigrams, they have entirely disappeared. What is in current use of John Wallis, the Franciscan, who acquired the name of the tree of life? Of William of Malmsbury; of Simeon of Durham; of Benedict of Peterborough; of John Hanvill of St. Albans, of . . ."

"Prithee, friend," cried the quarto, in a testy tone, "how old do you think me? You are talking of authors that lived long before my time, and wrote either in Latin or French, so that they in a manner expatriated themselves, and deserved to be forgotten;* but I, sir, was ushered into the world from the press of the renowned Wynkyn de Worde. I was written

---

*In Latin and French hath many soueraine wittes had great delyte to endite, and have many noble things fulfilde, but certes there ben some that speaken their poisye in French, or which speche the Frenchmen have as good a fantasye as we have in hearying of Frenchmen's Englishe.—*Chaucer's Testament of Love.*

in my own native tongue, at a time when the language had become fixed, and indeed I was considered a model of pure and elegant English."

(I should observe that these remarks were couched in such intolerably antiquated terms that I have had infinite difficulty in rendering them into modern phraseology.)

"I cry your mercy," said I, "for mistaking your age, but it matters little; almost all the writers of your time have likewise passed into forgetfulness, and De Worde's publications are mere literary rarities among book collectors. The purity and stability of language, too, on which you found your claims to perpetuity have been the fallacious dependence of authors of every age, even back to the times of the worthy Robert of Gloucester, who wrote his history in rhymes of mongrel Saxon.* Even now many talk of Spenser's 'well of pure English undefiled,' as if the language ever sprang from a well or fountainhead, and was not rather a mere confluence of various tongues, perpetually subject to changes and intermixtures. It is this which has made English literature so extremely mutable, and the reputation built upon it so fleeting. Unless thought can be committed to something more permanent and unchangeable than such a medium, even thought must share the fate of everything else and fall into decay. This should serve as a check upon the vanity and exultation of the most popular writer. He finds the language in which he has embarked his fame gradually altering, and subject to the dilapidations of time and the caprice of fashion. He looks back

---

*Holinshed, in his Chronicle, observes, "afterwards, also, by deligent travell of Geffry Chaucer and of John Gowre, in the time of Richard the Second, and after them of John Scogan and John Lydgate, monke of Berrie, our said toong was brought to an excellent passe, notwithstanding that it never came unto the type of perfection until the time of Queen Elizabeth, wherein John Jewell, Bishop of Sarum, John Fox, and sundrie learned and excellent writers, have fully accomplished the ornature of the same, to their great praise and immortal commendation."

and beholds the early authors of his country, once the favorites of their day, supplanted by modern writers. A few short ages have covered them with obscurity, and their merits can only be relished by the quaint taste of the bookworm. And such, he anticipates, will be the fate of his own work, which, however it may be admired in its day and held up as a model of purity, will in the course of years grow antiquated and obsolete, until it shall become almost as unintelligible in its native land as an Egyptian obelisk, or one of those Runic inscriptions said to exist in the deserts of Tartary. I declare," added I, with some emotion, "when I contemplate a modern library, filled with new works, in all the bravery of rich gilding and binding, I feel disposed to sit down and weep, like the good Xerxes, when he surveyed his army, pranked out in all the splendor of military array, and reflected that in one hundred years not one of them would be in existence!"

"Ah," said the little quarto, with a heavy sigh, "I see how it is; these modern scribblers have superseded all the good old authors. I suppose nothing is read nowadays but Sir Philip Sidney's *Arcadia,* Sackville's stately plays, and *Mirror for Magistrates,* or the fine-spun euphuisms of the 'unparalleled John Lyly.' "

"There you are again mistaken," said I. "The writers whom you suppose in vogue, because they happened to be so when you were last in circulation, have long since had their day. Sir Philip Sidney's *Arcadia,* the immortality of which was so fondly predicted by his admirers,* and which, in truth,

---

*Live ever sweete booke; the simple image of his gentle witt, and the golden-pillar of his noble courage; and ever notify unto the world that they writer was the secretary of eloquence, the breath of the muses, the honey-bee of the daintyest flowers of witt and arte, the pith of morale and intellectual virtues, the arme of Bellona in the field, the tonge of Suada in the chamber, the sprite of Practise in esse, and the paragon of excellency in print.—*Harvey Pierce's Supererogation.*

is full of noble thoughts, delicate images, and graceful turns of language, is now scarcely ever mentioned. Sackville has strutted into obscurity; and even Lyly, though his writings were once the delight of a court and apparently perpetuated by a proverb, is now scarcely known even by name. A whole crowd of authors who wrote and wrangled at the time have likewise gone down, with all their writings and their controversies. Wave after wave of succeeding literature has rolled over them, until they are buried so deep that it is only now and then that some industrious diver after fragments of antiquity brings up a specimen for the gratification of the curious.

"For my part," I continued, "I consider this mutability of language a wise precaution of Providence for the benefit of the world at large, and of authors in particular. To reason from analogy, we daily behold the varied and beautiful tribes of vegetables springing up, flourishing, adorning the fields for a short time, and then fading into dust, to make way for their successors. Were not this the case, the fecundity of nature would be a grievance instead of a blessing. The earth would groan with rank and excessive vegetation, and its surface become a tangled wilderness. In like manner the works of genius and learning decline and make way for subsequent productions. Language gradually varies, and with it fade away the writings of authors who have flourished their allotted time; otherwise, the creative powers of genius would overstock the world and the mind would be completely bewildered in the endless mazes of literature. Formerly there were some restraints on this excessive multiplication. Works had to be transcribed by hand, which was a slow and laborious operation; they were written either on parchment, which was expensive, so that one work was often erased to make way for another, or on papyrus, which was fragile and extremely perishable. Authorship was a limited and unprofitable craft, pursued chiefly by monks in the leisure and solitude of their cloisters. The accumulation of manuscripts was slow and costly and confined almost entirely to monasteries. To these circumstances it may, in some measure, be owing that we have not been inundated by the intellect of antiquity, that the fountains of thought have not been broken up and modern genius drowned in the deluge. But the inventions of paper and the press have put an end to all these restraints. They have made everyone a writer and enabled every mind to pour itself into print and diffuse itself over the whole intellectual world. The consequences are alarming. The stream of literature has swollen into a torrent—augmented into a river—expanded into a sea. A few centuries since, five or six hundred manuscripts constituted a great library; but what would you say to libraries such as actually exist, containing three or four hundred thousand volumes; legions of authors at the same time busy; and the press going on with fearfully increasing activity, to double and quadruple the number? Unless some unforeseen mortality should break out among the progeny of the muse, now that she has become so prolific, I tremble for posterity. I fear the mere fluctuation of language will not be sufficient. Criticism may do much. It increases with the increase of literature and resembles one of those salutary checks on population spoken of by economists. All possible encouragement, therefore, should be given to the growth of critics, good or bad. But I fear all will be in vain; let criticism do what it may, writers will write, printers will print, and the world will inevitably be overstocked with good books. It will soon be the employment of a lifetime merely to learn their names. Many a man of passable information, at the present day, reads scarcely anything but reviews; and before long a man of erudition will be little better than a mere walking catalogue."

"My very good sir," said the little quarto, yawning most drearily in my face, "excuse my interrupting you, but I perceive you are rather given to prose. I would ask the fate of an author who was making some noise just as I left the world. His reputation, however, was considered quite temporary. The learned shook their heads at him, for he was a poor, half-educated varlet who knew little of Latin and nothing of Greek and had been obliged to run the country for deer stealing. I think his name was Shakespeare. I presume he soon sank into oblivion."

"On the contrary," said I, "it is owing to that very man that the literature of his period has experienced a duration beyond the ordinary term of English literature. There rise authors now and then who seem proof against the mutability of language because they have rooted themselves in the unchanging principles of human nature. They are like gigantic trees that we sometimes see on the banks of a stream, which, by their vast and deep roots, penetrating through the mere surface and laying hold on the very foundations of the earth, preserve the soil around them from being swept away by the ever-flowing current and hold up many a neighboring plant and, perhaps, worthless weed to perpetuity. Such is the case with Shakespeare, whom we behold defying the encroachments of time, retaining in modern use the language and literature of his day, and giving duration to many an indifferent author, merely from having flourished in his vicinity. But even he, I grieve to say, is gradually assuming the tint of age, and his whole form is overrun by a profusion of commentators, who, like clambering vines and creepers, almost bury the noble plant that upholds them."

Here the little quarto began to heave his sides and chuckle, until at length he broke out in a plethoric fit of laughter that had well nigh choked him, by reason of his excessive corpulency. "Mighty well!" cried he, as soon as he could recover breath. "Mighty well! And so you would persuade me that the literature of an age is to be perpetuated by a vagabond deer stealer! By a man without learning; by a poet, forsooth—a poet!" And here he wheezed forth another fit of laughter.

I confess that I felt somewhat nettled at this rudeness, which, however, I pardoned on account of his having flourished in a less polished age. I determined, nevertheless, not to give up my point.

"Yes," resumed I, positively, "a poet; for of all writers he has the best chance for immortality. Others may write from the head, but he writes from the heart, and the heart will always understand him. He is the faithful portrayer of nature, whose features are always the same and always interesting. Prose writers are voluminous and unwieldy; their pages are crowded with commonplaces and their thoughts expanded into tediousness. But with the true poet everything is terse, touching, or brilliant. He gives the choicest thoughts in the choicest language. He illustrates them by everything that he sees most striking in nature and art. He enriches them by pictures of human life, such as it is passing before him. His writings, therefore, contain the spirit, the aroma, if I may use the phrase, of the age in which he lives. They are caskets which enclose within a small compass the wealth of the language— its family jewels, which are thus transmitted in a portable form to posterity. The setting may occasionally be antiquated and require now and then to be renewed, as in the case of Chaucer; but the brilliancy and intrinsic value of the gems continue unaltered. Cast a look back over the long reach of literary history. What vast valleys of dullness, filled with monkish legends and academical controversies! What bogs of theological speculations! What dreary wastes of metaphysics! Here and there only do we behold the heaven-illuminated bards, elevated like beacons on their widely separate heights, to transmit the pure light of poetical intelligence from age to age."*

> *Thorrow earth and waters deepe,*
>   *The pen by skill doth passe:*
> *And featly nyps the worldes abuse,*
>   *And shoes us in a glasse,*
> *The vertu and the vice*
>   *Of every wight alyve;*
> *The honey comb that bee doth make*
>   *Is not so sweet in hyve,*
> *As are the golden leves*
>   *That drop from poet's head!*
> *Which doth surmount our common talke*
>   *As farre as dross doth lead.*
>   Churchyard

I was just about to launch forth into eulogiums upon the poets of the day when the sudden opening of the door caused me to turn my head. It was the verger, who came to inform me that it was time to close the library. I sought to have a parting word with the quarto, but the worthy little tome was silent; the clasps were closed, and it looked perfectly unconscious of all that had passed. I have been to the library two or three times since, and have endeavored to draw it into further conversation, but in vain; and whether all this rambling colloquy actually took place or whether it was another of those odd day-dreams to which I am subject, I have never to this moment been able to discover.

RURAL FUNERALS

Here's a few flowers! but about midnight more:
The herbs that have on them cold dew o' the night;
Are strewings fitt'st for graves—
You were as flowers now wither'd; even so
These herblets shall, which we upon you strow.

CYMBELINE

Among the beautiful and simple-hearted customs of rural life which still linger in some parts of England are those of strewing flowers before the funerals and planting them at the graves of departed friends. These, it is said, are the remains of some of the rites of the primitive church; but they are of still higher antiquity, having been observed among the Greeks and Romans and frequently mentioned by their writers, and were, no doubt, the spontaneous tributes of unlettered affection, originating long before art had tasked itself to modulate sorrow into song, or story it on the monument. They are now only to be met with in the most distant and retired places of the kingdom, where fashion and innovation have not been able to throng in and trample out all the curious and interesting traces of the olden time.

In Glamorganshire, we are told, the bed whereon the corpse lies is covered with flowers, a custom alluded to in one of the wild and plaintive ditties of Ophelia:

> *White his shroud as the mountain snow*
> *Larded all with sweet flowers;*
> *Which be-wept to the grave did go,*
> *With true love showers.*

There is also a most delicate and beautiful rite observed in some of the remote villages of the south, at the funeral of a female who has died young and unmarried. A chaplet of white flowers is borne before the corpse by a young girl nearest in age, size, and resemblance, and is afterward hung up in the church over the accustomed seat of the deceased. These chaplets are sometimes made of white paper, in imitation of flowers, and inside of them is generally a pair of white gloves. They are intended as emblems of the purity of the deceased and the crown of glory which she has received in heaven.

In some parts of the country, also, the dead are carried to the grave with the singing of psalms and hymns: a kind of triumph, "to show," says Bourne, "that they have finished their course with joy, and are become conquerors." This, I am informed, is observed in some of the northern counties, particularly in Northumberland, and it has a pleasing though melancholy effect, to hear, of a still evening in some lonely country scene, the mournful melody of a funeral dirge swelling from a distance, and to see the train slowly moving along the landscape.

> *Thus, thus, and thus, we compass round*
> *Thy harmlesse and unhaunted ground,*
> *And as we sing thy dirge, we will*
>   *The daffodill*

And other flowers lay upon
The altar of our love, thy stone.

HERRICK

There is also a solemn respect paid by the traveler to the passing funeral in these sequestered places, for such spectacles, occurring among the quiet abodes of nature, sink deep into the soul. As the mourning train approaches, he pauses, uncovered, to let it go by; he then follows silently in the rear, sometimes quite to the grave, at other times for a few hundred yards, and, having paid this tribute of respect to the deceased, turns and resumes his journey.

The rich vein of melancholy which runs through the English character and gives it some of its most touching and ennobling graces is finely evidenced in these pathetic customs and in the solicitude shown by the common people for an honored and a peaceful grave. The humblest peasant, whatever may be his lowly lot while living, is anxious that some little respect may be paid to his remains. Sir Thomas Overbury, describing the "faire and happy milkmaid," observes, "thus lives she, and all her care is, that she may die in the spring-time, to have store of flowers stucke upon her windingsheet." The poets, too, who always breathe the feeling of a nation, continually advert to this fond solicitude about the grave. In *The Maid's Tragedy*, by Beaumont and Fletcher, there is a beautiful instance of the kind, describing the capricious melancholy of a broken-hearted girl:

When she sees a bank
Stuck full of flowers, she, with a sigh, will tell
Her servants, what a pretty place it were
To bury lovers in; and make her maids
Pluck 'em, and slew her over like a corse.

The custom of decorating graves was once universally prevalent; osiers were carefully bent over them to keep the turf uninjured, and about them were planted evergreens and flowers.

"We adorn their graves," says Evelyn, in his *Sylva,* "with flowers and redolent plants, just emblems of the life of man, which has been compared in Holy Scriptures to those fading beauties, whose roots being buried in dishonor, rise again in glory." This usage has now become extremely rare in England, but it may still be met with in the churchyards of retired villages, among the Welsh mountains; and I recollect an instance of it at the small town of Ruthen, which lies at the head of the beautiful vale of Clewyd. I have been told also by a friend, who was present at the funeral of a young girl in Glamorganshire, that the female attendants had their aprons full of flowers, which, as soon as the body was interred, they stuck about the grave.

He noticed several graves which had been decorated in the same manner. As the flowers had been merely stuck in the ground, and not planted, they had soon withered, and might be seen in various states of decay, some drooping, others quite perished. They were afterward to be supplanted by holly, rosemary, and other evergreens, which on some graves had grown to great luxuriance and overshadowed the tombstones.

There was formerly a melancholy fancifulness in the arrangement of these rustic offerings that had something in it truly poetical. The rose was sometimes blended with the lily, to form a general emblem of frail mortality. "This sweet flower," said Evelyn, "borne on a branch set with thorns and accompanied with the lily are natural hieroglyphics of our fugitive, umbratile, anxious, and transitory life, which, making so fair a show for a time, is not yet without its thorns and crosses." The nature and color of the flowers, and of the ribbons with which they were tied, had often a particular reference to the qualities or story of the deceased, or were expressive of the feelings of the mourner. In an old poem, entitled *Corydon's Doleful Knell,* a lover specifies the decorations he intends to use:

> *A garland shall be framed*
> *By art and nature's skill,*
> *Of sundry-color'd flowers,*
> *In token of good-will.*

> *And sundry-color'd ribands*
>   *On it I will bestow;*
> *But chiefly blacke and yellowe*
>   *With her to grave shall go.*
>
> *I'll deck her tomb with flowers,*
>   *The rarest ever seen;*
> *And with my tears as showers,*
>   *I'll keep them fresh and green.*

The white rose, we are told, was planted at the grave of a virgin; her chaplet was tied with white ribbons, in token of her spotless innocence, though sometimes black ribbons were intermingled, to bespeak the grief of the survivors. The red rose was occasionally used in remembrance of such as had been remarkable for benevolence, but roses in general were appropriated to the graves of lovers. Evelyn tells us that the custom was not altogether extinct in his time, near his dwelling in the county of Surrey, "where the maidens yearly planted and decked the graves of their defunct sweethearts with rosebushes." And Camden likewise remarks, in his *Britannia:* "Here is also a certain custom, observed time out of mind, of planting rose trees upon the graves, especially by the young men and maids who have lost their loves; so that this church-yard is now full of them."

When the deceased had been unhappy in their loves, emblems of a more gloomy character were used, such as the yew and cypress, and if flowers were strewn, they were of the most melancholy colors. Thus, in poems by Thomas Stanley, Esq. (published in 1651), is the following stanza:

>   *Yet strew*
> *Upon my dismall grave*
> *Such offerings as you have,*
>   *Forsaken cypresse and sad yewe;*
> *For kinder flowers can take no birth*
> *Or growth from such unhappy earth.*

In *The Maid's Tragedy*, a pathetic little air is introduced, illustrative of this mode of decorating the funerals of females who had been disappointed in love:

> *Lay a garland on my hearse.*
>   *Of the dismall yew,*
> *Maidens, willow branches wear,*
>   *Say I died true.*
>
> *My love was false, but I was firm,*
>   *From my hour of birth,*
> *Upon my buried body lie*
>   *Lightly, gentle earth.*

The natural effect of sorrow over the dead is to refine and elevate the mind, and we have a proof of it in the purity of sentiment and the unaffected elegance of thought which pervaded the whole of these funeral observances. Thus, it was an especial precaution that none but sweet-scented evergreens and flowers should be employed. The intention seems to have been to soften the horrors of the tomb, to beguile the mind from brooding over the disgraces of perishing mortality, and to associate the memory of the deceased with the most delicate and beautiful objects in nature. There is a dismal process going on in the grave, ere dust can return to its kindred dust, which the imagination sinks from contemplating; and we seek still to think of the form we have loved with those refined associations which it awakened when blooming before us in youth and beauty. "Lay her i' the earth," sayd Laertes, of his virgin sister,

> *And from her fair and unpolluted flesh*
> *May violets spring!*

Herrick, also, in his *Dirge of Jephtha*, pours forth a fragrant flow of poetical thought and image, which in a manner embalms the dead in the recollections of the living.

Sleep in thy peace, thy bed of spice,
And make this place all Paradise:
May sweets grow here! and smoke from hence
                              Fat frankincense.
Let balme and cassia send their scent
From out thy maiden monument.
* * * * * *
May all shie maids at wonted hours
Come forth to strew thy tombe with flowers!
May virgins, when they come to mourn,
                              Male incense burn
Upon thine altar! then return
And leave thee sleeping in thine urn.

I might crowd my pages with extracts from the older British poets who wrote when these rites were more prevalent, and delighted frequently to allude to them, but I have already quoted more than is necessary. I cannot, however, refrain from giving a passage from Shakespeare, even though it should appear trite, which illustrates the emblematical meaning often conveyed in these floral tributes, and at the same time possesses that magic of language and appositeness of imagery for which he stands pre-eminent.

                With fairest flowers,
Whilst summer lasts, and I live here, Fidele,
I'll sweeten thy sad grave; thou shalt not lack
The flower that's like thy face, pale primrose; nor
The azured harebell, like thy veins; no, nor
The leaf of eglantine; whom not to slander,
Outsweeten'd not thy breath.

There is certainly something more affecting in these prompt and spontaneous offerings of nature than in the most costly monuments of art; the hand strews the flower while the heart is warm and the tear falls on the grave as affection is binding the osier round the sod; but pathos expires under the slow labor of the chisel and is chilled among the cold conceits of sculptured marble.

It is greatly to be regretted that a custom so truly elegant and touching has disappeared from general use, and exists only in the most remote and insignificant villages. But it seems as if poetical custom always shuns the walks of cultivated society. In proportion as people grow polite they cease to be poetical. They talk of poetry, but they have learned to check its free impulses, to distrust its sallying emotions, and to supply its most affecting and picturesque usages by studied form and pompous ceremonial. Few pageants can be more stately and frigid than an English funeral in town. It is made up of show and gloomy parade; mourning carriages, mourning horses, mourning plumes, and hireling mourners, who make a mockery of grief. "There is a grave digged," says Jeremy Taylor, "and a solemn mourning, and a great talk in the neighborhood, and when the daies are finished, they shall be, and they shall be remembered no more." The associate in the gay and crowded city is soon forgotten; the hurrying succession of new intimates and new pleasures effaces him from our minds, and the very scenes and circles in which he moved are incessantly fluctuating. But funerals in the country are solemnly impressive. The stroke of death makes a wider space in the village circle, and is an awful event in the tranquil uniformity of rural life. The passing bell tolls its knell in every ear; it steals with its pervading melancholy over hill and vale, and saddens all the landscape.

The fixed and unchanging features of the country also perpetuate, the memory of the friend with whom we once enjoyed them, who was the companion of our most retired walks, and gave animation to every lonely scene. His idea is associated with every charm of nature; we hear his voice in the echo which he once delighted to awaken; his spirit haunts the grove which he once frequented; we think of him in the wild upland solitude or amidst the pensive beauty of the valley. In the freshness of joyous morning, we remember his beaming smiles and bounding gaiety; and when sober evening returns with its gathering shadows and subduing quiet, we call to mind many a twilight hour of gentle talk and sweet-souled melancholy.

> *Each lonely place shall him restore,*
> *For him the tear be duly shed;*
> *Belov'd, till life can charm no more;*
> *And mourn'd till pity's self be dead.*

Another cause that perpetuates the memory of the deceased in the country is that the grave is more immediately in sight of the survivors. They pass it on their way to prayer, it meets their eyes when their hearts are softened by the exercises of devotion; they linger about it on the Sabbath, when the mind is disengaged from worldly cares and most disposed to turn aside from present pleasures and present loves and to sit down among the solemn mementos of the past. In North Wales the peasantry kneel and pray over the graves of their deceased friends for several Sundays after the interment; and where the tender rite of strewing and planting flowers is still practiced, it is always renewed on Easter, Whisuntide, and other festivals, when the season brings the companion of former festivity more vividly to mind. It is also invariably performed by the nearest relatives and friends; no menials nor hirelings are employed; and if a neighbor yields assistance, it would be deemed an insult to offer compensation.

I have dwelled upon this beautiful rural custom because, as it is one of the last, so is it one of the holiest offices of love. The grave is the ordeal of true affection. It is there that the divine passion of the soul manifests its superiority to the instinctive impulse of mere animal attachment. The latter must be continually refreshed and kept alive by the presence of its object; but the love that is seated in the soul can live on long remembrance. The mere inclinations of sense languish and decline with the charms which excited them, and turn with shuddering disgust from the dismal precincts of the tomb;

but it is thence that truly spiritual affection rises, purified from every sensual desire, and returns, like a holy flame, to illumine and sanctify the heart of the survivor.

The sorrow for the dead is the only sorrow from which we refuse to be divorced. Every other wound we seek to heal—every other affliction to forget; but this wound we consider it a duty to keep open—this affliction we cherish and brood over in solitude. Where is the mother who would willingly forget the infant that perished like a blossom from her arms, though every recollection is a pang? Where is the child that would willingly forget the most tender of parents, though to remember be but to lament? Who, even in the hour of agony, would forget the friend over whom he mourns? Who, even when the tomb is closing upon the remains of her he most loved, when he feels his heart, as it were, crushed in the closing of its portal, would accept of consolation that must be bought by forgetfulness? No, the love which survives the tomb is one of the noblest attributes of the soul. If it has its woes, it has likewise its delights; and when the overwhelming burst of grief is calmed into the gentle tear of recollection, when the sudden anguish and the convulsive agony over the present ruins of all that we most loved are softened away into pensive meditation on all that it was in the days of its loveliness—who would root out such a sorrow from the heart? Though it may sometimes throw a passing cloud over the bright hour of gaiety, or spread a deeper sadness over the hour of gloom, yet who would exchange it even for the song of pleasure, or the burst of revelry? No, there is a voice from the tomb sweeter than song. There is a remembrance of the dead to which we turn even from the charms of the living. Oh, the grave! The grave! It buries every error—covers every defect—extinguishes every resentment! From its peaceful bosom spring none but fond regrets and tender recollections. Who can look down upon the grave even of an enemy and not feel a compunctious throb that he should ever have warred with the poor handful of earth that lies moldering before him.

But the grave of those we loved—what a place for meditation! There it is that we call up in long review the whole history of virtue and gentleness, and the thousand endearments lavished upon us almost unheeded in the daily intercourse of intimacy—there it is that we dwell upon the tenderness, the solemn, awful tenderness of the parting scene. The bed of death, with all its stifled griefs—its noiseless attendance—its mute, watchful assiduities. The last testimonies of expiring love! The feeble, fluttering, thrilling—oh! how thrilling!—pressure of the hand! The faint, faltering accents, struggling in death to give one more assurance of affection! The last fond look of the glazing eye, turned upon us even from the threshold of existence!

Ay, go to the grave of buried love and meditate! There settle the account with thy conscience for every past benefit unrequited—every past endearment unregarded, of that departed being, who can never, never, never return to be soothed by thy contrition!

If thou art a child and hast ever added a sorrow to the soul or a furrow to the silvered brow of an affectionate parent; if thou art a husband and hast ever caused the fond bosom that ventured its whole happiness in thy arms to doubt one moment of thy kindness or thy truth; if thou art a friend and hast ever wronged, in thought, or word, or deed, the spirit that generously confided in thee; if thou art a lover and hast ever given one unmerited pang to that true heart which now lies cold and still beneath thy feet—then be sure that every unkind look, every ungracious word, every ungentle action, will come thronging back upon thy memory, and knocking dolefully at thy soul—then be sure that thou wilt lie down sorrowing and repentant on the grave, and utter the unheard groan, and pour the unavailing tear, more deep, more bitter, because unheard and unavailing.

Then weave thy chaplet of flowers and strew the beauties of nature about the grave; console thy broken spirit, if thou canst, with these tender yet futile tributes of regret; but take warning by the bitterness of this thy contrite affliction over the dead, and henceforth be more faithful and affectionate in the discharge of thy duties to the living.

In writing the preceding article, it was not intended to give a full detail of the funeral customs of the English peasantry, but merely to furnish a few hints and quotations illustrative of particular rites, to be appended, by way of note, to another paper, which has been withheld. The article swelled insensibly into its present form, and this is mentioned as an apology for so brief and casual a notice of these usages, after they have been amply and learnedly investigated in other works.

I must observe, also, that I am well aware that this custom of adorning graves with flowers prevails in other countries besides England. Indeed, in some it is much more general, and is observed even by the rich and fashionable; but it is then apt to lose its simplicity, and to degenerate into affectation. Bright, in his travels in Lower Hungary, tells of monuments of marble and recesses formed for retirement, with seats placed among bowers of greenhouse plants; and that the graves generally are covered with the gayest flowers of the season. He gives a casual picture of filial piety, which I cannot but transcribe, for I trust it is as useful as it is delightful, to illustrate the amiable virtues of the sex. "When I was at Berlin," says he, "I followed the celebrated Iffland to the grave. Mingled with some pomp, you might trace much real feeling. In the midst of the ceremony, my attention was attracted by a young woman, who stood on a mound of earth, newly covered with turf, which she anxiously protected from the feet of the passing crowd. It was the tomb of her parent; and the figure of this affectionate daughter presented a monument more striking than the most costly work of art."

I will barely add an instance of sepulchral decoration that I once met with among the mountains of Switzerland. It was at the village of Gersau, which stands on the borders of the Lake of Lucerne, at the foot of Mount Rigi. It was once the capital of a miniature republic, shut up between the Alps and the lake, and accessible on the land side only by footpaths. The whole force of the republic did not exceed six hundred fighting men, and a few miles of circumference, scooped out as it were from the bosom of the mountains, comprised its territory. The village of Gersau seemed separated from the rest of the world, and retained the golden simplicity of a purer age. It had a small church, with a burying ground adjoining. At the heads of the graves were placed crosses of wood or iron. On some were affixed miniatures, rudely executed, but evidently attempts at likenesses of the deceased. On the crosses were hung chaplets of flowers, some withering, others fresh, as if occasionally renewed. I paused with interest at this scene; I felt that I was at the source of poetical description, for these were the beautiful but unaffected offerings of the heart which poets are fain to record. In a gayer and more populous place, I should have suspected them to have been suggested by factitious sentiment, derived from books; but the good people of Gersau knew little of books, there was not a novel nor a love poem in the village, and I question whether any peasant of the place dreamt, while he was twining a fresh chaplet for the grave of his mistress, that he was fulfilling one of the most fanciful rites of poetical devotion, and that he was practically a poet.

WESTMINSTER ABBEY

When I behold, with deep astonishment,
To famous Westminster how there resorte
Living in brasse or stoney monument,
The princes and the worthies of all sorte;
Doe not I see reformde nobilitie,
Without contempt, or pride, or ostentation,
And looke upon offenselesse majesty,
Naked of pomp or earthly domination?
And how a play-game of a painted stone
Contents the quiet now and silent sprites,
Whome all the world which late they stood upon
Could not content or quench their appetites.
    Life is a frost of cold felicitie,
    And death the thaw of all our vanitie.
        Christolero's Epigrams by T. B. 1598

On one of those sober and rather melancholy days, in the latter part of autumn, when the shadows of morning and evening almost mingle together and throw a gloom over the decline of the year, I passed several hours in rambling about Westminster Abbey. There was something congenial to the season in the mournful magnificence of the old pile; and, as I passed its threshold, seemed like stepping back into the regions of antiquity and losing myself among the shades of former ages.

I entered from the inner court of Westminster School, through a long, low, vaulted passage that had an almost subterranean look, being dimly lighted in one part by circular perforations in the massive walls. Through this dark avenue I had a distant view of the cloisters, with the figure of an old verger, in his black gown, moving along their shadowy vaults, and seeming like a specter from one of the neighboring tombs. The approach to the abbey through these gloomy monastic remains prepares the mind for its solemn contemplation. The cloisters still retain something of the quiet and seclusion of former days. The gray walls are discolored by damps and crumbling with age; a coat of hoary moss has gathered over the inscriptions of the mural monuments and obscured the death's heads and other funereal emblems. The sharp touches of the chisel are gone from the rich tracery of the arches; the roses which adorned the keystones have lost their leafy beauty; everything bears marks of the gradual dilapidations of time, which yet has something touching and pleasing in its very decay.

The sun was pouring down a yellow autumnal ray into the square of the cloisters, beaming upon a scanty plot of grass in the center and lighting up an angle of the vaulted passage with a kind of dusky splendor. From between the arcades, the eye glanced up to a bit of blue sky or a passing cloud, and beheld the sun-gilt pinnacles of the abbey towering into the azure heaven.

As I paced the cloisters, sometimes contemplating this mingled picture of glory and decay, and sometimes endeavoring to decipher the inscriptions on the tombstones, which formed the pavement beneath my feet, my eye was attracted to three figures, rudely carved in relief, but nearly worn away by the footsteps of many generations. They were the effigies of three of the early abbots; the epitaphs were entirely effaced; the names alone remained, having no doubt been renewed in later times. (Vitalis Abbas. 1082, and Gislebertus Crispinus. Abbas. 1114, and Laurentius. Abbas. 1176.) I remained some little while, musing over these casual relics of antiquity, thus left like wrecks upon this distant shore of time, telling no tale but that such beings had been and had perished; teaching no moral but the futility of that pride which hopes still to exact homage in its ashes, and to live in an inscription. A little longer and even these faint records will be obliterated, and the monument will cease to be a memorial. While I was yet looking down upon these gravestones, I was roused by the sound of the abbey clock, reverberating from buttress to buttress, and echoing among the cloisters. It is almost startling to hear this warning of departed time sounding among the tombs and telling the lapse of the hour, which, like a billow, has rolled us onward toward the grave. I pursued my walk to an arched door opening to the interior of the abbey. On entering here, the magnitude of the building breaks fully upon the mind, contrasted with the vaults of the cloisters. The eyes gaze with wonder at clustered columns of gigantic dimensions, with arches springing from them to such an amazing height; and man wandering about their bases, shrunk into insignificance in comparison with his own handiwork. The spaciousness and gloom of this vast edifice produce a profound and mysterious awe. We step cautiously and softly about, as if fearful of disturbing the hallowed silence of the tomb, while every footfall whispers along the walls and chatters among the sepulchers, making us more sensible of the quiet we have interrupted.

It seems as if the awful nature of the place presses down upon the soul, and hushes the beholder into noiseless reverence. We feel that we are surrounded by the congregated bones of the great men of past times, who have filled history with their deeds and the earth with their renown.

And yet it almost provokes a smile at the vanity of human ambition to see how they are crowded together and jostled in the dust; what parsimony is observed in doling out a scanty nook, a gloomy corner, a little portion of earth, to those, whom, when alive, kingdoms could not satisfy; and how many shapes, and forms, and artifices are devised to catch the casual notice of the passenger and save from forgetfulness for a few short years a name which once aspired to occupy ages of the world's thought and admiration.

I passed some time in Poets' Corner, which occupies an end of one of the transepts or cross aisles of the abbey. The monuments are generally simple, for the lives of literary men afford no striking themes for the sculptor. Shakespeare and Addison have statues erected to their memories, but the greater part have busts, medallions, and sometimes mere inscriptions. Notwithstanding the simplicity of these memorials, I have always observed that the visitors to the abbey remained longest about them. A kinder and fonder feeling takes the place of that cold curiosity or vague admiration with which they gaze on the splendid monuments of the great and the heroic. They linger about these as about the tombs of friends and companions, for indeed there is something of companionship between the author and the reader. Other men are known to posterity only through the medium of history, which is continually growing faint and obscure; but the intercourse between the author and his fellow men is ever new, active, and immediate. He has lived for them more than for himself; he has sacrificed surrounding enjoyments and shut himself up from the delights of social life that he might the more intimately commune with distant minds and distant ages. Well may the world cherish his renown, for it has been purchased, not by deeds of violence and blood, but by the diligent dispensation of pleasure. Well may posterity be grateful to his memory, for he has left it an inheritance, not of empty names and sounding actions, but whole treasures of wisdom, bright gems of thought, and golden veins of language.

From Poets' Corner I continued my stroll toward that part of the abbey which contains the sepulchers of the kings. I wandered among what once were chapels but which are now occupied by the tombs and monuments of the great. At every turn I met with some illustrious name, or the cognizance of some powerful house renowned in history. As the eye darts into these dusky chambers of death, it catches glimpses of quaint effigies; some kneeling in niches, as if in devotion; others stretched upon the tombs, with hands piously pressed together—warriors in armor, as if reposing after battle; prelates with crosiers and miters; and nobles in robes and coronets, lying as it were in state. In glancing over this scene, so strangely populous, yet where every form is so still and silent, it seems almost as if we were treading a mansion of that fabled city, where every being had been suddenly transmuted into stone.

I paused to contemplate a tomb on which lay the effigy of a knight in complete armor. A large buckler was on one arm; the hands were pressed together in supplication upon the breast: the face was almost covered by the morion; the legs were crossed, in token of the warrior's having been engaged in the holy war. It was the tomb of a crusader, of one of those military enthusiasts who so strangely mingled religion and romance and whose exploits form the connecting link between fact and fiction, between the history and the fairy tale. There is something extremely picturesque in the tombs of these adventurers, decorated as they are with rude armorial bearings and Gothic sculpture. They comport with the antiquated chapels in which they are generally found; and in considering them the imagination is apt to kindle with the legendary associations, the romantic fiction, the chivalrous pomp and pageantry which poetry has spread over the wars for the sepulcher of Christ. They are the relics of times utterly gone by, of beings passed from recollection, of customs and manners with which ours have no affinity. They are like objects from some strange and distant land, of which we have no certain knowledge and about which all our conceptions are vague and visionary. There is something extremely solemn and awful in those effigies on Gothic tombs, extended as if in the sleep of death, or in the supplication of the dying hour. They have an effect infinitely more impressive on my feelings than the fanciful attitudes, the overwrought conceits, and allegorical groups, which abound on modern monuments. I have been struck, also, with the superiority of many of the old sepulchral inscriptions. There was a noble way, in former times, of saying things simply, and yet saying them proudly; and I do not know an epitaph that breathes a loftier consciousness of family worth and honorable lineage than one which affirms, of a noble house, that "all the brothers were brave, and all the sisters virtuous."

In the opposite transept to Poets' Corner stands a monument which is among the most renowned achievements of modern art, but which to me appears horrible rather than sublime. It is the tomb of Mrs. Nightingale, by Roubillac. The bottom of the monument is represented as throwing open its marble doors, and a sheeted skeleton is starting forth. The shroud is falling from its fleshless frame as he launches his dart at his victim. She is sinking into her affrighted husband's arms, who strives, with vain and frantic effort, to avert the blow. The whole is executed with terrible truth and spirit; we almost fancy we hear the gibbering yell of triumph bursting from the distended jaws of the specter. But why should we thus seek to clothe death with unnecessary terrors, and to spread horrors around the tomb of those we love? The grave should be surrounded by everything that might inspire tenderness and veneration for the dead, or that might win the living to virtue. It is the place, not of disgust and dismay, but of sorrow and meditation.

While wandering about these gloomy vaults and silent aisles, studying the records of the dead, the sound of busy existence from without occasionally reaches the ear—the rumbling of the passing equipage, the murmur of the multitude, or perhaps the light laugh of pleasure. The contrast is striking with the deathlike repose around, and it has a strange effect upon the feelings, thus to hear the surges of active life hurrying along, and beating against the very walls of the sepulcher.

I continued in this way to move from tomb to tomb, and from chapel to chapel. The day was gradually wearing away; the distant tread of loiterers about the abbey grew less and less frequent; the sweet-tongued bell was summoning to evening prayers; and I saw at a distance the choristers, in their white surplices, crossing the aisle and entering the choir. I stood before the entrance to Henry the Seventh's chapel. A flight of steps lead up to it, through a deep and gloomy but magnificent arch. Great gates of brass, richly and delicately wrought, turn heavily upon their hinges, as if proudly reluctant to admit the feet of common mortals into this most gorgeous of sepulchers.

On entering, the eye is astonished by the pomp of architecture and the elaborate beauty of sculptured detail. The very walls are wrought into universal ornament, encrusted with tracery, and scooped into niches, crowded with the statues of saints and martyrs. Stone seems, by the cunning labor of the chisel, to have been robbed of its weight and density, suspended aloft, as if by magic, and the fretted roof achieved with the wonderful minuteness and airy security of a cobweb.

Along the sides of the chapel are the lofty stalls of the Knights of the Bath, richly carved of oak, though with the grotesque decorations of Gothic architecture. On the pinnacles of the stalls are affixed the helmets and crests of the knights, with their scarfs and swords; and above them are suspended their banners, emblazoned with armorial bearings, and contrasting the splendor of gold and purple and crimson with the cold gray fretwork of the roof. In the midst of this grand mausoleum stands the sepulcher of its founder—his effigy, with that of his queen, extended on a sumptuous tomb, and the whole surrounded by a superbly wrought brazen railing.

There is a sad dreariness in this magnificence, this strange mixture of tombs and trophies, these emblems of living and aspiring ambition, close beside mementos which show the dust and oblivion in which all must sooner or later terminate. Nothing impresses the mind with a deeper feeling of loneliness than to tread the silent and deserted scene of former throng and pageant. On looking around on the vacant stalls of the knights and their esquires and on the rows of dusty but gorgeous banners that were once borne before them, my imagination conjured up the scene when this hall was bright with the valor and beauty of the land, glittering with the splendor of jeweled rank and military array, alive with the tread of many feet and the hum of an admiring multitude. All had passed away; the silence of death had settled again upon the place, interrupted only by the casual chirping of birds, which had found their way into the chapel and built their nests among its friezes and pendants—sure signs of solitariness and desertion.

When I read the names inscribed on the banners, they were those of men scattered far and wide about the world, some tossing upon distant seas, some under arms in distant lands, some mingling in the busy intrigues of courts and cabinets; all seeking to deserve one more distinction in this mansion of shadowy honors—the melancholy reward of a monument.

Two small aisles on each side of this chapel present a touching instance of the equality of the grave, which brings down the oppressor to a level with the oppressed, and mingles the dust of the bitterest enemies together. In one is the sepulcher of the haughty Elizabeth; in the other is that of her victim, the lovely and unfortunate Mary. Not an hour in the day but some ejaculation of pity is uttered over the fate of the latter, mingled with indignation at her oppressor. The walls of Elizabeth's sepulcher continually echo with the sighs of sympathy heaved at the grave of her rival.

A peculiar melancholy reigns over the aisle where Mary lies buried. The light struggles dimly through windows darkened by dust. The greater part of the place is in deep shadow, and the walls are stained and tinted by time and weather. A marble figure of Mary is stretched upon the tomb, around which is an iron railing, much corroded, bearing her national emblem— the thistle. I was weary with wandering, and sat down to rest myself by the monument, revolving in my mind the checkered and disastrous story of poor Mary.

The sound of casual footsteps had ceased from the abbey. I could only hear, now and then, the distant voice of the priest repeating the evening service, and the faint responses of the choir; these paused for a time, and all was hushed. The stillness, the desertion and obscurity that were gradually prevailing around gave a deeper and more solemn interest to the place:

> *For in the silent grave no conversation,*
> *No joyful tread of friends, no voice of lovers,*
> *No careful father's counsel—nothing's heard,*
> *For nothing is, but all oblivion,*
> *Dust, and an endless darkness.*

Suddenly the notes of the deep-laboring organ burst upon the ear, falling with doubled and redoubled intensity, and rolling, as it were, huge billows of sound. How well do their volume and grandeur accord with this mighty building! With what pomp do they swell through its vast vaults, and breathe their awful harmony through these caves of death, and make the silent sepulcher vocal! And now they rise in triumph and acclamation, heaving higher and higher their accordant notes, and piling sound on sound. And now they pause, and the soft voices of the choir break out into sweet gushes of melody; they soar aloft, and warble along the roof, and seem to play about these lofty vaults like the pure airs of heaven. Again the pealing organ heaves its thrilling thunders, compressing air into music, and rolling it forth upon the soul. What long-drawn cadences! What solemn sweeping concords! It grows more and more dense and powerful—it fills the vast pile, and seems to jar the very walls—the ear is stunned—the senses are overwhelmed. And now it is winding up in full jubilee—it is rising from the earth to heaven—the very soul seems rapt away and floated upward on this swelling tide of harmony!

I sat for some time lost in that kind of reverie which a strain of music is apt sometimes to inspire; the shadows of evening were gradually thickening around me, the monuments began to cast deeper and deeper gloom, and the distant clock again gave token of the slowly waning day.

I rose and prepared to leave the abbey. As I descended the flight of steps which lead into the body of the building, my eye was caught by the shrine of Edward the Confessor, and I ascended the small staircase that conducts to it, to take from thence a general survey of this wilderness of tombs. The shrine is elevated upon a kind of platform, and close around it are the sepulchers of various kings and queens. From this eminence the eye looks down between pillars and funeral trophies to the chapels and chambers below, crowded with tombs, where warriors, prelates, courtiers and statesmen lie moldering in their "beds of darkness." Close by me stood the great chair of coronation, rudely carved of oak, in the barbarous taste of a remote and Gothic age. The scene seemed almost as if contrived, with theatrical artifice, to produce an effect upon the beholder. Here was a type of the beginning and the end of human pomp and power; here it was literally but a step from the throne to the sepulcher. Would not one think that these incongruous mementos had been gathered together as a lesson to living greatness?—to show it, even in the moment of its proudest exaltation, the neglect and dishonor to which it must soon arrive; how soon that crown which encircles its brow must pass away, and it must lie down in the dust and disgraces of the tomb, and be trampled upon by the feet of the meanest of the multitude. For, strange to tell, even the grave is here no longer a sanctuary. There is a shocking levity in some natures which leads them to sport with awful and hallowed things; and there are base minds, which delight to revenge on the illustrious dead the abject homage and groveling servility which they pay to the living. The coffin of Edward the Confessor has been broken open, and his remains despoiled of their funereal ornaments; the scepter has been stolen from the hand of the imperious Elizabeth, and the effigy of Henry the Fifth lies headless. Not a royal monument but bears some proof how false and fugitive is the homage of mankind. Some are plundered; some mutilated; some covered with ribaldry and insult—all more or less outraged and dishonored!

The last beams of day were now faintly streaming through the painted windows in the high vaults above me; the lower parts of the abbey were already wrapped in the obscurity of twilight. The chapels and aisles grew darker and darker. The effigies of the kings faded into shadows; the marble figures of the monuments assumed strange shapes in the uncertain light; the evening breeze crept through the aisles like the cold breath of the grave; and even the distant footfall of a verger, traversing the Poets' Corner, had something strange and dreary in its sound. I slowly retraced my morning's walk, and as I passed out at the portal of the cloisters, the door, closing with a jarring noise behind me, filled the whole building with echoes.

I endeavored to form some arrangement in my mind of the objects I had been contemplating, but found they were already fallen into indistinctness and confusion. Names, inscriptions, trophies, had all become confounded in my recollection, though I had scarcely taken my foot from off the threshold. What, thought I, is this vast assemblage of sepulchers but a treasury of humiliation; a huge pile of reiterated homilies on the emptiness of renown and the certainty of oblivion! It is, indeed, the empire of death; his great shadowy palace, where he sits in state, mocking at the relics of human glory, and spreading dust and forgetfulness on the monuments of princes. How idle a boast, after all, is the immortality of a name! Time is ever silently turning over his pages; we are too much engrossed by the story of the present to think of the characters and anecdotes that gave interest to the past; and each age is a volume thrown aside to be speedily forgotten. The idol of today pushes the hero of yesterday out of our recollection, and will, in turn, be supplanted by his successor of tomorrow. "Our fathers," says Sir Thomas Brown, "find their graves in our short memories, and sadly tell us how we may be buried in our survivors." History fades into fable; fact becomes clouded with doubt and controversy; the inscription molders from the tablet; the statue falls from the pedestal. Columns, arches, pyramids, what are they but heaps of sand; and their epitaphs, but characters written in the dust? What is the security of a tomb, or the perpetuity of an embalmment? The remains of Alexander the Great have been scattered to the wind, and his empty sarcophagus is now the mere curiosity of a museum. "The Egyptian mummies, which Cambyses or time hath spared, avarice now consumeth; Mizraim cures wounds, and Pharaoh is sold for balsams."*

What then is to insure this pile which now towers above me from sharing the fate of mightier mausoleums? The time must come when its gilded vaults, which now spring so loftily, shall lie in rubbish beneath the feet; when, instead of the sound of melody and praise, the wind shall whistle through the broken arches, and the owl hoot from the shattered tower; when the garish sunbeam shall break into these gloomy mansions of death, and the ivy twine around the fallen column, and the foxglove hang its blossoms about the nameless urn, as if in mockery of the dead. Thus man passes away; his name perishes from record and recollection; his history is as a tale that is told, and his very monument becomes a ruin.†

---

*Sir T. Brown.

†For notes on Westminster Abbey, see Appendix.

STRATFORD ON AVON

Thou soft-flowing Avon, by thy silver stream
Of things more than mortal sweet Shakespeare would
*   dream;*
The fairies by moonlight dance round his green bed,
For hallow'd the turf is which pillow'd his head.

GARRICK

To a homeless man, who has no spot on this wide world
which he can truly call his own, there is a momentary feeling
of something like independence and territorial consequence
when, after a weary day's travel, he kicks off his boots,
thrusts his feet into slippers, and stretches himself before an
inn fire. Let the world without go as it may; let kingdoms
rise or fall, so long as he has the wherewithal to pay his
bill, he is, for the time being, the very monarch of all he
surveys. The armchair is his throne, the poker his scepter,
and the little parlor, some twelve feet square, his undisputed
empire. It is a morsel of certainty, snatched from the midst
of the uncertainties of life; it is a sunny moment gleaming

out kindly on a cloudy day, and he who has advanced some way on the pilgrimage of existence knows the importance of husbanding even morsels and moments of enjoyment. "Shall I not take mine ease in mine inn?" thought I, as I gave the fire a stir, lolled back in my elbow chair, and cast a complacent look about the little parlor of the Red Horse, at Stratford on Avon.

The words of sweet Shakespeare were just passing through my mind as the clock struck midnight from the tower of the church in which he lies buried. There was a gentle tap at the door, and a pretty chambermaid, putting in her smiling face, inquired, with a hesitating air, whether I had rung. I understood it as a modest hint that it was time to retire. My dream of absolute dominion was at an end; so abdicating my throne, like a prudent potentate, to avoid being deposed, and putting the Stratford *Guide Book* under my arm as a pillow companion I went to bed, and dreamed all night of Shakespeare, the jubilee, and David Garrick.

The next morning was one of those quickening mornings which we sometimes have in early spring, for it was about the middle of March. The chills of a long winter had suddenly given way; the north wind had spent its last gasp; and a mild air came stealing from the west, breathing the breath of life into nature, and wooing every bud and flower to burst forth into fragrance and beauty.

I had come to Stratford on a poetical pilgrimage. My first visit was to the house where Shakespeare was born, and where, according to tradition, he was brought up to his father's craft of wool-combing. It is a small, mean-looking edifice of wood and plaster, a true nestling place of genius, which seems to delight in hatching its offspring in by-corners. The walls of its squalid chambers are covered with names and inscriptions in every language, by pilgrims of all nations, ranks, and conditions, from the prince to the peasant, and present a simple but striking instance of the spontaneous and universal homage of mankind to the great poet of nature.

The house is shown by a garrulous old lady, in a frosty

red face, lighted up by a cold blue anxious eye, and garnished with artificial locks of flaxen hair, curling from under an exceedingly dirty cap. She was peculiarly assiduous in exhibiting the relics with which this, like all other celebrated shrines, abounds. There was the shattered stock of the very match lock with which Shakespeare shot the deer on his poaching exploits. There, too, was his tobacco box, which proves that he was a rival smoker of Sir Walter Raleigh; the sword also with which he played Hamlet; and the identical lantern with which Friar Laurence discovered Romeo and Juliet at the tomb! There was an ample supply also of Shakespeare's mulberry tree, which seems to have as extraordinary powers of self-multiplication as the wood of the true cross, of which there is enough extant to build a ship of the line.

The most favorite object of curiosity, however, is Shakespeare's chair. It stands in the chimney nook of a small gloomy chamber, just behind what was his father's shop. Here he may many a time have sat when a boy, watching the slowly revolving spit with all the longing of an urchin, or of an evening, listening to the cronies and gossips of Stratford dealing forth churchyard tales and legendary anecdotes of the troublesome times of England. In this chair it is the custom of everyone that visits the house to sit: whether this be done with the hope of imbibing any of the inspiration of the bard I am at a loss to say, I merely mention the fact; and mine hostess privately assured me that, though built of solid oak, such was the fervent zeal of devotees that the chair had to be new bottomed at least once in three years. It is worthy of notice also, in the history of this extraordinary chair, that it partakes something of the volatile nature of the Santa Casa of Loretto, or the flying chair of the Arabian enchanter, for though sold some few years since to a northern princess, yet, strange to tell, it has found its way back again to the old chimney corner.

I am always of easy faith in such matters, and am ever willing to be deceived where the deceit is pleasant and costs nothing. I am therefore a ready believer in relics, legends, and local anecdotes of goblins and great men, and would advise all travelers who travel for their gratification to be the same. What is it to us whether these stories be true or false, so long as we can persuade ourselves into the belief of them, and enjoy all the charm of the reality? There is nothing like resolute good-humored credulity in these matters; and on this occasion I went even so far as willingly to believe the claims of mine hostess to a lineal descent from the poet, when, luckily, for my faith, she put into my hands a play of her own composition, which set all belief in her consanguinity at defiance.

From the birthplace of Shakespeare a few paces brought me to his grave. He lies buried in the chancel of the parish church, a large and venerable pile, moldering with age, but richly ornamented. It stands on the banks of the Avon, on an embowered point, and separated by adjoining gardens from the suburbs of the town. Its situation is quiet and retired; the river runs murmuring at the foot of the churchyard, and the elms which grow upon its banks droop their branches into its clear bosom. An avenue of limes, the boughs of which are curiously interlaced so as to form in summer an arched way of foliage, leads up from the gate of the yard to the church porch. The graves are overgrown with grass; the gray tombstones, some of them nearly sunk into the earth, are half covered with moss, which has likewise tinted the reverend old building. Small birds have built their nests among the cornices and fissures of the walls, and keep up a continual flutter and chirping; and rooks are sailing and cawing about its lofty gray spire.

In the course of my rambles I met with the gray-headed sexton, Edmonds, and accompanied him home to get the key of the church. He had lived in Stratford, man and boy, for eighty years, and seemed still to consider himself a vigorous man, with the trivial exception that he had nearly lost the use of his legs for a few years past. His dwelling was a cottage looking out upon the Avon and its bordering meadows, and was a

picture of that neatness, order, and comfort which pervade
the humblest dwellings in this country. A low white-washed
room with a stone floor carefully scrubbed served for parlor,
kitchen, and hall. Rows of pewter and earthen dishes glittered
along the dresser. On an old oaken table, well rubbed and
polished, lay the family Bible and prayerbook, and the drawer
contained the family library, composed of about half a score
of well-thumbed volumes. An ancient clock, that important
article of cottage furniture, ticked on the opposite side of
the room, with a bright warming pan hanging on one side
of it, and the old man's horn-handled Sunday cane on the
other. The fireplace, as usual, was wide and deep enough to
admit a gossip knot within its jambs. In one corner sat the
old man's granddaughter sewing, a pretty blue-eyed girl—and
in the opposite corner was a superannuated crony, whom he
addressed by the name of John Ange, and who, I found, had
been his companion from childhood. They had played together
in infancy; they had worked together in manhood; they were
now tottering about and gossiping away the evening of life;
and in a short time they will probably be buried together in
the neighboring churchyard. It is not often that we see two
streams of existence running thus evenly and tranquilly side
by side; it is only in such quiet "bosom scenes" of life that
they are to be met with.

I had hoped to gather some traditionary anecdotes of the
bard from these ancient chroniclers, but they had nothing
new to impart. The long interval during which Shakespeare's
writings lay in comparative neglect has spread its shadow
over his history, and it is his good or evil lot that scarcely
anything remains to his biographers but a scanty handful of
conjectures.

The sexton and his companion had been employed as car-
penters on the preparations for the celebrated Stratford jubilee,
and they remembered Garrick, the prime mover of the fete,
who superintended the arrangements, and who, according to
the sexton, was "a short punch man, very lively and bustling."
John Ange had assisted also in cutting down Shakespeare's

mulberry tree, of which he had a morsel in his pocket for sale, no doubt a sovereign quickener of literary conception.

I was grieved to hear these two worthy wights speak very dubiously of the eloquent dame who shows the Shakespeare house. John Ange shook his head when I mentioned her valuable collection of relics, particularly her remains of the mulberry tree, and the old sexton even expressed a doubt as to Shakespeare having been born in her house. I soon discovered that he looked upon her mansion with an evil eye, as a rival to the poet's tomb, the latter having comparatively but few visitors. Thus it is that historians differ at the very outset, and mere pebbles make the stream of truth diverge into different channels even at the fountainhead.

We approached the church through the avenue of limes, and entered by a Gothic porch, highly ornamented, with carved doors of massive oak. The interior is spacious, and the architecture and embellishments superior to those of most country churches. There are several ancient monuments of nobility and gentry, over some of which hang funeral escutcheons, and banners dropping piecemeal from the walls. The tomb of Shakespeare is in the chancel. The place is solemn and sepulchral. Tall elms wave before the pointed windows, and the Avon, which runs at a short distance from the walls, keeps up a low perpetual murmur. A flat stone marks the spot where the bard is buried. There are four lines inscribed on it, said to have been written by himself, and which have in them something extremely awful. If they are indeed his own, they show that solicitude about the quiet of the grave which seems natural to fine sensibilities and thoughtful minds.

> *Good friend, for Jesus' sake forbeare*
> *To dig the dust enclosed here.*
> *Blessed be he that spares these stones,*
> *And curst be he that moves my bones.*

Just over the grave, in a niche of the wall, is a bust of Shakespeare, put up shortly after his death, and considered as a resemblance. The aspect is pleasant and serene, with a finely arched forehead, and I thought I could read in it clear indications of that cheerful, social disposition by which he was as much characterized among his contemporaries as by the vastness of his genius. The inscription mentions his age at the time of his decease—fifty-three years; an untimely death for the world, for what fruit might not have been expected from the golden autumn of such a mind, sheltered as it was from the stormy vicissitudes of life and flourishing in the sunshine of popular and royal favor.

The inscription on the tombstone has not been without its effect. It has prevented the removal of his remains from the bosom of his native place to Westminster Abbey, which was at one time contemplated. A few years since also, as some laborers were digging to make an adjoining vault, the earth caved in, so as to leave a vacant space almost like an arch, through which one might have reached into his grave. No one, however, presumed to meddle with his remains so awfully guarded by a malediction; and lest any of the idle or the curious or any collector of relics should be tempted to commit depredations, the old sexton kept watch over the place for two days until the vault was finished and the aperture closed again. He told me that he had made bold to look in at the hole, but could see neither coffin nor bones; nothing but dust. It was something, I thought, to have seen the dust of Shakespeare.

Next to this grave are those of his wife, his favorite daughter, Mrs. Hall, and others of his family. On a tomb close by, also, is a full-length effigy of his old friend John Combe of usurious memory, on whom he is said to have written a ludicrous epitaph. There are other monuments around, but the mind refuses to dwell on anything that is not connected with Shakespeare. His idea pervades the place; the whole pile seems but as his mausoleum. The feelings, no longer checked and thwarted by doubt, here indulge in perfect confidence; other traces of him may be false or dubious, but

here is palpable evidence and absolute certainty. As I trod the
sounding pavement there was something intense and thrilling
in the idea that, in very truth, the remains of Shakespeare were
moldering beneath my feet. It was a long time before I could
prevail upon myself to leave the place; and as I passed through
the churchyard I plucked a branch from one of the yew trees,
the only relic that I have brought from Stratford.

I had now visited the usual objects of a pilgrim's devotion,
but I had a desire to see the old family seat of the Lucys, at
Charlecot, and to ramble through the park where Shakespeare,
in company with some of the roysters of Stratford, committed his youthful offence of deer stealing. In this harebrained
exploit we are told that he was taken prisoner and carried to
the keeper's lodge, where he remained all night in doleful
captivity. When brought into the presence of Sir Thomas Lucy,
his treatment must have been galling and humiliating, for it so
wrought upon his spirit as to produce a rough pasquinade,
which was affixed to the park gate at Charlecot.*

This flagitious attack upon the dignity of the knight so
incensed him that he applied to a lawyer at Warwick to put
the severity of the laws in force against the rhyming deer
stalker. Shakespeare did not wait to brave the united puissance
of a knight of the shire and a country attorney. He forthwith

---

*The following is the only stanza extant of this lampoon:

> A parliament member, a justice of peace,
> At home a poor scarecrow, at London an asse,
> If lowsie is Lucy, as some volke miscalle it,
> Then Lucy is lowsie, whatever befall it.
>   He thinks himself great;
>   Yet an asse in his state,
> We allow by his ears but with asses to mate,
> If Lucy is lowsie, as some volke miscalle it,
> Then sing lowsie Lucy whatever befall it.

abandoned the pleasant banks of the Avon and his paternal trade, wandered away to London, became a hanger-on to the theaters, then an actor, and, finally, wrote for the stage; and thus, through the persecution of Sir Thomas Lucy, Stratford lost an indifferent wool comber and the world gained an immortal poet. He retained, however, for a long time a sense of the harsh treatment of the Lord of Charlecot, and revenged himself in his writings, but in the sportive way of a good-natured mind. Sir Thomas is said to be the original Justice Shallow, and the satire is slyly fixed upon him by the justice's armorial bearings, which, like those of the knight, had white luces* in the quarterings.

Various attempts have been made by his biographers to soften and explain away this early transgression of the poet, but I look upon it as one of those thoughtless exploits natural to his situation and turn of mind. Shakespeare, when young, had doubtless all the wildness and irregularity of an ardent, undisciplined, and undirected genius. The poetic temperament has naturally something in it of the vagabond. When left to itself it runs loosely and wildly, and delights in everything eccentric and licentious. It is often a turn-up of a die, in the gambling freaks of fate, whether a natural genius shall turn out a great rogue or a great poet; and had not Shakespeare's mind fortunately taken a literary bias, he might have as daringly transcended all civil as he has all dramatic laws.

I have little doubt that, in early life, when running, like an unbroken colt, about the neighborhood of Stratford, he was to be found in the company of all kinds of odd anomalous characters, that he associated with all the madcaps of the place, and was one of those unlucky urchins at mention of whom old men shake their heads and predict that they will one day come to the gallows. To him the poaching in Sir Thomas Lucy's park was doubtless like a foray to a Scottish

---

*The luce is a pike or jack, and abounds in the Avon about Charlecot.

knight, and struck his eager and as yet untamed imagination as something delightfully adventurous.*

The old mansion of Charlecot and its surrounding park still remain in the possession of the Lucy family, and are pecu-

---

*A proof of Shakespeare's random habits and associates in his youthful days may be found in a traditionary anecdote, picked up at Stratford by the elder Ireland, and mentioned in his *Picturesque Views on the Avon.*

About seven miles from Stratford lies the thirsty little market town of Bedford, famous for its ale. Two societies of the village yeomanry used to meet, under the appellation of the Bedford topers, and to challenge the lovers of good ale of the neighboring villages to a contest of drinking. Among others, the people of Stratford were called out to prove the strength of their heads; and in the number of the champions was Shakespeare, who, in spite of the proverb that "they who drink beer will think beer," was as true to his ale as Falstaff to his sack. The chivalry of Stratford was staggered at the first onset, and sounded a retreat while they had yet legs to carry them off the field. They had scarcely marched a mile when, their legs failing them, they were forced to lie down under a crabtree, where they passed the night. It is still standing, and goes by the name of Shakespeare's tree.

In the morning his companions awaked the bard, and proposed returning to Bedford, but he declined, saying he had had enough, having drank with

> Piping Pebworth, Dancing Marston,
> Haunted Hilbro', Hungry Grafton,
> Dudging Exhall, Papist Wicksford,
> Beggarly Broom, and Drunken Bedford.

"The villages here alluded to," says Ireland, "still bear the epithets thus given them: the people of Pebworth are still famed for their skill on the pipe and tabor; Hilborough is now called Haunted Hilborough; and Grafton is famous for the poverty of its soil."

liarly interesting from being connected with this whimsical but eventful circumstance in the scanty history of the bard. As the house stood but little more than three miles' distance from Stratford, I resolved to pay it a pedestrian visit, that I might stroll leisurely through some of those scenes from which Shakespeare must have derived his earliest ideas of rural imagery.

The country was yet naked and leafless, but English scenery is always verdant, and the sudden change in the temperature of the weather was surprising in its quickening effects upon the landscape. It was inspiring and animating to witness this first awakening of spring, to feel its warm breath stealing over the senses, to see the moist mellow earth beginning to put forth the green sprout and the tender blade, and the trees and shrubs, in their reviving tints and bursting buds, giving the promise of returning foliage and flower. The cold snowdrop, that little borderer on the skirts of winter, was to be seen with its chaste white blossoms in the small gardens before the cottages. The bleating of the new-dropped lambs was faintly heard from the fields. The sparrow twittered about the thatched eaves and budding hedges; the robin threw a livelier note into his late querulous wintry strain; and the lark, springing up from the reeking bosom of the meadow, towered away into the bright fleecy cloud, pouring forth torrents of melody. As I watched the little songster, mounting up higher and higher until his body was a mere speck on the white bosom of the cloud, while the ear was still filled with his music, it called to mind Shakespeare's exquisite little song in *Cymbeline:*

> *Hark! hark! the lark at heaven's gate sings,*
> *And Phoebus 'gins arise,*
> *His steeds to water at those springs,*
> *On chaliced flowers that lies.*

> *And winking mary-buds begin*
> *To ope their golden eyes;*
> *With every thing that pretty bin,*
> *My lady sweet arise!*

Indeed the whole country about here is poetic ground: every-thing is associated with the idea of Shakespeare. Every old cottage that I saw, I fancied into some resort of his boyhood, where he had acquired his intimate knowledge of rustic life and manners, and heard those legendary tales and wild super-stitions which he has woven like witchcraft into his dramas. For in his time, we are told, it was a popular amusement in winter evenings "to sit round the fire, and tell merry tales of errant knights, queens, lovers, lords, ladies, giants, dwarfs, thieves, cheaters, witches, fairies, goblins, and friars."*

My route for a part of the way lay in sight of the Avon, which made a variety of the most fancy doublings and wind-ings through a wide and fertile valley, sometimes glittering from among willows which fringed its borders, sometimes disappearing among groves or beneath green banks, and some-times rambling out into full view, and making an azure sweep around a slope of meadow land. This beautiful bosom of country is called the Vale of the Red Horse. A distant line of undulating blue hills seems to be its boundary, while all the soft intervening landscape lies in a manner enchained in the silver links of the Avon.

After pursuing the road for about three miles, I turned off into a footpath which led along the borders of fields and under hedgerows to a private gate of the park; there was a stile, however, for the benefit of the pedestrian, there being a public right of way through the grounds. I delight in these hospitable

---

*Scott, in his *Discoverie of Witchcraft,* enumerates a host of these fireside fancies. "And they have so fraid us with bull-beggars, spirits, witches, urchins, elves, hags, fairies, satyrs, pans, faunes, syrens, kit with the can sticke, tritons, centaurs, dwarfes, giantes, imps, calcars, conjurors, nymphes, changelings, incubus, Robin-good-fellow, the spoorne, the mare, the man in the oke, the hell-waige, the fier-drake, the puckle, Tom Thombe, hobgoblins, Tom Tumbler, boneless, and such other bugs, that we were afraid of our own shadowes."

estates, in which everyone has a kind of property—at least as far as the footpath is concerned. It in some measure reconciles a poor man to his lot, and, what is more, to the better lot of his neighbor thus to have parks and pleasure grounds thrown open for his recreation. He breathes the pure air as freely and lolls as luxuriously under the shade as the lord of the soil; and if he has not the privilege of calling all that he sees his own, he has not, at the same time, the trouble of paying for it and keeping it in order.

I now found myself among noble avenues of oaks and elms, whose vast size bespoke the growth of centuries. The wind sounded solemnly among their branches, and the rooks cawed from their hereditary nests in the tree tops. The eye ranged through a long lessening vista, with nothing to interrupt the view but a distant statue, and a vagrant deer stalking like a shadow across the opening.

There is something about these stately old avenues that has the effect of Gothic architecture, not merely from the pretended similarity of form, but from their bearing the evidence of long duration, and of having had their origin in a period of time with which we associate ideas of romantic grandeur. They betoken also the long-settled dignity and proudly concentrated independence of an ancient family; and I have heard a worthy but aristocratic old friend observe, when speaking of the sumptuous palaces of modern gentry, that "money could do much with stone and mortar, but, thank Heaven, there was no such thing as suddenly building up an avenue of oaks."

It was from wandering in early life among this rich scenery and about the romantic solitudes of the adjoining park of Fullbroke, which then formed a part of the Lucy estate, that some of Shakespeare's commentators have supposed he derived his noble forest meditations of Jaques, and the enchanting woodland pictures in *As You Like It*. It is in lonely wanderings through such scenes that the mind drinks deep but quiet drafts of inspiration, and becomes intensely sensible of the beauty and majesty of nature. The imagination kindles into reverie and rapture; vague but exquisite images and ideas keep breaking upon it; and we revel in a mute and almost incommunicable luxury of thought. It was in some such mood, and perhaps under one of those very trees before me which threw their broad shades over the grassy banks and quivering waters of the Avon that the poet's fancy may have sallied forth into that little song which breathes the very soul of a rural voluptuary:

> *Under the greenwood tree,*
> *Who loves to lie with me,*
> *And tune his merry throat*
> *Unto the sweet bird's note,*
> *Come hither, come hither, come hither.*
> *Here shall he see*
> *No enemy,*
> *But winter and rough weather.*

I had now come in sight of the house. It is a large building of brick, with stone quoins, and is in the Gothic style of Queen Elizabeth's day, having been built in the first year of her reign. The exterior remains very nearly in its original state, and may be considered a fair specimen of the residence of a wealthy country gentleman of those days. A great gateway opens from the park into a kind of courtyard in front of the house, ornamented with a grass plot, shrubs, and flower beds. The gateway is in imitation of the ancient barbacan, being a kind of outpost and flanked by towers, though evidently for mere ornament instead of defence. The front of the house is completely in the old style, with stone-shafted casements, a great bow window of heavy stonework, and a portal with armorial bearings over it, carved in stone. At each corner of the building is an octagon tower, surmounted by a gilt ball and weathercock.

The Avon, which winds through the park, makes a bend just at the foot of a gently sloping bank, which sweeps down from the rear of the house. Large herds of deer were feeding or reposing upon its borders, and swans were sailing majestically upon its bosom. As I contemplated the venerable old mansion, I called to mind Falstaff's encomium on Justice Shallow's abode, and the affected indifference and real vanity of the latter:

"*Falstaff.* You have a goodly dwelling and a rich.
Shallow. Barren, barren, barren; beggars all, beggars all, Sir John:—marry, good air."

What may have been the joviality of the old mansion in the days of Shakespeare, it had now an air of stillness and solitude. The great iron gateway that opened into the courtyard was locked; there was no show of servants bustling about the place; the deer gazed quietly at me as I passed, being no longer harried by the moss troopers of Stratford. The only sign of domestic life that I met with was a white cat, stealing with wary look and stealthy pace toward the stables, as if on some nefarious expedition. I must not omit to mention the carcass of a scoundrel crow which I saw suspended against the barn wall, as it shows that the Lucys still inherit that lordly abhorrence of poachers and maintain that rigorous exercise of territorial power which was so strenuously manifested in the case of the bard.

After prowling about for some time, I at length found my way to a lateral portal, which was the everyday entrance to the mansion. I was courteously received by a worthy old housekeeper, who, with the civility and communicativeness of her order, showed me the interior of the house. The greater part has undergone alterations and been adapted to modern tastes and modes of living; there is a fine old oaken staircase, and the great hall, that noble feature in an ancient manor house, still retains much of the appearance it must have had in the days of Shakespeare. The ceiling is arched and lofty, and at one end is a gallery in which stands an organ. The weapons and trophies of the chase, which formerly adorned the hall of a country gentleman, have made way for family portraits. There is a wide hospitable fireplace, calculated for an ample old-fashioned wood fire, formerly the rallying place of winter festivity. On the opposite side of the hall is the huge Gothic bow window, with stone shafts, which looks out upon the courtyard. Here are emblazoned in stained glass the armorial bearings of the Lucy family for many generations, some being dated in 1558. I was delighted to observe in the quarterings the three *white luces,* by which the character of Sir Thomas was first identified with that of Justice Shallow. They are mentioned in the first scene of *The Merry Wives of Windsor,* where the Justice is in a rage with Falstaff for having "beaten his men, killed his deer, and broken into his lodge." The poet had no doubt the offenses of himself and his comrades in mind at the time, and we may suppose the family pride and vindictive threats of the puissant Shallow to be a caricature of the pompous indignation of Sir Thomas.

"*Shallow.* Sir Hugh, persuade me not: I will make a Star-Chamber matter of it; if he were twenty John Falstaffs, he shall not abuse Sir Robert Shallow, Esq.

Slender. In the county of Gloster, justice of peace, and *coram.*

Shallow. Ay, cousin Slender, and *custalorum.*

Slender. Ay, and *ratalorum* too, and a gentleman born, master parson; who writes himself *Armigero* in any bill, warrant, quittance, or obligation, *Armigero.*

Shallow. Ay, that I do; and have done any time these three hundred years.

Slender. All his successors gone before him have done't, and all his ancestors that come after him may; they may give the dozen *white luces* in their coat.*****

Shallow. The council shall hear it; it is a riot.

Evans. It is not meet the council hear of a riot; there is no fear of Got in a riot; the council, hear you, shall desire to hear the fear of Got, and not to hear a riot; take your vizaments in that.

Shallow. Ha! o' my life, if I were young again, the sword should end it!"

Near the window thus emblazoned hung a portrait by Sir Peter Lely, of one of the Lucy family, a great beauty of the time of Charles the Second; the old housekeeper shook her head as she pointed to the picture, and informed me that this lady had been sadly addicted to cards, and had gambled away a great portion of the family estate, among which was that part of the park where Shakespeare and his comrades had killed the deer. The lands thus lost had not been entirely regained by the family even at the present day. It is but justice to this recreant dame to confess that she had a surpassingly fine hand and arm.

The picture which most attracted my attention was a great painting over the fireplace, containing likenesses of Sir Thomas Lucy and his family, who inhabited the hall in the latter part of Shakespeare's lifetime. I at first thought that it was the vindictive knight himself, but the housekeeper assured me that it was his son, the only likeness extant of the former being an effigy upon his tomb in the church of the neighboring hamlet of Charlecot.* The picture gives a lively idea of the costume and

---

*This effigy is in white marble, and represents the knight in complete armor. Near him lies the effigy of his wife, and on her tomb is the following inscription, which, if really composed by her husband, places him quite above the intellectual level of Master Shallow:

Here lyeth the Lady Joyce Lucy wife of Sir Thomas Lucy of Charlecot in ye county of Warwick, Knight, Daughter and heir of Thomas Acton of Sutton in ye county of Worcester Esquire who departed out of this wretched world to her heavenly kingdom ye 10 day of February in ye yeare of our Lord God 1595 and of her age 60 and three. All the time of her lyfe a true and faythful servant of her good God, never detected of any cryme or vice. In religion most sounde, in love to her husband most faythful and true. In friendship most constant; to what in trust was committed unto her most secret. In wisdom excelling. In governing of her

manners of the time.* Sir Thomas is dressed in ruff and doublet, white shoes with roses in them, and has a peaked yellow, or, as Master Slender would say, "a cane-colored beard." His lady is seated on the opposite side of the picture, in wide ruff and long stomacher, and the children have a most venerable stiffness and formality of dress. Hounds and spaniels are mingled in the family group; a hawk is seated on his perch in the foreground, and one of the children holds a bow—all intimating the knight's skill in hunting, hawking, and archery, so indispensable to an accomplished gentleman in those days.†

I regretted to find that the ancient furniture of the hall had disappeared, for I had hoped to meet with the stately elbow chair of carved oak in which the country squire of former

---

*house, bringing up of youth in ye fear of God that did converse with her moste rare and singular. A great maintayner of hospitality. Greatly esteemed of her betters; misliked of none unless of the envyous. When all is spoken that can be saide a woman so garnished with virtue as not to be bettered and hardly to be equalled by any. As shee lived most virtuously so shee died most Godly. Set downe by him yt best did knowe what hath byn written to be true.   Thomas Lucye.

†Bishop Earle, speaking of the country gentleman of his time, observes, "his housekeeping is seen much in the different families of dogs, and servingmen attendant on their kennels; and the deepness of their throats is the depth of his discourse. A hawk he esteems the true burden of nobility, and is exceedingly ambitious to seem delighted with the sport, and have his fist gloved with his jesses." And Gilpin, in his description of a Mr. Hastings, remarks, "he kept all sorts of hounds that run buck, fox, hare, otter, and badger; and had hawks of all kinds both long and short winged. His great hall was commonly strewed with marrow bones, and full of hawk perches, hounds, spaniels, and terriers. On a broad hearth, paved with brick, lay some of the choicest terriers, hounds, and spaniels."

days was wont to sway the scepter of empire over his rural domains, and in which it might be presumed the redoubted Sir Thomas sat enthroned in awful state when the recreant Shakespeare was brought before him. As I like to deck out pictures for my own entertainment, I pleased myself with the idea that this very hall had been the scene of the unlucky bard's examination on the morning after his captivity in the lodge. I fancied to myself the rural potentate, surrounded by his bodyguard of butler, pages, and blue-coated servingmen, with their badges, while the luckless culprit was brought in, forlorn and chopfallen, in the custody of gamekeepers, huntsmen, and whippers-in, and followed by a rabble rout of country clowns. I fancied bright faces of curious housemaids peeping from the half-opened doors, while from the gallery the fair daughters of the knight leaned gracefully forward, eying the youthful prisoner with that pity "that dwells in womanhood." Who would have thought that this poor varlet, thus trembling before the brief authority of a country squire, and the sport of rustic boors, was soon to become the delight of princes, the theme of all tongues and ages, the dictator to the human mind, and was to confer immortality on his oppressor by a caricature and a lampoon!

I was now invited by the butler to walk into the garden, and I felt inclined to visit the orchard and arbor where the justice treated Sir John Falstaff and Cousin Silence "to a last year's pippin of his own grafting, with a dish of caraways"; but I had already spent so much of the day in my ramblings that I was obliged to give up any further investigations. When about to take my leave I was gratified by the civil entreaties of the housekeeper and butler that I would take some refreshment, an instance of good old hospitality which, I grieve to say, we castle hunters seldom meet with in modern days. I make no doubt it is a virtue which the present representative of the Lucys inherits from his ancestors, for Shakespeare, even in his caricature, makes Justice Shallow importunate in this respect, as witness his pressing instances to Falstaff.

"By cock and pye, sir, you shall not away to-night***I will not excuse you; you shall not be excused; excuses shall not be admitted; there is no excuse shall serve; you shall not be excused***. Some pigeons, Davy; a couple of short-legged hens; a joint of mutton; and any pretty little tiny kickshaws, tell William Cook."

I now bade a reluctant farewell to the old hall. My mind had become so completely possessed by the imaginary scenes and characters connected with it that I seemed to be actually living among them. Everything brought them as it were before my eyes, and as the door of the dining room opened I almost expected to hear the feeble voice of Master Silence quavering forth his favorite ditty:

> " 'Tis merry in hall, when beards wag all,
>   And welcome merry shrove-tide!"

On returning to my inn, I could not but reflect on the singular gift of the poet; to be able thus to spread the magic of his mind over the very face of nature; to give to things and places a charm and character not their own, and to turn this "working-day world" into a perfect fairyland. He is indeed the true enchanter, whose spell operates, not upon the senses, but upon the imagination and the heart. Under the wizard influence of Shakespeare I had been walking all day in a complete delusion. I had surveyed the landscape through the prism of poetry, which tinged every object with the hues of the rainbow. I had been surrounded with fancied beings, with mere airy nothings, conjured up by poetic power, yet which, to me, had all the charm of reality. I had heard Jaques soliloquize beneath his oak; had beheld the fair Rosalind and her companion adventuring through the woodlands; and, above all, had been once more present in spirit with fat Jack Falstaff and his contemporaries, from the august Justice Shallow, down to the gentle Master Slender and the sweet Anne Page. Ten thousand honors and blessings on the bard who has thus gilded the dull realities of life with innocent illusions; who has spread exquisite and unbought pleasures in my checkered path; and beguiled my spirit in many a lonely hour with all the cordial and cheerful sympathies of social life!

As I crossed the bridge over the Avon on my return, I paused to contemplate the distant church in which the poet lies buried, and could not but exult in the malediction which has kept his ashes undisturbed in its quiet and hallowed vaults. What honor could his name have derived from being mingled in dusty companionship with the epitaphs and escutcheons and venal eulogiums of a titled multitude? What would a crowded corner in Westminster Abbey have been, compared with this reverend pile, which seems to stand in beautiful loneliness as his sole mausoleum! The solicitude about the grave may be but the offspring of an overwrought sensibility; but human nature is made up of foibles and prejudices, and its best and tenderest affections are mingled with these factitious feelings. He who has sought renown about the world and has reaped a full harvest of worldly favor will find, after all, that there is no love, no admiration, no applause, so sweet to the soul as that which springs up in his native place. It is there that he seeks to be gathered in peace and honor among his kindred and his early friends. And when the weary heart and failing head begin to warn him that the evening of life is drawing on, he turns as fondly as does the infant to the mother's arms, to sink to sleep in the bosom of the scene of his childhood.

How would it have cheered the spirit of the youthful bard when, wandering forth in disgrace upon a doubtful world, he cast back a heavy look upon his paternal home, could he have foreseen that, before many years, he should return to it covered with renown; that his name should become the boast and glory of his native place; that his ashes should be religiously guarded as its most precious treasure; and that its lessening spire, on which his eyes were fixed in tearful contemplation, should one day become the beacon, towering amidst the gentle landscape, to guide the literary pilgrim of every nation to his tomb!

TRAITS OF INDIAN CHARACTER

"I appeal to any white man if ever he entered Logan's cabin hungry, and he gave him not to eat; if ever he came cold and naked, and he clothed him not."

SPEECH OF AN INDIAN CHIEF

There is something in the character and habits of the North American savage, taken in connection with the scenery over which he is accustomed to range, its vast lakes, boundless forests, majestic rivers, and trackless plains, that is, to my mind, wonderfully striking and sublime. He is formed for the wilderness as the Arab is for the desert. His nature is stern, simple, and enduring; fitted to grapple with difficulties, and to support privations. There seems but little soil in his heart for the support of the kindly virtues, and yet, if we would but take the trouble to penetrate through that proud stoicism and habitual taciturnity which lock up his character from casual observation we should find him linked to his fellowman of civilized life by more of those sympathies and affections than are usually ascribed to him.

It has been the lot of the unfortunate aborigines of America, in the early periods of colonization, to be doubly wronged by the white men. They have been dispossessed of their hereditary possessions by mercenary and frequently wanton warfare, and their characters have been traduced by bigoted and interested writers. The colonist often treated them like beasts of the forest, and the author has endeavored to justify him in his outrages. The former found it easier to exterminate than to civilize, the latter to vilify than to discriminate. The appellations of savage and pagan were deemed sufficient to sanction the hostilities of both; and thus the poor wanderers of the forest were persecuted and defamed, not because they were guilty, but because they were ignorant.

The rights of the savage have seldom been properly appreciated or respected by the white man. In peace he has too often been the dupe of artful traffic; in war he has been regarded as a ferocious animal whose life or death was a question of mere precaution and convenience. Man is cruelly wasteful of life when his own safety is endangered, and he is sheltered by impunity; and little mercy is to be expected from him when he feels the sting of the reptile and is conscious of the power to destroy.

The same prejudices, which were indulged thus early, exist in common circulation at the present day. Certain learned societies have, it is true, with laudable diligence endeavored to investigate and record the real characters and manners of the Indian tribes; the American government, too, has wisely and humanely exerted itself to inculcate a friendly and forbearing spirit toward them, and to protect them from fraud and injustice.* The current opinion of the Indian character, however, is

------

*The American government has been indefatigable in its exertions to ameliorate the situation of the Indians, and to introduce among them the arts of civilization, and civil and religious knowledge. To protect them from the frauds of the white traders, no purchase of land from them by individuals is permitted; nor is any person allowed to receive lands from them as a present, without the express sanction of government. These precautions are strictly enforced.

too apt to be formed from the miserable hordes which infest the frontiers and hang on the skirts of the settlements. These are too commonly composed of degenerate beings, corrupted and enfeebled by the vices of society without being benefited by its civilization. That proud independence, which formed the main pillar of savage virtue, has been shaken down, and the whole moral fabric lies in ruins. Their spirits are humiliated and debased by a sense of inferiority, and their native courage cowed and daunted by the superior knowledge and power of their enlightened neighbors. Society has advanced upon them like one of those withering airs that will sometimes breed desolation over a whole region of fertility. It has enervated their strength, multiplied their diseases, and superinduced upon their original barbarity the low vices of artificial life. It has given them a thousand superfluous wants, while it has diminished their means of mere existence. It has driven before it the animals of the chase, who fly from the sound of the axe and the smoke of the settlement and seek refuge in the depths of remoter forests and yet untrodden wilds. Thus do we too often find the Indians on our frontiers to be the mere wrecks and remnants of once powerful tribes who have lingered in the vicinity of the settlements and sunk into precarious and vagabond existence. Poverty, repining and hopeless poverty, a canker of the mind unknown in savage life, corrodes their spirits and blights every free and noble quality of their natures. They become drunken, indolent, feeble, thievish, and pusillanimous. They loiter like vagrants about the settlements, among spacious dwellings replete with elaborate comforts which only render them sensible of the comparative wretchedness of their own condition. Luxury spreads its ample board before their eyes; but they are excluded from the banquet. Plenty revels over the fields; but they are starving in the midst of its abundance: the whole wilderness has blossomed into a garden; but they feel as reptiles that infest it.

How different was their state while yet the undisputed lords of the soil! Their wants were few, and the means of gratification within their reach. They saw everyone around them sharing the same lot, enduring the same hardships, feeding on the same ailments, arrayed in the same rude garments. No roof then rose but was open to the homeless stranger; no smoke curled among the trees but he was welcome to sit down by its fire and join the hunter in his repast. "For," says an old historian of New England, "their life is so void of care, and they are so loving also that they make use of those things they enjoy as common goods, and are therein so compassionate that rather than one should starve through want, they would starve all; thus they pass their time merrily, not regarding our pomp, but are better content with their own, which some men esteem so meanly of." Such were the Indians while in the pride and energy of their primitive natures; they resembled those wild plants which thrive best in the shades of the forest but shrink from the hand of cultivation and perish beneath the influence of the sun.

In discussing the savage character, writers have been too prone to indulge in vulgar prejudice and passionate exaggeration, instead of the candid temper of true philosophy. They have not sufficiently considered the peculiar circumstances in which the Indians have been placed, and the peculiar principles under which they have been educated. No being acts more rigidly from rule than the Indian. His whole conduct is regulated according to some general maxims early implanted in his mind. The moral laws that govern him are, to be sure, but few, but then he conforms to them all; the white man abounds in laws of religion, morals, and manners, but how many does he violate?

A frequent ground of accusation against the Indians is their disregard of treaties, and the treachery and wantonness with which, in time of apparent peace, they will suddenly fly to hostilities. The intercourse of the white men with the Indians, however, is too apt to be cold, distrustful, oppressive, and insulting. They seldom treat them with that confidence and frankness which are indispensable to real friendship; nor is sufficient caution observed not to offend against those feelings of pride or superstition which often prompt the Indian to hostility quicker than mere considerations of interest. The solitary savage feels silently, but acutely. His sensibilities are not diffused over so wide a surface as those of the white man, but they run in steadier and deeper channels. His pride, his affections, his superstitions, are all directed toward fewer objects; but the wounds inflicted on them are proportionably severe, and furnish motives of hostility which we cannot sufficiently appreciate. Where a community is also limited in number, and forms one great patriarchal family, as in an Indian tribe, the injury of an individual is the injury of the whole, and the sentiment of vengeance is almost instantaneously diffused. One council fire is sufficient for the discussion and arrangement of a plan of hostilities. Here all the fighting men and sages assemble. Eloquence and superstition combine to inflame the minds of the warriors. The orator awakens their martial ardor, and they are wrought up to a kind of religious desperation by the visions of the prophet and the dreamer.

An instance of one of those sudden exasperations, arising from a motive peculiar to the Indian character, is extant in an old record of the early settlement of Massachusetts. The planters of Plymouth had defaced the monuments of the dead at Passonagessit, and had plundered the grave of the Sachem's mother of some skins with which it had been decorated. The Indians are remarkable for the reverence which they entertain for the sepulchers of their kindred. Tribes that have passed generations exiled from the abodes of their ancestors, when by chance they have been traveling in the vicinity, have been known to turn aside from the highway, and, guided by wonderfully accurate tradition, have crossed the country for miles to some tumulus, buried perhaps in woods, where the bones of their tribe were anciently deposited, and there have passed hours in silent meditation. Influenced by this sublime and holy feeling, the Sachem, whose mother's tomb had been violated, gathered his men together, and addressed them in the following beautifully simple and pathetic harangue, a curious specimen of Indian eloquence and an affecting instance of filial piety in a savage.

"When last the glorious light of all the sky was underneath this globe, and birds grew silent, I began to settle, as my custom is, to take repose. Before mine eyes were fast closed, methought I saw a vision, at which my spirit was much troubled; and trembling at that doleful sight, a spirit cried aloud, 'Behold, my son, whom I have cherished, see the breasts that gave thee suck, the hands that lapped thee warm, and fed thee oft. Canst thou forget to take revenge of those wild people who have defaced my monument in a despiteful manner, disdaining our antiquities and honorable customs? See, now, the Sachem's grave lies like the common people, defaced by an ignoble race. Thy mother doth complain, and implore thy aid against this thievish people, who have newly intruded on our land. If this be suffered, I shall not rest quiet in my everlasting habitation.' This said, the spirit vanished, and I, all in a sweat, not able scarce to speak, began to get some strength, and recollect my spirits that were fled, and determined to demand your counsel and assistance."

I have adduced this anecdote at some length, as it tends to show how these sudden acts of hostility, which have been attributed to caprice and perfidy, may often arise from deep and generous motives, which our inattention to Indian character and customs prevents our properly appreciating.

Another ground of violent outcry against the Indians is their barbarity to the vanquished. This had its origin partly in policy and partly in superstition. The tribes, though sometimes called nations, were never so formidable in their numbers but that the loss of several warriors was sensibly felt; this was particularly the case when they had frequently been engaged in warfare; and many an instance occurs in Indian history where a tribe that had long been formidable to its neighbors has been broken up and driven away by the capture and massacre of its principal fighting men. There was a strong temptation, therefore, to the victor to be merciless, not so much to gratify any cruel revenge as to provide for future security. The Indians had also the superstitious belief, frequent among barbarous nations and prevalent also among the ancients, that the manes of their friends who had fallen in battle were soothed by the blood of the captives. The prisoners, however, who are not thus sacrificed are adopted into their families in the place of the slain and are treated with the confidence and affection of relatives and friends; nay, so hospitable and tender is their entertainment that when the alternative is offered them, they will often prefer to remain with their adopted brethren rather than return to the home and the friends of their youth.

The cruelty of the Indians toward their prisoners has been heightened since the colonization of the whites. What was formerly a compliance with policy and superstition has been exasperated into a gratification of vengeance. They cannot but be sensible that the white men are the usurpers of their ancient dominion, the cause of their degradation, and the gradual destroyers of their race. They go forth to battle, smarting with injuries and indignities which they have individually suffered, and they are driven to madness and despair by the wide-spreading desolation and the overwhelming ruin of European warfare. The whites have too frequently set them an example of violence by burning their villages and laying waste their slender means of subsistence; and yet they wonder that savages do not show moderation and magnanimity toward those who have left them nothing but mere existence and wretchedness.

We stigmatize the Indians, also, as cowardly and treacherous, because they use stratagem in warfare in preference to open force; but in this they are fully justified by their rude code of honor. They are early taught that stratagem is praiseworthy; the bravest warrior thinks it no disgrace to lurk in silence and take every advantage of his foe: he triumphs in the superior craft and sagacity by which he has been enabled to surprise and destroy an enemy. Indeed, man is naturally more prone to subtilty than open valor, owing to his physical weakness in comparison with other animals. They are endowed with natural weapons of defense: with horns, with tusks, with hoofs, and talons; but man has to depend on his superior sagacity. In all his encounters with these, his proper enemies, he resorts to stratagem; and when he perversely turns his hostility against his fellow-man, he at first continues the same subtle mode of warfare.

The natural principle of war is to do the most harm to our enemy with the least harm to ourselves, and this of course is to be effected by stratagem. That chivalrous courage which induces us to despise the suggestions of prudence and to rush in the face of certain danger is the offspring of society and produced by education. It is honorable because it is in fact the triumph of lofty sentiment over an instinctive repugnance to pain and over those yearnings after personal ease and security which society has condemned as ignoble. It is kept alive by pride and the fear of shame; and thus the dread of real evil is overcome by the superior dread of an evil which exists but in the imagination. It has been cherished and stimulated also by various means. It has been the theme of spirit-stirring song and chivalrous story. The poet and minstrel have delighted to shed round it the splendors of fiction; and even the historian has forgotten the sober gravity of narration and broken forth into enthusiasm and rhapsody in its praise. Triumphs and gorgeous pageants have been its reward: monuments, on which art has exhausted its skill and opulence its treasures, have been erected to perpetuate a nation's gratitude and admiration. Thus artificially excited, courage has risen to an extraordinary and factitious degree of heroism; and arrayed in all the glorious "pomp and circumstance of war," this turbulent quality has even been able to eclipse many of those quiet but invaluable virtues which silently ennoble the human character and swell the tide of human happiness.

But if courage intrinsically consists in the defiance of danger and pain, the life of the Indian is a continual exhibition of it. He lives in a state of perpetual hostility and risk. Peril and adventure are congenial to his nature, or rather seem necessary to arouse his faculties and to give an interest to his existence. Surrounded by hostile tribes, whose mode of warfare is by ambush and surprisal, he is always prepared for fight, and lives with his weapons in his hands. As the ship careers in fearful singleness through the solitudes of ocean; as the bird mingles among clouds and storms, and wings its way, a mere speck, across the pathless fields of air; so the Indian holds his course, silent, solitary, but undaunted, through the boundless bosom of the wilderness. His expeditions may vie in distance and danger with the pilgrimage of the devotee, or the crusade of the knight-errant. He traverses vast forests, exposed to the hazards of lonely sickness, of lurking enemies, and pining famine. Stormy lakes, those great inland seas, are no obstacles to his wanderings; in his light canoe of bark he sports, like a feather, on their waves, and darts, with the swiftness of an arrow, down the roaring rapids of the rivers. His very subsistence is snatched from the midst of toil and peril. He gains his food by the hardships and dangers of the chase; he wraps himself in the spoils of the bear, the panther, and the buffalo, and sleeps among the thunders of the cataract.

No hero of ancient or modern days can surpass the Indian in his lofty contempt of death, and the fortitude with which he sustains its cruelest infliction. Indeed we here behold him rising superior to the white man, in consequence of his peculiar education. The latter rushes to glorious death at the cannon's mouth; the former calmly contemplates its approach, and triumphantly endures it, amid the varied torments of surrounding foes and the protracted agonies of fire. He even takes a pride in taunting his persecutors and provoking their ingenuity of torture; and as the devouring flames prey on his very vitals, and the flesh shrinks from the sinews, he raises his last song of triumph, breathing the defiance of an unconquered heart and invoking the spirits of his fathers to witness that he dies without a groan.

Notwithstanding the obloquy with which the early historians have overshadowed the characters of the unfortunate natives, some bright gleams occasionally break through, which throw a degree of melancholy luster on their memories. Facts are occasionally to be met with in the rude annals of the eastern provinces, which, though recorded with the coloring of prejudice and bigotry, yet speak for themselves, and will be dwelt on with applause and sympathy when prejudice shall have passed away.

In one of the homely narratives of the Indian wars in New England, there is a touching account of the desolation carried into the tribe of the Pequod Indians. Humanity shrinks from the cold-blooded detail of indiscriminate butchery. In one place we read of the surprisal of an Indian fort in the night, when the wigwams were wrapped in flames, and the miserable inhabitants shot down and slain in attempting to escape, "all being despatched and ended in the course of an hour." After a series of similar transactions, "our soldiers," as the historian piously observes, "being resolved by God's assistance to make a final destruction of them," the unhappy savages being hunted from their homes and fortresses and pursued with fire and sword, a scanty but gallant band, the sad remnant of the Pequod warriors, with their wives and children, took refuge in a swamp.

Burning with indignation and rendered sullen by despair, with hearts bursting with grief at the destruction of their tribe and spirits galled and sore at the fancied ignominy of their defeat, they refused to ask their lives at the hands of an insulting foe, and preferred death to submission.

As the night drew on they were surrounded in their dismal retreat, so as to render escape impracticable. Thus situated, their enemy "plied them with shot all the time, by which means many were killed and buried in the mire." In the darkness and fog that preceded the dawn of day some few broke through the besiegers and escaped into the woods; "the rest were left to the conquerors, of which many were killed in the swamp, like sullen dogs who would rather, in their self-willedness and madness, sit still and be shot through, or cut to pieces," than implore for mercy. When the day broke upon this handful of forlorn but dauntless spirits, the soldiers, we are told, entering the swamp, "saw several heaps of them sitting close together, upon whom they discharged their pieces, laden with ten or twelve pistol bullets at a time, putting the muzzles of the pieces under the boughs, within a few yards of them; so as, besides those that were found dead, many more were killed and sunk into the mire, and never were minded more by friend or foe."

Can anyone read this plain unvarnished tale without admiring the stern resolution, the unbending pride, the loftiness of spirit that seemed to nerve the hearts of these self-taught heroes and to raise them above the instinctive feelings of human nature? When the Gauls laid waste the city of Rome, they found the senators clothed in their robes, and seated with stern tranquility in their curule chairs; in this manner they suffered death without resistance or even supplication. Such conduct was, in them, applauded as noble and magnanimous; in the hapless Indian it was reviled as obstinate and sullen! How truly are we the dupes of show and circumstance! How different is virtue, clothed in purple and enthroned in state, from virtue, naked and destitute, and perishing obscurely in a wilderness!

But I forbear to dwell on these gloomy pictures. The eastern tribes have long since disappeared; the forests that sheltered them have been laid low, and scarce any traces remain of them in the thickly settled states of New England, excepting here and there the Indian name of a village or a stream. And such must, sooner or later, be the fate of those other tribes which skirt the frontiers, and have occasionally been inveigled from their forests to mingle in the wars of white men. In a little while, and they will go the way that their brethren have gone before. The few hordes which still linger about the shores of Huron and Superior and the tributary streams of the Mississippi will share the fate of those tribes that once spread over Massachusetts and Connecticut and lorded it along the proud banks of the Hudson, of that gigantic race said to have existed on the borders of the Susquehanna, and of those various nations that flourished about the Potomac and the Rappahannock and that peopled the forests of the vast valley of Shenandoah. They will vanish like a vapor from the face of the earth; their very history will be lost in forgetfulness, and "the places that now know them will know them no more for ever." Or if, perchance, some dubious memorial of them should survive, it may be in the romantic dreams of the poet, to people in imagination his glades and groves, like the fauns and satyrs and sylvan deities of antiquity. But should he venture upon the dark story of their wrongs and wretchedness; should he tell how they were invaded, corrupted, despoiled, driven from their native abodes and the sepulchers of their fathers, hunted like wild beasts about the earth, and sent down with violence and butchery to the grave, posterity will either turn with horror and incredulity from the tale, or blush with indignation at the inhumanity of their forefathers. "We are driven back," said an old warrior, "until we can retreat no farther—our hatchets are broken, our bows are snapped, our fires are nearly extinguished: a little longer and the white man will cease to persecute us—for we shall cease to exist!"

ENGLISH AND FRENCH CHARACTER

As I am a mere looker-on in Europe, and hold myself as much as possible aloof from its quarrels and prejudices, I feel something like one overlooking a game, who, without any great skill of his own, can occasionally perceive the blunders of much abler players. This neutrality of feeling enables me to enjoy the contrasts of character presented in this time of general peace, when the various people of Europe, who have so long been sundered by wars, are brought together and placed side by side in this great gathering-place of nations. No greater contrast, however, is exhibited than that of the French and English. The peace has deluged this gay capital with English visitors of all ranks and conditions. They throng every place of curiosity and amusement; fill the public gardens, the galleries, the *cafés*, saloons, theatres; always herding together, never associating with the French. The two nations are like two threads of different colors, tangled together, but never blended.

In fact, they present a continual antithesis, and seem to value themselves upon being unlike each other; yet each have their peculiar merits, which should entitle them to each other's esteem. The French intellect is quick and active. It flashes its way into a subject with the rapidity of lightning, seizes upon remote conclusion with a sudden bound, and its deductions are almost intuitive. The English intellect is less rapid, but more persevering; less sudden, but more sure in deductions. The quickness and mobility of the French enable them to find enjoyment in the multiplicity of sensations. They speak and act more from immediate impressions than from reflection and meditation. They are therefore more social and communicative, more fond of society and of places of public resort and amusement. An Englishman is more reflective in his habits. He lives in the world of his own thoughts, and seems more self-existent and self-dependent. He loves the quiet of his own apartment; even when abroad, he in a manner makes a little solitude around him by his silence and reserve; he moves about shy and solitary, and, as it were, buttoned up, body and soul.

The French are great optimists; they seize upon every good as it flies, and revel in the passing pleasure. The Englishman is too apt to neglect the present good in preparing against the possible evil. However adversities may lower, let the sun shine but for a moment, and forth sallies the mercurial Frenchman, in holiday dress and holiday spirits, gay as a butterfly, as though his sunshine were perpetual; but let the sun beam never so brightly, so there be but a cloud in the horizon, the wary Englishman ventures forth distrustfully, with his umbrella in his hand.

The Frenchman has a wonderful facility at turning small things to advantage. No one can be gay and luxurious on smaller means; no one requires less expense to be happy. He practises a kind of gilding in his style of living, and hammers out every guinea into gold-leaf. The Englishman, on the contrary, is expensive in his habits and expensive in his enjoyments. He values everything, whether useful or ornamental, by what it costs. He has no satisfaction in show, unless it be solid and complete. Everything goes with him by the square foot. Whatever display he makes, the depth is sure to equal the surface.

The Frenchman's habitation, like himself, is open, cheerful, bustling, and noisy. He lives in a part of a great hotel, with wide portal, paved court, a spacious dirty stone staircase, and a family on every floor. All is clatter and chatter. He is good-humored and talkative with his servants, sociable with his neighbors, and complaisant to all the world. Anybody has access to himself and his apartments; his very bedroom is open to visitors, whatever may be its state of confusion; and all this not from any peculiarly hospitable feeling, but from that communicative habit which predominates over his character.

The Englishman, on the contrary, ensconces himself in a snug brick mansion, which he has all to himself; locks the front door; puts broken bottles along his walls, and spring-guns and man-traps in his gardens; shrouds himself with trees and window-curtains; exults in his quiet and privacy, and seems disposed to keep out noise, daylight, and company. His house, like himself, has a reserved, inhospitable exterior; yet whoever gains admittance is apt to find a warm heart and warm fireside within.

The French excel in wit, the English in humor; the French have gayer fancy, the English richer imaginations. The former are full of sensibility, easily moved, and prone to sudden and great excitement: but their excitement is not durable; the English are more phlegmatic, not so readily affected, but capable of being aroused to great enthusiasm. The faults of these opposite temperaments are, that the vivacity of the French is apt to sparkle up and be frothy, the gravity of the English to settle down and grow muddy. When the two characters can be fixed in a medium, the French kept from effervescence and the English from stagnation, both will be found excellent.

This contrast of character may also be noticed in the great concerns of the two nations. The ardent Frenchman is all for military renown: he fights for glory, that is to say, for success in arms. For, provided the national flag be victorious, he cares little about the expense, the injustice, or the inutility of the war. It is wonderful how the poorest Frenchman will revel on a triumphant bulletin; a great victory is meat and drink to him;

and at the sight of a military sovereign, bringing home captured cannon and captured standards, he throws up his greasy cap in the air, and is ready to jump out of his wooden shoes for joy.

John Bull, on the contrary, is a reasoning, considerate person. If he does wrong, it is in the most rational way imaginable. He fights because the good of the world requires it. He is a moral person, and makes war upon his neighbor for the maintenance of peace and good order, and sound principles. He is a money-making personage, and fights for the prosperity of commerce and manufactures. Thus the two nations have been fighting, time out of mind, for glory and good. The French, in pursuit of glory, have had their capital twice taken; and John, in pursuit of good, has run himself over head and ears in debt.

THE TUILERIES AND WINDSOR CASTLE

I have sometimes fancied I could discover national characteristics in national edifices. In the Château of the Tuileries, for instance, I perceive the same jumble of contrarieties that marks the French character; the same whimsical mixture of the great and the little, the splendid and the paltry, the sublime and the grotesque. On visiting this famous pile, the first thing that strikes both eye and ear is military display. The courts glitter with steel-clad soldiery, and resound with tramp of horse, the roll of drum, and the bray of trumpet. Dismounted guardsmen patrol its arcades, with loaded carbines, jingling spurs, and clanking sabres. Gigantic grenadiers are posted about its staircases; young officers of the guards loll from the balconies, or lounge in groups upon the terraces; and the gleam of bayonet from window to window shows that sentinels are pacing up and down the corridors and ante-chambers. The first floor is brilliant with the splendors of a court. French taste has tasked itself in adorning the sumptuous suites of apartments; nor are the gilded chapel and splendid theatre forgotten, where Piety and Pleasure are next-door neighbors, and harmonize together with perfect French *bienséance*.

Mingled up with all this regal and military magnificence is a world of whimsical and makeshift detail. A great part of the huge edifice is cut up into little chambers and nestling-places for retainers of the court, dependants on retainers and hangers-on of dependants. Some are squeezed into narrow *entre-sols*, those low, dark, intermediate slices of apartments between floors, the inhabitants of which seem shoved in edgewise, like books between narrow shelves; others are perched, like swallows, under the eaves; the high roofs, too, which are tall and steep as a French cocked hat, have rows of little dormer-windows, tier above tier, just large enough to admit light and air for some dormitory, and to enable its occupant to peep out at the sky. Even to the very ridge of the roof may be seen, here and there, one of these air-holes, with a stove-pipe beside it, to carry off the smoke from the handful of fuel with which its weazen-faced tenant simmers his *demi-tasse* of coffee.

On approaching the palace from the Pont Royal, you take in at a glance all the various strata of inhabitants: the garreteer in the roof, the retainer in the *entre-sol*, the courtiers at the casement of the royal apartments; while on the ground-floor a steam of savory odors, and a score or two of cooks, in white caps, bobbing their heads about the windows, betray that scientific and all-important laboratory, the royal kitchen.

Go into the grand antechamber of the royal apartments on Sunday, and see the mixture of Old and New France: the *émigrés*, returned with the Bourbons; little, withered, spindle-shanked old noblemen, clad in court-dresses that figured in these saloons before the revolution, and have been carefully treasured up during their exile; with the solitaires and *ailes de pigeon* of former days, and the court-swords strutting out behind, like pins stuck through dry beetles. See them haunting the scenes of their former splendor, in hopes of a restitution of estates, like ghosts haunting the vicinity of buried treasure; while around them you see Young France, grown up in the fighting school of Napoleon, equipped *en militaire*: tall, hardy, frank, vigorous, sun-burnt, fierce-whiskered; with tramping boots, towering crests, and glittering breastplates.

It is incredible the number of ancient and hereditary feeders on royalty said to be housed in this establishment. Indeed, all the royal palaces abound with noble families returned from exile, and who have nestling-places allotted them while they await the restoration of their estates, or the much-talked-of law indemnity. Some of them have fine quarters, but poor living. Some families have but five or six hundred francs a year, and all their retinue consists of a servant-woman. With all this, they maintain their old aristocratical *hauteur*, look down with vast contempt upon the opulent families which have risen since the revolution; stigmatize them all as *parvenus*, or upstarts, and refuse to visit them.

In regarding the exterior of the Tuileries, with all its outward signs of internal populousness, I have often thought what a rare sight it would be to see it suddenly unroofed, and all its nooks and corners laid open to the day. It would be like turning up the stump of an old tree, and dislodging the world of grubs and ants and beetles lodged beneath. Indeed, there is a scandalous anecdote current, that, in the time of one of the petty plots, when petards were exploded under the windows of the Tuileries, the police made a sudden investigation of the palace at four o'clock in the morning, when a scene of the most whimsical confusion ensued. Hosts of super-numerary inhabitants were found foisted into the huge edifice: every rat-hole had its occupant; and places which had been considered as tenanted only by spiders, were found crowded with a surreptitious population. It is added, that many ludicrous accidents occurred; great scampering and slamming of doors, and whisking away in night-gowns and slippers; and several persons, who were found by accident in their neighbor's chambers, evinced indubitable astonishment at the circumstance.

As I have fancied I could read the French character in the national palace of the Tuileries, so I have pictured to myself some of the traits of John Bull in his royal abode of Windsor Castle. The Tuileries, outwardly a peaceful palace, is in effect a swaggering military hold; while the old castle, on the contrary, in spite of its bullying look, is completely under petticoat government. Every corner and nook is built up into some snug, cosy nestling-place, some "procreant cradle," not tenanted by meagre expectants or whiskered warriors, but by sleek placemen; knowing realizers of present pay and present pudding; who seemed placed there not to kill and destroy, but to breed and multiply. Nursery-maids and children shine with rosy faces at the windows, and swarm about the courts and terraces. The very soldiery have a pacific look, and, when off duty, may be seen loitering about the place with the nursery-maids; not making love to them in the gay gallant style of the French soldiery, but with infinite *bonhomie* aiding them to take care of the broods of children.

Though the old castle is in decay, everything about it thrives; the very crevices of the walls are tenanted by swallows, rooks, and pigeons, all sure of quiet lodgment; the ivy strikes its roots deep in the fissures, and flourishes about the mouldering tower.* Thus it is with honest John: according to his own account, he is ever going to ruin, yet everything that lives on him thrives and waxes fat. He would fain be a soldier, and swagger like his neighbors; but his domestic, quiet-loving, uxorious nature continually gets the upper hand; and though he may mount his helmet and gird on his sword, yet he is apt to sink into the plodding, painstaking father of a family, with a troop of children at his heels, and his women-kind hanging on each arm.

---

*The above sketch was written before the thorough repairs and magnificent additions made of late years to Windsor Castle.

THE GUESTS FROM GIBBET ISLAND

A Legend of Communipaw
Found among the Knickerbocker Papers at Wolfert's Roost.

Whoever has visited the ancient and renowned village of
Communipaw may have noticed an old stone building, of most
ruinous and sinister appearance. The doors and window-shutters
are ready to drop from their hinges; old clothes are stuffed in the
broken panes of glass, while legions of half-starved dogs prowl
about the premises, and rush out and bark at every passer-by,
for your beggarly house in a village is most apt to swarm with
profligate and ill-conditioned dogs. What adds to the sinister
appearance of this mansion is a tall frame in front, not a
little resembling a gallows, and which looks as if waiting
to accommodate some of the inhabitants with a well-merited
airing. It is not a gallows, however, but an ancient sign-post;
for this dwelling in the golden days of Communipaw was one
of the most orderly and peaceful of village taverns, where public
affairs were talked and smoked over. In fact, it was in this very
building that Oloffe the Dreamer and his companions concert-
ed that great voyage of discovery and colonization in which
they explored Buttermilk Channel, were nearly shipwrecked
in the strait of Hell Gate, and finally landed on the island of

Manhattan, and founded the great city of New Amsterdam.

Even after the province had been cruelly wrested from the sway of their High Mightinesses by the combined forces of the British and the Yankees, this tavern continued its ancient loyalty. It is true, the head of the Prince of Orange disappeared from the sign, a strange bird being painted over it, with the explanatory legend of "DIE WILDE GANS," or, The Wild Goose; but this all the world knew to be a sly riddle of the landlord, the worthy Teunis Van Gieson, a knowing man, in a small way, who laid his finger beside his nose and winked, when any one studied the signification of his sign, and observed that his goose was hatching, but would join the flock whenever they flew over the water; an enigma which was the perpetual recreation and delight of the loyal but fat-headed burghers of Communipaw.

Under the sway of this patriotic, though discreet and quiet publican, the tavern continued to flourish in primeval tranquility, and was the resort of true-hearted Nederlanders, from all parts of Pavonia; who met here quietly and secretly, to smoke and drink the downfall of Briton and Yankee, and success to Admiral Van Tromp.

The only drawback on the comfort of the establishment was a nephew of mine host, a sister's son, Yan Yost Vanderscamp by name, and a real scamp by nature. This unlucky whipster showed an early propensity to mischief, which he gratified in a small way by playing tricks upon the frequenters of the Wild Goose—putting gunpowder in their pipes, or squibs in their pockets, and astonishing them with an explosion, while they sat nodding around the fireplace in the bar-room; and if perchance a worthy burgher from some distant part of Pavonia lingered until dark over his potation, it was odds but young Vanderscamp would slip a brier under his horse's tail, as he mounted, and send him clattering along the road, in neck-or-nothing style, to the infinite astonishment and discomfiture of the rider.

It may be wondered at, that mine host of the Wild Goose did not turn such a graceless varlet out of doors; but Teunis Van Gieson was an easy-tempered man, and, having no child of his own, looked upon his nephew with almost parental indulgence. His patience and good-nature were doomed to be tried by another inmate of his mansion. This was a cross-grained curmudgeon of a Negro, named Pluto, who was a kind of enigma in Communipaw. Where he came from, nobody knew. He was found one morning, after a storm, cast like a sea-monster on the strand, in front of the Wild Goose, and lay there, more dead than alive. The neighbors gathered round, and speculated on this production of the deep; whether it were fish or flesh, or a compound of both, commonly yclept a merman. The kind-hearted Teunis Van Gieson, seeing that he wore the human form, took him into his house, and warmed him into life. By degrees, he showed signs of intelligence, and even uttered sounds very much like language, but which no one in Communipaw could understand. Some thought him a Negro just from Guinea, who had either fallen overboard, or escaped from a slave-ship. Nothing, however, could ever draw from him any account of his origin. When questioned on the subject, he merely pointed to Gibbet Island, a small rocky islet which lies in the open bay, just opposite Communipaw, as if that were his native place, though everybody knew it had never been inhabited.

In the process of time, he acquired something of the Dutch language; that is to say, he learnt all its vocabulary of oaths and maledictions, with just words sufficient to string them together. "*Donder en blicksem!*" (thunder and lightning) was the gentlest of his ejaculations. For years he kept about the Wild Goose, more like one of those familiar spirits, or household goblins, we read of, than like a human being. He acknowledged allegiance to no one, but performed various domestic offices, when it suited his humor; waiting occasionally on the guests, grooming the horses, cutting wood, drawing water; and all this without being ordered. Lay any command on him, and the stubborn sea-urchin was sure to rebel. He was never so much at home, however, as when on the water, plying about in skiff or canoe, entirely alone, fishing, crabbing, or grabbing for oysters, and would bring home quantities for the larder of the Wild Goose, which he would throw down at the kitchen-door, with a growl. No wind nor weather deterred him from launching forth on his favorite element; indeed, the wilder the weather, the more he seemed to enjoy it. If a storm was brewing, he was sure to put off from shore; like a feather on the waves, when sea and sky were in a turmoil, and the stoutest ships were fain to lower their sails. Sometimes on such occasions he would be absent for days together. How he weathered the tempest, and how and where he subsisted, no one could divine, nor did any one venture to ask, for all had an almost superstitious awe of him. Some of the Communipaw oystermen declared they had more than once seen him suddenly disappear, canoe and all, as if plunged beneath the waves, and after a while come up again, in quite a different part of the bay; whence they concluded that he could live under water like that notable species of wild-duck commonly called the hell-diver. All began to consider him in the light of a foul-weather bird, like the Mother Carey's chicken, or stormy petrel; and whenever they saw him putting far out in his skiff, in cloudy weather, made up their minds for a storm.

The only being for whom he seemed to have any liking was Yan Yost Vanderscamp, and him he liked for his very wickedness. He in a manner took the boy under his tutelage, prompted him to all kinds of mischief, aided him in every wild harum-scarum freak, until the lad became the complete scapegrace of the village, a pest to his uncle and to every one else. Nor were his pranks confined to the land; he soon learned to accompany old Pluto on the water. Together these worthies would cruise about the broad bay, and all the neighboring straits and rivers; poking around in skiffs and canoes; robbing the set nets of the fishermen; landing on remote coasts, and laying waste orchards and water-melon patches; in short, carrying on a complete system of piracy, on a small scale. Piloted by Pluto, the youthful Vanderscamp soon became acquainted with all the bays, rivers, creeks, and inlets of the watery world around him; could navigate from the Hook to Spiting Devil on the darkest night, and learned to set even the terrors of Hell Gate at defiance.

At length Negro and boy suddenly disappeared, and days and weeks elapsed, but without tidings of them. Some said they must have run away and gone to sea; others jocosely hinted that old Pluto, being no other than his namesake in disguise, had spirited away the boy to the nether regions. All, however, agreed in one thing, that the village was well rid of them.

In the process of time, the good Teunis Van Gieson slept with his fathers, and the tavern remained shut up, waiting for a claimant, for the next heir was Yan Yost Vanderscamp, and he had not been heard of for years. At length, one day, a boat was seen pulling for shore, from a long, black, rakish-looking schooner, that lay at anchor in the bay. The boat's crew seemed worthy of the craft from which they debarked. Never had such a set of noisy roistering, swaggering varlets landed in peaceful Communipaw. They were outlandish in garb and demeanor, and were headed by a rough, burly, bully ruffian, with fiery whiskers, a copper nose, a scar across his face, and a great Flaunderish beaver slouched on one side of his head, in whom, to their dismay, the quiet inhabitants were made to recognize their early pest, Yan Yost Vanderscamp. The rear of this hopeful gang was brought up by old Pluto, who had lost an eye, grown grizzly-headed, and looked more like a devil than ever. Vanderscamp renewed his acquaintance with the old burghers, much against their will, and in a manner not at all to their taste. He slapped them familiarly on the back, gave them an iron grip of the hand, and was hail-fellow well met. According to his own account, he had been all the world over, had made money by bags full, had ships in every sea, and now meant to turn the Wild Goose into a country-seat, where he and his comrades, all rich merchants from foreign parts, might enjoy themselves in the interval of their voyages.

Sure enough, in a little while there was a complete metamorphose of the Wild Goose. From being a quiet, peaceful Dutch public-house, it became a most riotous, uproarious private dwelling; a complete rendezvous for boisterous men of the seas, who came here to have what they called a "blow-out" on dry land, and might be seen at all hours, lounging about the door, or lolling out of the windows, swearing among themselves and cracking rough jokes on every passer-by. The house was fitted up, too, in so strange a manner: hammocks slung to the walls, instead of bedsteads; odd kinds of furniture, of foreign fashion; bamboo couches, Spanish chairs; pistols, cutlasses, and blunderbusses, suspended on every peg; silver crucifixes on the mantle-pieces, silver candle-sticks and porringers on the tables, contrasting oddly with the pewter and Delf ware of the original establishment. And then the strange amusements of these sea-monsters! Pitching Spanish dollars, instead of quoits; firing blunderbusses out of the window; shooting at a mark, or at any unhappy dog, or cat, or pig, or barn-door fowl, that might happen to come within reach.

The only being who seemed to relish their rough waggery was old Pluto; and yet he led but a dog's life of it, for they practised all kinds of manual jokes upon him, kicked him about like a foot-ball, shook him by his grizzly mop of wool, and never spoke to him without coupling a curse by way of adjective, to his name, and consigning him to the infernal regions. The old fellow, however, seemed to like them the better the more they cursed him, though his utmost expression of pleasure never amounted to more than the growl of a petted bear, when his ears are rubbed.

Old Pluto was the ministering spirit at the orgies of the Wild Goose; and such orgies as took place there! Such drinking, singing, whooping, swearing; with an occasional interlude of quarrelling and fighting. The noisier grew the revel, the more old Pluto plied the potations, until the guests would become frantic in their merriment, smashing everything to pieces, and throwing the house out of the windows. Sometimes, after a drinking bout, they sallied forth and scoured the village, to the dismay of the worthy burghers, who gathered their women within doors, and would have shut up the house. Vanderscamp, however, was not to be rebuffed. He insisted on renewing acquaintance with his old neighbors, and on introducing his friends, the merchants, to their families; swore he was on the lookout for a wife, and meant, before he stopped, to find husbands for all their daughters. So, will-ye, nill-ye, sociable he was; swaggered about their best parlors, with his hat on one side of his head; sat on the good-wife's nicely waxed mahogany table, kicking his heels against the carved and polished leg; kissed and tousled the young *vrows*; and, if they frowned and pouted, gave them a gold rosary, or a sparkling cross, to put them in good-humor again.

Sometimes nothing would satisfy him, but he must have some of his old neighbors to dinner at the Wild Goose. There was no refusing him, for he had the complete upper hand of the community, and the peaceful burghers all stood in awe of him. But what a time would the quiet, worthy men have, among these rake-hells, who would delight to astound them with the most extravagant gunpowder tales, embroidered with all kinds of foreign oaths, clink the can with them, pledge them in deep potations, bawl drinking-songs in their ears, and occasionally fire pistols over their heads, or under the table, and then laugh in their faces, and ask them how they liked the smell of gunpowder.

Thus was the little village of Communipaw for a time like the unfortunate wight possessed with devils; until Vanderscamp and his brother merchants would sail on another trading voyage, when the Wild Goose would be shut up and everything relapse into quiet, only to be disturbed by his next visitation.

The mystery of all these proceedings gradually dawned upon the tardy intellects of Communipaw. These were the times of the notorious Captain Kidd, when the American harbors were the resorts of piratical adventurers of all kinds, who, under pretext of mercantile voyages, scoured the West Indies, made plundering descents upon the Spanish Main, visited even the remote Indian Seas, and then came to dispose of their booty, have their revels, and fit out new expeditions in the English colonies.

Vanderscamp had served in this hopeful school, and, having risen to importance among the buccaneers, had pitched upon his native village and early home, as a quiet, out-of-the-way, unsuspected place, where he and his comrades, while anchored at New York, might have their feasts, and concert their plans, without molestation.

At length the attention of the British government was called to these piratical enterprises, that were becoming so frequent and outrageous. Vigorous measures were taken to check and punish them. Several of the most noted freebooters were caught and executed, and three of Vanderscamp's chosen comrades, the most riotous swash-bucklers of the Wild Goose, were hanged in chains on Gibbet Island, in full sight of their favorite resort. As to Vanderscamp himself, he and his man Pluto again disappeared, and it was hoped by the people of Communipaw that he had fallen in some foreign brawl, or been swung on some foreign gallows.

For a time, therefore, the tranquility of the village was restored; the worthy Dutchmen once more smoked their pipes in peace, eying with peculiar complacency their old pests and terrors, the pirates, dangling and drying in the sun, on Gibbet Island.

This perfect calm was doomed at length to be ruffled. The fiery persecution of the pirates gradually subsided. Justice was satisfied with the examples that had been made, and there was no more talk of Kidd, and the other heroes of like kidney. On a calm summer evening, a boat, somewhat heavily laden, was seen pulling into Communipaw. What was the surprise and disquiet of the inhabitants to see Yan Yost Vanderscamp seated at the helm, and his man Pluto tugging at the oar! Vanderscamp, however, was apparently an altered man. He brought home with him a wife, who seemed to be a shrew, and to have the upper hand of him. He no longer was the swaggering, bully ruffian, but affected the regular merchant, and talked of retiring from business, and settling down quietly, to pass the rest of his days in his native place.

The Wild Goose mansion was again opened, but with diminished splendor, and no riot. It is true, Vanderscamp had frequent nautical visitors, and the sound of revelry was occasionally overheard in his house; but everything seemed to be done under the rose, and old Pluto was the only servant that officiated at these orgies. The visitors, indeed, were by no means of the turbulent stamp of their predecessors; but quiet mysterious traders; full of nods, and winks, and hieroglyphic signs, with whom, to use their cant phrase, "everything was smug." There ships came to anchor at night, in the lower bay; and, on a private signal, Vanderscamp would launch his boat, and, accompanied solely by his man Pluto, would make them mysterious visits. Sometimes boats pulled in at night, in front of the Wild Goose, and various articles of merchandise were landed in the dark, and spirited away, nobody knew whither. One of the more curious of the inhabitants kept watch, and caught a glimpse of the features of some of these night visitors, by the casual glance of a lantern, and declared that he recognized more than one of the freebooting frequenters of the Wild Goose, in former times; whence he concluded that Vanderscamp was at his old game, and that this mysterious merchandise was nothing more nor less than piratical plunder. The more charitable opinion, however, was, that Vanderscamp and his comrades, having been driven from their old line of business by the "oppressions of government," had resorted to smuggling to make both ends meet.

Be that as it may, I come now to the extraordinary fact which is the butt-end of this story. It happened, late one night, that Yan Yost Vanderscamp was returning across the broad bay, in his light skiff, rowed by his man Pluto. He had been carousing on board of a vessel, newly arrived, and was somewhat obfuscated in intellect, by the liquor he had imbibed. It was a still, sultry night; a heavy mass of lurid clouds was rising in the west, with the low muttering of distant thunder. Vanderscamp called on Pluto to pull lustily, that they might get home before the gathering storm. The old Negro made no reply, but shaped his course so as to skirt the rocky shores of Gibbet Island. A faint creaking overhead caused Vanderscamp to cast up his eyes, when, to his horror, he beheld the bodies of his three pot companions and brothers in iniquity dangling in the moonlight, their rags fluttering, and their chains creaking, as they were slowly swung backward and forward by the rising breeze.

"What do you mean, you blockhead!" cried Vanderscamp, "by pulling so close to the island?"

"I thought you'd be glad to see your old friends once more," growled the Negro; "you were never afraid of a living man, what do you fear from the dead?"

"Who's afraid?" hiccoughed Vanderscamp, partly heated by liquor, partly nettled by the jeer of the Negro; "who's afraid? Hang me, but I would be glad to see them once more, alive or dead, at the Wild Goose. Come, my lads in the wind!" continued he, taking a draught and flourishing the bottle above his head, "here's fair weather to you in the other world; and if you should be walking the rounds to-night, odds fish! but I'll be happy if you will drop in to supper."

A dismal creaking was the only reply. The wind blew loud and shrill, and as it whistled round the gallows, and among the bones, sounded as if they were laughing and gibbering in the air. Old Pluto chuckled to himself, and now pulled for home. The storm burst over the voyagers, while they were yet far from shore. The rain fell in torrents, the thunder crashed and pealed, and the lightning kept up an incessant blaze. It was stark midnight before they landed at Communipaw.

Dripping and shivering, Vanderscamp crawled homeward. He was completely sobered by the storm, the water soaked from without having diluted and cooled the liquor within. Arrived at the Wild Goose, he knocked timidly and dubiously at the door; for he dreaded the reception he was to experience from his wife. He had reason to do so. She met him at the threshold, in a precious ill-humor.

"Is this a time," said she, "to keep people out of their beds, and to bring home company, to turn the house upside down?"

"Company?" said Vanderscamp, meekly; "I have brought no company with me, wife."

"No, indeed! they have got here before you, but by your invitation; and blessed-looking company they are, truly!"

Vanderscamp's knees smote together. "For the love of heaven, where are they, wife?"

"Where?—why in the blue room, up-stairs, making themselves as much at home as if the house were their own."

Vanderscamp made a desperate effort, scrambled up to the room, and threw open the door. Sure enough, there at a table, on which burned a light as blue as brimstone, sat the three guests from Gibbet Island, with halters round their necks, and bobbing their cups together, as if they were hob-or-nobbing, and trolling the old Dutch freebooter's glee, since translated into English:

> "For three merry lads be we,
> And three merry lads be we;
> I on the land, and thou on the sand,
> And Jack on the gallows-tree."

Vanderscamp saw and heard no more. Starting back with horror; he missed his footing on the landing-place, and fell from the top of the stairs to the bottom. He was taken up speechless, either from the fall or the fright, and was buried in the yard of the little Dutch church at Bergen, on the following Sunday.

From that day forward the fate of the Wild Goose was sealed. It was pronounced a *haunted house*, and avoided accordingly. No one inhabited it but Vanderscamp's shrew of a widow and old Pluto, and they were considered but little better than its hobgoblin visitors. Pluto grew more and more haggard and morose, and looked more like an imp of darkness than a human being. He spoke to no one, but went about muttering to himself; or, as some hinted, talking with the devil, who, though unseen, was ever at his elbow. Now and then he was seen pulling about the bay alone in his skiff, in dark weather, or at the approach of night-fall; nobody could tell why, unless, on an errand to invite more guests from the gallows. Indeed, it was affirmed that the Wild Goose still continued to be a house of entertainment for such guests, and that on stormy nights the blue chamber was occasionally illuminated, and sounds of diabolical merriment were overheard, mingling with the howling of the tempest. Some treated these as idle stories, until on one such night, it was about the time of the equinox, there was a horrible uproar in the Wild Goose, that could not be mistaken. It was not so much the sound of revelry, however, as strife, with two or three piercing shrieks, that pervaded every part of the village. Nevertheless, no one thought of hastening to the spot. On the contrary, the honest burghers of Communipaw drew their nightcaps over their ears, and buried their heads under the bedclothes, at the thoughts of Vanderscamp and his gallows companions.

The next morning some of the bolder and more curious undertook to reconnoitre. All was quiet and lifeless at the Wild Goose. The door yawned wide open, and had evidently been open all night, for the storm had beaten into the house. Gathering more courage from the silence and apparent desertion, they gradually ventured over the threshold. The house had indeed the air of having been possessed by devils. Everything was topsy-turvy; trunks had been broken open, and chests of drawers and corner cupboards turned inside out, as in a time of general sack and pillage; but the most woful sight was the widow of Yan Yost Vanderscamp, extended a corpse on the floor of the blue chamber, with the marks of a deadly gripe on the windpipe.

All now was conjecture and dismay at Communipaw; and the disappearance of old Pluto, who was nowhere to be found, gave rise to all kinds of wild surmises. Some suggested that the Negro had betrayed the house to some of Vanderscamp's buccaneering associates, and that they had decamped together with the booty; others surmised that the Negro was nothing more nor less than a devil incarnate, who had now accomplished his ends, and made off with his dues.

Events, however, vindicated the Negro from this last implication. His skiff was picked up, drifting about the bay, bottom upward, as if wrecked in a tempest; and his body was found, shortly afterward, by some Communipaw fishermen, stranded among the rocks of Gibbet Island, near the foot of the pirates' gallows. The fishermen shook their heads and observed that old Pluto had ventured once too often to invite guests from Gibbet Island.

THE LEGEND OF
DON MUNIO SANCHO DE HINOJOSA

In the cloisters of the ancient Benedictine convent of San Domingo, at Silos, in Castile, are the mouldering yet magnificent monuments of the once powerful and chivalrous family of Hinojosa. Among these reclines the marble figure of a knight, in complete armor, with the hands pressed together, as if in prayer. On one side of his tomb is sculptured, in relief, a band of Christian cavaliers capturing a cavalcade of male and female Moors; on the other side, the same cavaliers are represented kneeling before an altar. The tomb, like most of the neighboring monuments, is almost in ruins, and the sculpture is nearly unintelligible, excepting to the keen eye of the antiquary. The story connected with the sepulchre, however, is still preserved in the old Spanish chronicles, and is to the following purport:

In old times, several hundred years ago, there was a noble Castilian cavalier, named Don Munio Sancho de Hinojosa, lord of a border castle, which had stood the brunt of many a Moorish foray. He had seventy horsemen as his household troops, all of the ancient Castilian proof, stark warriors, hard riders, and men of iron; with these he scoured the Moorish lands, and made his name terrible throughout the borders. His castle hall was covered with banners and scimetars and Moslem helms, the trophies of his prowess. Don Munio was, moreover, a keen huntsman; and rejoiced in hounds of all kinds, steeds for the chase, and hawks for the towering sport of falconry. When not engaged in warfare, his delight was to beat up the neighboring forests; and scarcely ever did he ride forth without hound and horn, a boar-spear in his hand, or a hawk upon his fist, and an attendant train of huntsmen.

His wife, Doña Maria Palacin, was of a gentle and timid nature, little fitted to be the spouse of so hardy and adventurous a knight; and many a tear did the poor lady shed when he sallied forth upon his daring enterprises, and many a prayer did she offer up for his safety.

As this doughty cavalier was one day hunting, he stationed himself in a thicket, on the borders of a green glade of the forest, and dispersed his followers to rouse the game and drive it towards his stand. He had not been here long when a caval-cade of Moors, of both sexes, came prancing over the forest lawn. They were unarmed, and magnificently dressed in robes of tissue and embroidery, rich shawls of India, bracelets and anklets of gold, and jewels that sparkled in the sun.

At the head of this gay cavalcade rode a youthful cavalier, superior to the rest in dignity and loftiness of demeanor, and in splendor of attire; beside him was a damsel, whose veil, blown aside by the breeze, displayed a face of surpassing beauty, and eyes cast down in maiden modesty, yet beaming with tender-ness and joy.

Don Munio thanked his stars for sending him such a prize, and exulted at the thought of bearing home to his wife the glittering spoils of these infidels. Putting his hunting-horn to his lips, he gave a blast that rung through the forest. His huntsmen came running from all quarters, and the astonished Moors were surrounded and made captives.

The beautiful Moor wrung her hands in despair, and her female attendants uttered the most piercing cries. The young

Moorish cavalier alone retained self-possession. He inquired the name of the Christian knight who commanded this troop of horsemen. When told that it was Don Munio Sancho de Hinojosa, his countenance lighted up. Approaching that cavalier, and kissing his hand, "Don Munio Sancho," said he, "I have heard of your fame as a true and valiant knight, terrible in arms, but schooled in the noble virtues of chivalry. Such do I trust to find you. In me you behold Abadil, son of a Moorish alcaid. I am on the way to celebrate my nuptials with this lady; chance has thrown us in your power, but I confide in your magnanimity. Take all our treasure and jewels; demand what ransom you think proper for our persons, but suffer us not to be insulted or dishonored."

When the good knight heard this appeal and beheld the beauty of the youthful pair, his heart was touched with tenderness and courtesy. "God forbid," said he, "that I should disturb such happy nuptials. My prisoners in troth shall ye be, for fifteen days, and immured within my castle, where I claim, as conqueror, the right of celebrating your espousals."

So saying, he despatched one of his fleetest horsemen in advance, to notify Doña Maria Palacin of the coming of this bridal party; while he and his huntsmen escorted the cavalcade, not as captors, but as a guard of honor. As they drew near to the castle, the banners were hung out, and the trumpets sounded from the battlements, and on their nearer approach, the drawbridge was lowered, and Doña Maria came forth to meet them, attended by her ladies and knights, her pages and her minstrels. She took the young bride, Allifra, in her arms, kissed her with the tenderness of a sister, and conducted her into the castle. In the meantime, Don Munio sent forth missives in every direction, and had viands and dainties of all kinds collected from the country round; and the wedding of the Moorish lovers was celebrated with all possible state and festivity. For fifteen days the castle was given up to joy and revelry. There were tiltings and jousts at the ring, and bull-fights, and banquets, and dances to the sound of minstrelsy. When the fifteen days were at an end, he made the bride and bridegroom magnificent presents, and conducted them and their attendants safely beyond the borders. Such, in old times, were the courtesy and generosity of a Spanish cavalier.

Several years after this event, the king of Castile summoned his nobles to assist him in a campaign against the Moors. Don Munio Sancho was among the first to answer the call, with seventy horsemen, all stanch and well-tried warriors. His wife, Doña Maria, hung about his neck. "Alas, my lord!" exclaimed she, "how often wilt thou tempt thy fate, and when wilt thy thirst for glory be appeased?"

"One battle more," replied Don Munio, "one battle more, for the honor of Castile, and I here make a vow that when this is over, I will lay by my sword, and repair with my cavaliers in pilgrimage to the Sepulchre of our Lord at Jerusalem." The cavaliers all joined with him in the vow, and Doña Maria felt in some degree soothed in spirit; still, she saw with a heavy heart the departure of her husband, and watched his banner with wistful eyes until it disappeared among the trees of the forest.

The king of Castile led his army to the plains of Salmanara, where they encountered the Moorish host, near to Ucles. The battle was long and bloody. The Christians repeatedly wavered, and were as often rallied by the energy of their commanders. Don Munio was covered with wounds, but refused to leave the field. The Christians at length gave way, and the king was hardly pressed, and in danger of being captured.

Don Munio called upon his cavaliers to follow him to the rescue. "Now is the time," cried he, "to prove your loyalty. Fall to, like brave men! We fight for the true faith, and if we lose our lives here, we gain a better life hereafter."

Rushing with his men between the king and his pursuers, they checked the latter in their career, and gave time for their monarch to escape; but they fell victims to their loyalty. They all fought to the last gasp. Don Munio was singled out by a powerful Moorish knight, but having been wounded in the right arm, he fought to disadvantage, and was slain. The battle being over, the Moor paused to possess himself of the spoils of this redoubtable Christian warrior. When he unlaced the helmet, however, and beheld the countenance of Don Munio, he gave a great cry, and smote his breast. "Woe is me!" cried he, "I have slain my benefactor! the flower of knightly virtue! the most magnanimous of cavaliers!"

While the battle had been raging on the plain of Salmanara, Doña Maria Palacin remained in her castle, a prey to the keenest anxiety. Her eyes were ever fixed on the road that led from the country of the Moors, and often she asked the watchman of the tower, "What seest thou?"

One evening, at the shadowy hour of twilight, the warden sounded his horn. "I see," cried he, "a numerous train winding up the valley. There are mingled Moors and Christians. The banner of my lord is in the advance. Joyful tidings!" exclaimed the old seneschal; "my lord returns in triumph, and brings captives!" Then the castle courts rang with shouts of joy; and the standard was displayed, and the trumpets were sounded, and the drawbridge was lowered, and Doña Maria went forth with her ladies, and her knights, and her pages, and her minstrels, to welcome her lord from the wars. But as the train drew nigh, she beheld a sumptuous bier, covered with black velvet, and on it lay a warrior, as if taking his repose; he lay in his armor, with his helmet on his head, and his sword in his hand, as one who had never been conquered, and around the bier were the escutcheons of the house of Hinojosa.

A number of Moorish cavaliers attended the bier, with emblems of mourning and with dejected countenances; and their leader cast himself at the feet of Doña Maria, and hid his face in his hands. She beheld in him the gallant Abadil, whom she had once welcomed with his bride to her castle, but who now came with the body of her lord, whom he had unknowingly slain in battle!

The sepulchre erected in the cloisters of the Convent of San Domingo was achieved at the expense of the Moor Abadil, as a feeble testimony of his grief for the death of the good knight

Don Munio, and his reverence for his memory. The tender and faithful Doña Maria soon followed her lord to the tomb. On one of the stones of a small arch, beside his sepulchre, is the following simple inscription: "*Hic jacet Maria Palacin, uxor Munonis Sancif de Hinojosa*": Here lies Maria Palacin, wife of Munio Sancho de Hinojosa.

The legend of Don Munio Sancho does not conclude with his death. On the same day on which the battle took place on the plain of Salmanara, a chaplain of the Holy Temple at Jerusalem, while standing at the outer gate, beheld a train of Christian cavaliers advancing, as if in pilgrimage. The chaplain was a native of Spain, and as the pilgrims approached, he knew the foremost to be Don Munio Sancho de Hinojosa, with whom he had been well acquainted in former times. Hastening to the patriarch, he told him of the honorable rank of the pilgrims at the gate. The patriarch, therefore, went forth with a grand procession of priests and monks, and received the pilgrims with all due honor. There were seventy cavaliers, beside their leader, all stark and lofty warriors. They carried their helmets in their hands, and their faces were deadly pale. They greeted no one, nor looked either to the right or to the left, but entered the chapel, and kneeling before the Sepulchre of our Saviour, performed their orisons in silence. When they had concluded, they rose as if to depart, and the patriarch and his attendants advanced to speak to them, but they were no more to be seen. Every one marvelled what could be the meaning of this prodigy. The patriarch carefully noted down the day, and sent to Castile to learn tidings of Don Munio Sancho de Hinojosa. He received for reply, that on the very day specified that worthy knight, with seventy of his followers, had been slain in battle. These, therefore, must have been the blessed spirits of those Christian warriors, come to fulfil their vow of a pilgrimage to the Holy Sepulchre at Jerusalem. Such was Castilian faith in the olden time, which kept its word even beyond the grave.

If any one should doubt of the miraculous apparition of these phantom knights, let him consult the *History of the Kings of Castile and Leon* by the learned and pious Fray Prudencio de

Sandoval, Bishop of Pamplona, where he will find it recorded in the *History of the King Don Alonzo VI.*, on the hundred and second page. It is too precious a legend to be lightly abandoned to the doubter.